"Are you suggesting I'm crazy?"

As Remy waited for Jonas's answer she seethed. He knew her well enough to not make those kinds of comments.

"Absolutely not. I know crazy." He paused. "But you are slightly cracked."

Remy couldn't say for certain whose scowl gave way to a smile first, but a second later they were both laughing. And a second after that, kissing.

She wanted to blame the Kraken—or the intensity of the situation—but she wasn't a liar. She'd been thinking about kissing him from the moment he showed up on her doorstep.

He broke it off first. "Damn. I promised myself I wasn't going to do that."

"Me, too," she said, touching her fingers to her lips. She'd kissed a dozen boys and men over the years but not a single one had left the sort of impression on her mouth that Jonas Galloway had.

Dear Reader,

I didn't set out to write a nine-book series. In fact, the very idea probably would have left me paralyzed with writer's block. But here we are at the ninth and final story in the Spotlight on Sentinel Pass series. In my proposal, I told my editor, oh, so casually, "And Remy's story will probably lead us away from the Black Hills."

That sounded logical and relatively simple in theory. But saying goodbye to my Sentinel Pass family hasn't been easy. Luckily, I really liked Remy when I met her in her sister Jessie's book, *Return to the Black Hills.* I wanted to tell her story, and it was clear her roots—and her heart—were in Louisiana.

When you meet Jonas Galloway, you'll understand why. He's the guy who got away—or rather was driven away by an outrageous and hurtful lie. Remy is poised to reinvent herself, and is determined to find a way to break free of the past and live her life fully. The last thing she wants or needs is a living, breathing ghost from her past showing up on her front porch to ask for her help in finding his missing daughter, Birdie. Help Remy can't give him because to do so would prove once and for all that she's a fake and fraud or, worse, that she's become her mother—a woman who wasted her life waiting for a man she could never have. But Jonas refuses to take no for an answer. His daughter is in trouble and he'll risk everything—even the love he's tried most of his life to deny—to find her.

In researching Remy's so-called gift—a facility for interpreting dreams—I learned a lot about lucid dreaming. Two websites in particular— dreammoods.com and lucidity.com—were helpful in understanding the brain's processing of dreams and attributing certain meanings and symbolism to dreams. The brain is a fascinating, complex and relatively unmapped frontier.

Dream on!

Debra Salonen

A Father's Quest
Debra Salonen

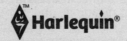

TORONTO NEW YORK LONDON
AMSTERDAM PARIS SYDNEY HAMBURG
STOCKHOLM ATHENS TOKYO MILAN MADRID
PRAGUE WARSAW BUDAPEST AUCKLAND

Recycling programs
for this product may
not exist in your area.

ISBN-13: 978-0-373-71704-0

A FATHER'S QUEST

Copyright © 2011 by Debra K. Salonen

This edition published by arrangement with Harlequin Books S.A.

For questions and comments about the quality of this book please contact us at Customer_eCare@Harlequin.ca.

www.eHarlequin.com

Printed in U.S.A.

ABOUT THE AUTHOR

Debra Salonen is a firm believer that dreams do come true...if you're willing to put in the time and effort to make them happen. For Debra, her dream of getting published became a reality *after* she consulted a psychic. A coincidence? Perhaps, but the psychic also predicted that Debra would live to be eightysomething, she'd be healthy and happy and have grandchildren she would adore. Like Debra, you'll have to wait awhile to find out about the eighty years part of the prediction, but the rest is...well, a dream come true. Visit her online at www.DebraSalonen.com.

Books by Debra Salonen

HARLEQUIN SUPERROMANCE

1196—A COWBOY SUMMER
1238—CALEB'S CHRISTMAS WISH
1279—HIS REAL FATHER
1386—A BABY ON THE WAY
1392—WHO NEEDS CUPID?
    "The Max Factor"
1434—LOVE, BY GEORGE
1452—BETTING ON SANTA
1492—BABY BY CONTRACT#
1516—HIS BROTHER'S SECRET#
1540—DADDY BY SURPRISE#
1564—PICTURE-PERFECT MOM#
1588—FINDING THEIR SON#
1633—UNTIL HE MET RACHEL#
1662—THE GOOD PROVIDER#
1698—RETURN TO THE BLACK HILLS#

#Spotlight on Sentinel Pass

SIGNATURE SELECT SAGA

BETTING ON GRACE

HARLEQUIN AMERICAN ROMANCE

1114—ONE DADDY TOO MANY
1126—BRINGING BABY HOME
1139—THE QUIET CHILD

For Malte, Rya and Daisy—
my inspiration and then some.

PROLOGUE

BIRDIE GALLOWAY WAS good at hiding. None of the other kids were half as good as her. That meant when it was her turn to hide, the others would search and search and search but not find her. Then they'd give up and go play some other game without letting her know the game was over. She hated that. She told them they were lazy, but they were little kids. They didn't listen.

Birdie was seven and a half. Six months older than David, the kid closest to her in age. His mother was Brother Thom's most special friend. Birdie's mother wanted to be that special, but she wasn't. She was only a friend. Like all the other GoodFriends who traveled with Brother Thom.

Mommy called them gypsies because the Friends all drove motor homes or pulled campers behind their trucks. When she and her mother first joined the group, there were a lot of trailers. Now, there were only two.

"Hard times," Mommy said. "Fewer donations. Less money for gas. Less of Thom to go around."

Birdie wasn't sure what that meant but she knew they were eating more cereal and beans now than when she and Mommy first ran away from home.

That's not what Mommy called what they were doing.

Mommy said they left their apartment in Memphis to answer God's call. Birdie didn't like thinking about God. He was big and scary. Birdie didn't want God to call. The only person she wanted to talk to was her daddy, but the more they drove around, the more afraid Birdie was that Daddy might never be able to find her.

Mommy said they didn't need Daddy anymore because they had Brother Thom and the Good Lord. But Birdie didn't like Brother Thom. He never looked her in the eye the way her daddy did. He never picked her up or carried her piggyback. And he was the reason they were driving around so much. So he could spread the good word. But sometimes he said bad words. She'd heard him.

He was also the reason she wasn't able to go to school. She missed school almost as much as she missed her daddy. Some days she was so sad it hurt to breathe. She'd play hide-and-seek alone so she could cry without anybody telling her to grow up or shut up or pray for forgiveness.

The GoodFriends spent a lot of time praying for forgiveness. Her mommy, too.

She turned her head to the side to listen for the other children. She should have known they'd never look under the motor home. Their mothers didn't let them play near the vehicles, because some kid supposedly got run over before Birdie and her mother joined the Friends.

Birdie's mother didn't tell her where not to play. Mommy was sick again. Not throw-up sick; sad-in-her-head sick. She didn't pay much attention to Birdie when she was sad-in-the-head sick, so Birdie could play any-place she wanted.

But being under the motor home was getting boring. She yawned and was about to crawl out of her hidey-hole when suddenly the floor above her moved with a loud *thud, thud, thud.* A man's footsteps.

Her heart started to beat faster. This was Brother Thom's motor home. The one he shared with David's mom, and sometimes one or two of the other ladies. Her mommy visited him here every once in a while, but not lately. A fact that made her mother sad. Mommy had been crying a lot lately, and nobody told her to shut up and pray for forgiveness.

Birdie knew she'd be in big trouble if someone heard her—especially Brother Thom. And she was certain he could hear her, since she could hear the musical jingle of his phone followed by his voice—a voice that reached to the very back of the big Sunday meetings tent without him needing a microphone. Mommy said that would have made him seem too common.

"What is it with you people? What part of I don't have the money don't you get?"

Birdie closed her eyes to listen better. She knew it was wrong to listen to private conversations, but Birdie did it anyway. Her daddy once told her, "You have to listen to what people mean, Birdie. Not just what they say."

"Listen, asshole. I've sold everything we own. What am I supposed to do? Sell the children?"

Birdie swallowed hard. Her hands trembled and she

nearly lost her grip on the dirty metal thing she was holding to keep from falling.

"Yeah," Brother Thom said with a laugh. Not a happy-sounding laugh. "Well, if I thought I could get enough to be worth the bother, I might consider it. Even God wouldn't fault me for dumping Cheryl. She barely lifts a finger around here. All she does is read the Bible and cry. She stopped taking her meds because she's convinced God will heal her...through me, of course."

Cheryl was Birdie's mommy's name. She believed Brother Thom was the SecondComing. Whatever that meant.

"And that kid of hers," he added with a tone that made tears well up in Birdie's eyes. "Don't get me started. She's like a ghost, always hanging in the background, watching and listening. A redheaded ghost."

Birdie couldn't hold on to the metal bar anymore. She slipped to the ground but didn't move until she heard Brother Thom leave. She watched him walk to the cooking tent, where the mothers spent their afternoons.

She rolled out from under the trailer and raced into the bushes at the edge of the clearing. She didn't go far. Mommy said the woods were full of alligators and poisonous snakes. Birdie crawled under a bush and curled into a tight ball, trying her best to keep her sobs as quiet as possible. But one word wouldn't stay silent.

"Daddy."

CHAPTER ONE

REMY BOUCHARD STRETCHED with the sweet pleasure of awakening in her own bed. A cool Louisiana breeze drifted through her window, carrying the scent of magnolias and the sputtering hum of a neighbor's mower. She smiled even before she opened her eyes to the rich magenta hue of her ceiling.

"Home," she murmured, with a contented sigh.

Not that the past few weeks hadn't been an adventure she'd always remember. The Black Hills of South Dakota had left a mark on her heart, and with her twin sister, Jessie, relocating there, Remy knew she'd return to the area soon.

But not too soon.

First, she needed to figure out exactly what she wanted to do with the rest of her life. She'd left Louisiana a few weeks earlier intending to use the time and distance to get some perspective on her life. She was thirty-two years old, unmarried, unemployed, un…everything. And the worst part of all was she had no idea what she wanted to accomplish.

She'd had dreams once. A long time ago. She'd planned to marry the love of her life, settle right here in Baylorville to be near her mother and sisters, raise a family and become a teacher. A normal life. That's all she'd ever craved.

Normal. Like that was even possible, given my family.

She sat up, rubbed the sleep from her eyes and hopped out of bed. Her toes curled up from contact with the chilly wood surface. She'd let her sisters take whatever possessions of their mother's they wanted after Mama passed. Someone must have wanted the throw rug that had always been beside the bed.

"Are you finally awake, sleepyhead?" a voice called from somewhere on the first floor. Jessie. Her sister. Her twin.

"I'm awake, but I'm not coming down until I smell the coffee percolating," Remy hollered back. "Don't tell me you've forgotten how to brew real Louisiana coffee."

The best thing about Jessie was she'd never dodged a challenge in her life.

But given the lateness of the hour—good heavens, it was after eight—there was a chance the coffee was already made and transferred to the thermal carafe Mama had kept filled most every day of her life. A life that had ended some ten months earlier.

Tiptoeing to the closet, Remy threw open the double doors and stepped inside. This was the only closet of decent size in the house. Mama had speculated that it was originally planned as a nursery, but since the lone window was a tiny, nonfunctioning oval with leaded glass, Remy had her doubts.

There were two smaller bedrooms and one bath on

the second floor. The 1940s–era home wasn't a true New Orleans's shotgun because it had a second floor, but Baylorville wasn't N'Awlins, either. The quiet hamlet was made up of an old downtown with a few surviving businesses, such as Marlene's House of Beauty and a newly renamed Dollar Shoppe, which replaced the old Five and Ten. There was also a school and the post office. Outside town was Catfish Haven, which was, perhaps, Baylorville's only claim to fame. All in all, the town was nothing fancy—that's what New Orleans, some forty-odd miles to the southeast, was for.

She pulled her Donna Karan nightgown over her head and folded it neatly before putting it away in the chest of drawers.

"Is this fast enough for you?"

The smell of chicory beat Jessie through the door.

Remy popped her head out of the closet. "Wow. Your ankle must be a whole lot better if you can climb the stairs, carrying two cups."

"It's amazing what really good painkillers can do," Jessie responded. "But I already had my coffee with Cade and Shiloh before they took off to rent a truck, so I only had to carry one cup. Where do you want this?"

Remy quickly pulled on a pair of panties. "Set it on the dresser while I get presentable."

Jessie made a raspberry. "*Presentable*. That's so Mama. As long as we all looked presentable, people wouldn't know we were eating grits and greens instead of steak."

"You like grits," Remy reminded her, fastening her bra.

She grabbed the first thing she spotted in her closet. A simple, scoop-neck dress. The gauzy material was a muted floral print that was both feminine and pretty. She'd loved it once.

After slipping it over her head, she turned sideways to study her reflection in the full-length mirror as she buttoned the small, pearl-like buttons of the bodice.

"Does this make me look fey?"

"*Fey?* What the...fey is that?" Jessie grinned at her own wit. She was dressed in capri-length black yoga pants and an oversize Girlz On Fire T-shirt.

"You know. Odd. Different. A bit off."

Jessie hobbled to the bed with a pronounced limp. She plumped up a couple of pillows against the headboard, then sat and swung her leg around to rest her Ace-bandaged ankle on the cushioned softness of the white, eyelet comforter.

"The dress is fine. It's not something I'd wear, but it looks like you." She pointed at the cup she'd left on the nightstand. "Better drink that while it's hot. I added cocoa and steamed milk, the way you like it."

"Yum. Thanks."

"No problem. It's the least I could do for the hospitality. Now, tell me what's going on with you. What's this fey thing about?"

Remy took a sip before answering. "Perfect," she declared, sitting opposite her sister at the foot of the bed. She wasn't sure how to express her current sense of self-doubt without sounding like a complainer, or—worse—making Jessie feel somehow responsible for this sudden onset of ennui because Jessie's life, by comparison, was so full of promise.

"So…" she said, curling her foot under her so she could lean forward a bit. "Here's the deal. You know I'm happy for you and Cade, right?"

"Of course. You've told me about a million times since you got here and you keep trying to palm off furniture on me—a sure sign of love in our family."

"You're going to be glad I did. Someday. When you have more kids to pass these antiques down to, but that's not my point. The fact that you've found your significant other and are setting forth on the road to happily-ever-after—"

"In our rented moving van, towing Yota." Yota was the nickname affectionately given to the beloved Toyota Land Cruiser Jessie had owned since high school.

Remy brushed aside the comment. "With your lovely future stepdaughter and a new dog. Perfect. My point exactly. All of that makes my life look pretty pathetic by comparison."

Jessie opened her eyes wide with surprise. "Really? Is that what you think? Wow. I was so wrapped up in everything going on in my life, I never even considered… damn. I'm sorry for being so self-absorbed, Rem. What can I do?"

Remy rolled her eyes. "Nothing. This is why I haven't said anything to you, Jess. You should be self-absorbed. You're in love and you're moving forward in your life and I couldn't be happier. I don't want you to worry about me or fixate on how to fix things here when you're in South Dakota."

Jessie's furrowed brow told Remy her sister wasn't jumping at the chance to distance herself from this announcement, so she decided to spell out her plans a bit more clearly. Well, as clearly as possible, given the fact she wasn't certain what her life would look like in the future—near or distant.

"I plan to make some changes. Career, for sure. I love working with the elderly, but nursing homes aren't exactly the most happening place, you know," she said, trying to keep her tone light.

Jessie snickered softly in agreement.

"And I'm rethinking my plan to stay in Baylorville."

"No way. You've always loved it here."

Remy shrugged. "Probably because I felt accepted. Mama made sure of that. I was Marlene Bouchard's odd daughter, but that was okay. This is the South. Families are expected to have one or two slightly off members, right?"

Before Jessie could protest that Remy wasn't odd, Remy rushed to add, "I'm not feeling sorry for myself. I simply don't want to be known as that dream girl anymore. I want to be normal and have a normal life. And I don't think I can do that here."

Jessie's expression turned to pure horror. "Remy, you can't change who you are. Nobody wants you to. You're a wonderful person. I've always wished I was more like you. Everyone wished I was more like you.

You're even-tempered and kind and sweet. You're the family peacemaker."

Remy finished her coffee then stared at the bottom of her empty mug. That was exactly how she'd felt lately— empty. Useless. Unfulfilled. "Yeah," she said, looking up. "And do you know what my psychology teacher used to say about peacemakers? They use other people's drama to avoid facing their own problems. And it's true. Did I or did I not travel two days by bus to South Dakota to involve myself in the middle of your extremely dramatic business?"

"But you told me you had a dream. It woke you up and you knew I was in trouble. And you were right. How can that be a bad thing?"

Remy got up, set her cup on the bedside table, then walked to the French doors that led to a tiny, ridiculously impractical balcony that one of Mama's suitors built for her. She opened the doors with a flourish. But she didn't step outside. Instead, she looked at her sister.

"I lied. There, I said it. I lied about the dream, Jessie. I've always lied. I don't dream any more or any less than anyone else. I may remember my dreams a wee bit more clearly than most people, but that comes from practice. It certainly doesn't make me clairvoyant or psychic or gifted."

Jessie's expression turned stormy. And belligerent. Jess was always Remy's most fervent defender. More than one little boy went home from school with a fat lip after calling Remy "crazy" or "weird." "That's not true. You are gifted. You inherited your gift from—"

"Our great-great-aunt, the witch." Remy made a no-no motion with her hands. "Jess, there was never a witchy great-aunt. Mama made that up. She told me so before she died."

"What?"

"Oh, please, don't look so surprised. Everyone knew Mama bent the truth when it suited her needs."

"But she told people you could see things in your dreams. And you did, Rem," Jessie argued. "I remember all sorts of times when you saw stuff in your dreams and it turned out exactly the way you said it would. And... and what about Jonas Galloway? You saved his life when he fell down that well. You can't deny that."

Remy had known this conversation wasn't going to be easy—changing a lifetime's belief never was with someone as stubborn as Jessie—but now that she'd finally brought up the subject, her knees felt wobbly and her palms were starting to sweat. She stepped outside for a breath of fresh air and to grasp the wrought-iron railing.

"I can't say for sure what happened with Jonas," she said, raising her voice so Jessie didn't have to get up. "I was only eight at the time. Maybe I dreamed something or maybe Mama elaborated on my lucky guess. Maybe she made the whole thing up. I don't know."

"Well, I do. I was in the beauty parlor when you woke up from that nap, sobbing and wailing. All the ladies gathered around Mama to comfort you and find out what was wrong. When you finally quit crying so much, you told them you saw the little boy at the bottom of a well."

Remy had no memory of that whatsoever, but she'd heard it repeated often enough over the years that she could imagine it quite clearly. She also knew from her college courses on psychology and aging that memory changed over the years. Nothing was ever quite as clear as you thought it was.

"The human brain is an amazing thing. There are a number of explanations for what happened, if, in fact, you're recalling a true scene and not something your mind thinks happened."

Jessie sat up, angrily. "Are you calling me a liar?"

"No. Not at all. I'm saying there's a lot we don't understand about the mind and our subconscious. As an impressionable little kid, my brain might have filed away all the details I overheard the ladies in the beauty parlor talking about and suddenly put those facts together in a dream."

Jessie didn't say anything, but Remy could tell she remained unconvinced.

"Lucid dreaming has been around a long time, Jess. People can train themselves to remember their dreams. There are books to explain what the imagery means. It's like breaking a code. Maybe I've developed my inherent ability a bit more than most people over the years because Mama and her friends made such a big deal about what I supposedly saw. Then Mama added the witchy great-aunt element to turn me into a sort of minor celebrity. I don't know. But you have to admit I've never claimed to have any psychic abilities."

Jessie was silent for long enough that Remy thought she would have to drag out more evidence to persuade her twin she had no special talents. Then Jessie asked, "Why are you bringing this up now? Is it because Mama's gone and you don't have to pretend for her sake? Now, that I do understand."

"Maybe. Or maybe I'm tired of living up to other people's expectations. Sweet, demure, dreamy...*fey*. I'm not any of those things, Jess."

"Well, who are you then?"

Remy threw out her hands. "I don't know. But I'm going to find out. Starting today. My first order of business is finding a job. A new, exciting, interesting job that could be anywhere in the world."

"Travel? *You?* The girl who took a bus to South Dakota because planes cost too much and sometimes fall out of the sky?"

She stuck out her tongue. "I never said that last part. I'm not a hick, you know. I'd just lost my job. I was being thrifty. And responsible."

"Okay. You're not afraid to fly, but my point is you're a homebody. You've always loved this town. You couldn't wait to get back here when we left Nashville. I, on the other hand, immediately split for the West Coast. Are we doing some kind of role reversal here? I'm the one who's supposed to be footloose and fancy-free and you're the hearth-and-home kind of girl. What happened?"

Time for honesty. "I learned from watching you fall in love with Cade."

"Really? Like what?"

"I decided a real relationship—the kind that's going to last—has to be built on trust. When you cut that rope on the climbing tower and fell into Cade's arms, you trusted him to catch you."

Jessie made a face. "Sorta. I mean, it's not like I had a lot of choices at the time. But, you're right, he did catch me and I do trust him."

"What I'm saying is I will never be able to find that around here because nobody in this town knows who I really am." *Including me.*

Remy could tell by the widening of Jessie's eyes that she understood. "Wow. That's insightful, Rem. So, what does that mean, exactly? You're moving?"

"Maybe. Probably. All I know for sure is I'm done pretending. My whole life has been one big pretense."

"No. I don't agree."

"Yes, it has. I pretended not to be angry with Mama for what she did to me and Jonas. I was the good girl in the family, for heaven's sake. The freakin' peacemaker." It was hard for her to even think the word *peacemaker* without contempt. Who wanted to use other people's problems to deny the existence of their own? "A good girl wouldn't hate her mother for doing what she thought was best for her daughter, right?"

"You hated Mama, too?" Jessie's voice was so quiet Remy almost didn't hear the question.

"Why do you think I went to Nashville with you? I

was so mad I couldn't stand to be in the same room with her, let alone live in her house. But I couldn't admit that out loud."

Jessie let out a low whistle. "I knew you were upset, but I thought you were pissed off at Jonas. The way he went to Europe instead of sticking around to make sure you were okay."

It had been a double whammy of hurt. First, her mother broke up Remy and Jonas; then, Jonas broke Remy's heart by running away as if she were contemptible—toxic—because she was her mother's daughter. Reinforcing, she realized later, the deep inner self-doubt she'd always harbored.

"What Mama told us that night confirmed something I'd always suspected."

"What?" Despite her obvious reluctance, Jessie rose and approached the balcony—a clear sign she wouldn't abandon this discussion.

"That our family isn't normal. Mama was a slut. And we're bastards. Not only that, but she admitted to depriving of us of a chance to know our father. All those years she pretended he was dead, he wasn't. We could have had a relationship with him. But by the time she told us, he was gone. That's pretty damn low, wouldn't you say?"

"But you came home again, after Nashville."

"I wanted to go to college, and Mama offered to let me live here free of charge while I went to school. And she apologized for everything, tried to explain and justify her choices." She shrugged. "You know how persuasive she could be. And you were in California by then, so there went my backbone."

"The brains and the brawn," Jessie said wistfully. "Isn't that what it said under our yearbook pictures?"

Remy was still thinking about her mother, the choices Mama made and how they affected her daughters. "Don't you ever wonder what our lives would have been like if we'd had a real father—not a string of Mama's boyfriends, who often happened to be someone else's dad?"

"Not really. Did you talk to Mom about this when you sat with her at the hospital?"

Remy shook her head. "It was too late by then. I didn't want her to feel bad."

Jessie took a step closer and touched Remy's shoulder in a supportive way. "See? You can't help yourself, Rem. You're nice. You care about people. That's why you tried to help Mama's clients by telling them about your dreams."

"Maybe. I don't know. I'm done with all of that. I've decided to be more like you."

Jessie made a skeptical sound. "Me?"

"Yes. You do what you want and to hell with what people think. When we were little, everybody cut you slack because of your burns, but you know as well as I do that you had a chip on your shoulder before you were injured. I probably tried a little too hard to be easygoing to make up for your attitude."

Jessie looked aghast. "You were sweet because I wasn't? Really? That's wild. Because I actually used to resent you for being so nice. I should have known you weren't as perfect as you pretended to be. After all—" she winked "—you're my twin."

Remy smiled. She felt better after getting some of her pent-up feelings off her chest. She still didn't have a plan, per se, but telling Jessie about her intentions was a big first step. She'd have to explain her position to their three older sisters at some point.

Or, not. Maybe she'd take a page from the Jessie Bouchard playbook and act first, explain later.

Jessie hobbled into the room and resumed her seated position to rest her ankle. "So, what does this epiphany mean exactly? Are you going to sell Mama's house and move? I'd love to have you closer to me."

Remy followed her inside but left the doors open. "We can't sell it. The market is too depressed. Maybe I'll rent it out. First I have to finish fixing it up." She nodded toward her walls, which she'd painted a brilliant shade of ruby. In a way, choosing such a bold color—something her mother would not have chosen—had been Remy's first act of rebellion.

"But, don't worry. Whatever I decide, I'll keep you informed," she said. "We do own this place together."

Their mother had been so proud to be able to give her daughters a tangible legacy. As she rightly should. She'd started her own hair salon, expanded to include two other locations, paid off this house and raised five daughters almost entirely on her own. Whatever her faults—and there were many—Marlene had provided financially for her children.

Remy and Jessie talked about some much lighter

topics for a few minutes longer until a loud, insistent barking interrupted.

"Is that my dog?" Jessie asked, returning to the balcony.

Beau, Jessie's foundling, was ordinarily calm and quiet. The mature Catahoula hound rarely made a sound. She leaned past Remy to check out the side yard where the dog was able to run free.

"Hey, boy, what are you upset about?"

The leggy tricolor mutt paced along the hedge.

Jessie frowned. "I thought it might be Cade and Shiloh, but there's no sign of a big orange truck in the drive. Only Yota."

Remy's gaze was drawn to the nose of a shiny black car parked across the street. She couldn't identify the make or model because the hedge blocked her view, but the pristine paint job sparkled in the morning light.

"There's someone in the car across the street."

Jessie tensed visibly. A predictable reaction given the fact she'd recently faced down a hit man who had been causing her grief. "Who?"

"I don't know. The hedge is in the way. But I'm guessing your dog can sense that someone's there."

"Do you want me to go check this out? Maybe you have a stalker of your own."

Remy put a hand on her sister's arm. "Chill, Kung Fu Panda. I'll finish dressing and put on some makeup, then meet you downstairs. Once I'm presentable, we can take a stroll and check out the car—together."

Jessie rolled her eyes. "Get *presentable* and *take a stroll*. My God, you do sound like Mama."

Remy waited for Jessie to go inside before she closed and locked the French doors. "You know, Jess, despite comments like that, I'm going to miss you. I've really enjoyed these past few weeks together."

"Me, too. It was almost like the old days in Nashville."

They'd worked crappy jobs to fund their living expenses while they played heartfelt songs about love and loss—and fire—in out-of-the-way joints. Everyone said that was what you had to do to get big. But apparently their out-of-the-way joints were never frequented by scouts for the legitimate record labels. They lasted three years and had some wonderful memories between them, but no recording contract.

"Except for the waiting-tables part," Remy returned with a smile. "You really, really hated that."

"True. I was easily the worst waitress on the planet. Thank God you made enough in tips for both of us." Jessie laughed but turned serious almost immediately. "Remy, I wish you didn't think you had to change to make your life better. I love you just the way you are. I mean that."

Remy could tell her sister was speaking from the heart. She gave her a hug then picked up her cosmetic bag and started toward the door. "Don't worry. My psychology professor liked to say that personality was formed in the womb. Knowing me, I probably ushered the way for you to exit first. 'Please, Jessie, be my guest.

Yell extra loud and make a big fuss, then I'll come out nice and quiet so everyone likes me best.'"

They looked at each other for a moment in silence. Remy hadn't planned for quite that much frankness, but she didn't retract the comment, either.

Jessie threw back her head and laughed. "You know, you're probably right. That is too funny. And a little sad, but I'm not going to think about what I can't change." She grabbed Remy's empty cup on her way to the door. "Hey, I meant to ask. I found Mama's glass cake plate in the cupboard. You know I can't bake for squat, but I thought I might take it if you don't care. It reminds me of her. In a good way."

"It's yours. Take it."

Jessie looked at her a moment, then grinned. "Thanks. You're a nice person, Remy. Whatever big changes you decide to make, try not to lose that part of your personality."

Remy didn't reply. Instead, she walked into the bathroom and closed the door. She felt like a traveler at a giant crossroads. Seeing her sister in love—really, truly, head-over-heels in love with Cade—had been the tipping point for Remy. Their completeness made her realize she wanted a full life, not the half-life she'd allowed herself. Not the kind their mother had lived, always holding back a part of her heart because the one love of her life left, never to return.

Remy knew how difficult it was to change old patterns. Her teacher had called this an addiction to the familiar. If Remy didn't initiate a change, she might very easily become her mother—filling up the hours of her day with other people's worries and drama and filling her nights with unavailable men who conveniently made themselves available to take the place of the only man she ever loved.

CHAPTER TWO

JONAS GALLOWAY SLUMPED down in the seat of his Dodge Challenger and drummed his fingers on the steering wheel. He wasn't the indecisive type. Normally. But nothing about his life had been normal for twenty-plus months.

Being dropped into the middle of the Iraq desert with his National Guard unit was craziness in and of itself. He still hadn't quite come to grips with everything he'd seen and dealt with there. The heat, the dust, the death, the fear, frustration and anxiety—24/7—was just a start. But he'd survived in one piece and brought his entire squad back alive. Something to be proud of. And he would have gladly embraced the praise of his coworkers and friends if he'd come home to find Birdie waiting for him.

Birdie. His nickname for his seven-and-a-half-year-old daughter, Brigitte Leann Galloway.

He glanced at the small, colorful frame attached to his dash. A treasure from her preschool days, adorned with globs of primary paint and bursts of purple glitter, it was one of the most tangible reminders he had of his creative, delightfully imaginative, gifted child.

"Purple is your special color, Daddy. I see it when I close my eyes and think of you," she'd told him at the time.

Although the frame was several years old, the photo it held was the most current he had. He'd cropped and printed it from an email Cheryl, his ex-wife, had sent him in Iraq. The pixel quality wasn't great, but the image had the power to bring him to the brink of tears. His daughter's wide smile showed an age-appropriate mix of baby teeth, recently lost gaps in the gum line and a couple of new, gigantic-looking permanent teeth.

The picture was his most valued possession at the moment. It was the last one he had of the little girl who, along with her mother, had vanished five months earlier.

He shifted uneasily. The heat was starting to build inside the car, despite the fact he had all the windows lowered. He was killing time, waiting for what his mother would have called a "decent" hour before knocking on the door of the house across the street.

His mother had always preached good manners and etiquette while Jonas was growing up. He knew she would have been appalled if he went visiting before nine in the morning. Bad enough he was showing up unannounced.

"Manners say a lot about a person, Jonas," his mother often said. "And the person who raised him."

The person who raised him—nearly single-handedly, Jonas acknowledged—was Charlotte Gainsford Galloway of the Mobile Gainsfords. Mother had tacked on that qualifier until the day he asked why he'd never met any of the Mobile Gainsfords. Tearfully, she'd explained that her parents had disowned her when she ran away with his father—a movie-star handsome, smooth-talking car salesman—instead of going to college, as planned. In the years that followed, she made numerous attempts to re-establish contact with family members, but after her parents died, she lost touch with her siblings completely.

Jonas had thought about tracking down her older brother and baby sister using the internet, but it hardly seemed worth the effort at this point. His mother was suffering from Alzheimer's or early onset dementia. Two diagnoses that seemed to mean the same thing—his mother's cognitive, thinking functions were sporadic, at best, and on the decline. In a way, she was as lost to him as he feared his baby girl might become if he didn't locate Birdie soon.

He'd never felt more alone and helpless. Well, except for that one time, when he was eight.

He closed his eyes and let his head fall against the headrest. The memory remained one of the most vivid of his childhood. Not surprising, he imagined, given he'd nearly died.

His parents were still married at the time, but his father was gone a lot. When Dad was around, the tension between his parents was tangible; Jonas would lie in bed at night with a pillow over his head to block the sound of their fights. Not gentle arguments befitting his society-conscious mother, but loud, skillet-throwing skirmishes that made him want to run away.

So, one day, he did.

He rose before dawn, made himself a peanut butter sandwich and headed into the woods behind his house. He'd been exploring the area the week before with some friends from school. Sorta friends. Boys Jonas wanted to be his friends. Two were older. They knew everything, including the location of an old well that had gotten covered up and forgotten near an abandoned farm that Jonas's mother had forbidden him to go near.

They'd tossed rocks at the rotten boards until one cracked in half, then they'd dared the youngest of the group—Jonas—to make a wish and drop a quarter into the abyss.

He'd been too afraid to accept the challenge and had run home. Naturally, the other boys had teased him mercilessly the next day. So, his first stop on the road to his new life would be the well—to prove that he was brave enough to go on.

He even knew exactly what he'd drop into the well when he made his wish—a small oval St. Christopher medal that belonged to his father. Jonas had carefully removed the medallion from the cheap chain—converted dog tags from last year's G.I. Joe Halloween costume—then knelt on the soft, moist ground near the yawn of an opening. He'd had to stretch out a long way because the medal was so small—no bigger than some of the fishing lures Jonas had seen in the hardware store. He'd leaned closer, straining to hear a splash, but unfortunately, that extra bit of weight on the well opening had proved too much for the rotted timbers.

He didn't remember falling. He didn't remember hitting bottom, but he could still recall with surprising clarity waking up in a black pit with a small uneven oval of blue above him and a wet, sandy, dead-leaf-lined well floor below him.

The walls were slick with moisture. Roots stuck out in places, but none were low enough for him to reach. He now had a new definition of *alone*.

It took rescuers twenty-nine hours to find him. He'd later learned that most of that time was spent dealing with his hysterical mother and organizing a search party. The actual finding was made simple once the men in charge took heed of a local beautician who insisted they listen to her daughter. A child Jonas's age.

"He's at the bottom of a well," Remy Bouchard was reputed to have said.

Jonas looked at the house on the corner lot across from where he was parked.

He hadn't known Remy at the time he fell in the well. They were in the same grade but had different teachers. He'd seen her on the playground, but one of his friends— Tommy Fergen, he thought—told him she was queer in the head and could put a hex on you if you looked at her funny. Jonas had kept his distance.

He didn't meet her the day of the rescue, either. But his mother had dragged him to the Bouchards'—a different house, not this place—to thank them. Remy wasn't at all what he'd been expecting. She was tiny, for one thing. With a halo of white-blond hair that looked too perfect to be real. And she still had her baby teeth. He remembered that strange fact way too clearly.

He remembered a lot about that day because it was the day he fell in love with Remy Bouchard. He never told anyone, of course. He never acted on his feelings until that night in high school when they bumped into each other at a hayride and wound up holding hands.

They'd done more than that eventually. They'd kissed until their lips were puffy and numb. They'd explored each other's body with joyful curiosity and a certain amount of pride. And, then, mere days away from their planned "first time" date, Remy's mother dropped the bomb of a lifetime in their laps, changing everything.

Jonas's mother had unwittingly provided the ultimate escape from the nightmare he'd been forbidden to tell her about. As a graduation gift she took him on a whirlwind tour of Europe. Upon his return, he did the responsible thing. Instead of going after Remy, who had moved to Nashville with her sister, he joined the National Guard to help pay for college.

He hadn't seen her since that fateful day. How many years? Fifteen? He'd never attended any of their class reunions. The only person he would have wanted to see was the one person he had no business in the world seeing.

The same person he was now about to beg for help.

He glanced at his watch. It was time.

He got out of the car and marched across the street, grateful for the breeze that touched the dampness across his back, producing an odd chill. He plucked at the fabric of his black, short-sleeve cotton shirt and rolled his shoulders, collecting himself. He looked down at his knee-length shorts and rugged, waterproof sandals.

Did he look like a tourist? Probably, but readapting to Louisiana humidity after his stay in a desert was taking time. Plus, he was on leave from his job. His suit and ties were retired until he found Birdie.

He knocked on the old-fashioned wood screen door. The sound echoed through the home's entry and elicited an excited barking from the rear of the house. The dog he'd heard earlier when he first pulled up, he assumed.

There were voices—including a loud, "Quiet, Beau"—coming from what he supposed was the kitchen. He'd been in homes like this one on the job. Insurance adjusters saw everything imaginable in the course of a day—even outright stupidity. He'd also been attacked at least twice by dogs that should have known better, since he was a huge improvement over their owners.

The buzz of female chatter made its way down the corridor, followed by footsteps. Two women. He recognized them both immediately. Remy and Jessie. As different as twins could be, but still alike in so many ways.

The moment they reached the openness of the entry and had a good look at him they froze. Jessie threw an arm across her sister's chest, like a mother trying to keep her child from flying forward in a car coming to a stop too fast.

Remy tilted her head and blinked, as if not quite believing her eyes. "Jonas? Jonas Galloway?"

"Yep. It's me. How are you doing, Remy? Jessie?" He shuffled his feet, wishing he'd used the time in the car to prepare what he needed to say. "I'm sorry to bother you so early on a Saturday. Would you happen to have a few minutes for an old friend?"

Jessie stepped forward, crossing her arms. "An old friend?" she repeated. "Jonas Galloway, you're the reason my sister is all alone and never married. You can't sashay back into her life like nothing happened."

The revelation was both painful and enlightening. He had no idea what to say to that.

Remy did. She shoved her sister aside with a force that seemed to surprise them both. Jessie staggered slightly. "That's the dumbest thing you've ever said. Where the heck is Cade with your moving van? I swear, girl." She shook her head.

Amazingly, her hair was still long, still blond and still gorgeous, Jonas couldn't help noticing when she opened the door for him.

"Pretend you didn't hear that, Jonas. I'm not the loser my sister has made me out to be, and you did not ruin my life. Just to be clear."

Jessie's mouth opened and closed a few times but whatever she'd hoped to offer in her own defense was put on hold by the sound of a truck pulling into the driveway.

"They're back," she exclaimed, grinning as she headed for the door. He noticed she had an odd gait and he realized her ankle was wrapped. Even so, she managed a good speed and Jonas had no choice but to step inside or be mowed over—gimpy foot or no gimpy foot.

"Hi, you two," she called, hobbling toward the moving van, where a man and teenage girl waited. "You took long enough."

"Jessie's married?"

Remy shook her head. "Not yet. She and Cade have to decide a few details, but I think everything will work out great in the end."

"And if anyone would know, it would be you, right?

You're the Dream Girl of Baylorville, Louisiana. Aren't you?"

"Oh, for heaven's sake," she shouted, clamping her hands to her hips, which made the flowing material of her dress dance around her knees. "See? This is exactly what Jessie and I were just talking about. Once you get a reputation in a small town, it is impossible to change people's minds."

She pivoted on one heel and stomped to the edge of the porch. She leaned over the railing, as if addressing the entire town, and yelled at the top of her voice, "I am not a psychic."

The hem of her skirt came up, revealing the very legs he'd never stopped dreaming about. Still as gorgeous as they had been fifteen years ago. He couldn't help but look. And remember. Until she spun around and caught him staring.

Her eyes narrowed and she advanced on him with the sort of intensity he'd witnessed in combat. If looks could kill…

A second later, the realization struck him that he was turned on. Good grief. His mind had snapped. Not only was he here on a mission of life and death, he wasn't over her. He still wanted her.

Remy.

His goddamned sister.

CHAPTER THREE

"OKAY," REMY SAID, returning from her outburst to stop a foot in front of him. "I don't know why you're here, but let's get one thing straight. I don't read tarot cards. I don't predict the future. And I don't see dead people."

Jonas was still trying to collect his highly valued, completely absent equanimity, so before he could respond, she added, "If you want to know where someone is buried, call a cadaver dog."

The thought made a chill run down his spine. "But you do find people. You found me."

Her green eyes narrowed with anger or frustration, he couldn't tell which. Whatever emotion it was, she felt it passionately. A memory of kissing her jumped into his brain and wouldn't leave. They'd come within a single layer of silk panties from consummating their feelings for each other. And they'd set the date for that, too. Until her mother intervened.

"So everybody says," she snapped. "But the only person who really knows for sure what happened that day at the beauty parlor is dead."

Her mother. Marlene Bouchard, the woman he considered the Machiavelli of Baylorville. He'd read the obit online.

"And like I said, I don't have a direct line to the great beyond." She paused and gave him a serious look, her lips pressed together. "Is that why you're here? To talk to someone who has crossed over? Oh, my God, your mother—"

"No. Mom's still with us...more or less."

She put a hand to her breast. She looked relieved. This was more like the Remy he remembered. Kind and concerned about people. Nice. Jessie was the fly-off-the-handle kind of person. Touchy.

"So, why are you here?"

A reasonable question.

"My daughter is missing. I need your help to find her."

There. A reasonable answer. Simple. A small favor for an old friend.

Remy took a step back. Could she read the desperation and fear he tried his level best to keep pushed way, way down below the surface? She'd been good at reading him. Did she guess how close he was to losing it?

"I'm sorry to hear that, Jonas. Really, I am. But I can't help you. I wish I could, but I can't."

No. That was not the truthful answer. She *could* help but was choosing not to. Was this a way to pay him back for running away when her mother sabotaged their lives?

"She's only seven. She's in trouble. I can feel it. Please, Remy, don't punish Birdie because you hate me."

"Hate?" she repeated softly.

She turned, as if preparing to run or call for help. He

didn't blame her. He probably sounded crazy. Desperate. He was both. He stepped in her path to block her escape and grabbed both her arms. Partly to steady himself. Partly to beg for her help.

"Jonas, let go of me. Stop. What—"

He pulled her to him, hard. As though she was the last person standing in a fight to the death. To let go would mean giving up everything he'd fought so hard to hold on to. He couldn't…not now.

He put his mouth close to her ear and whispered, "My little girl is missing. Something bad is going to happen. I know it. You're the one person in the world I didn't think I'd have to explain that to. Please, Rem, please. Help me."

"Holy moly," a voice exclaimed. "Jonas, let her go. Did you forget something? Like the fact you guys are related?"

REMY HEARD HER SISTER'S voice. She couldn't quite make out the words, though, because her head was reeling from a lack of oxygen. And she hoped panic—not the fact that the breath in her lungs evaporated the moment Jonas touched her—was to blame for her giddiness. Even after Jonas let go of her and dropped his arms, Remy struggled to remember how to breathe.

"Rem," Jessie said, taking her arm. "Are you okay? You're white as a ghost. Let's go inside and sit down. What did he do to you? One minute you're yelling at the neighbors and the next you're making out with him."

Remy put the brakes on, glancing over her shoulder at

Jonas. He looked so lost, shell-shocked and helpless. Her heart twisted in a way she hadn't felt since she watched her mother pass away.

"No. We didn't. He didn't." She brushed off her sister's hand. "I'm okay, Jess. Really. It's Jonas who is in trouble."

His back was to her but she could tell he was struggling to regain control over his emotions. She'd never known him to lose control—ever. Even that night when her mother delivered the most gut-wrenching news of their young lives—that she'd had an affair with Jonas's father nine months before Jessie and Remy were born—Jonas had been a pillar. No tears. No ranting. He'd held Remy's hand as they walked to his car. He'd told her they should sleep on it, maybe look into some kind of test or something. Of course, his *or something* turned out to be a trip to Europe with his mother.

"Everybody has their unique way of mourning," Jessie had said facetiously when they found out he was gone.

Remy had taken his leaving as proof that he didn't love her as much as she'd loved him. Or worse, that he considered her to be her mother's daughter.

But that was old news. Water long under the bridge. The pain she heard in his voice now told her how much he loved his daughter and feared for her safety.

"Jonas's daughter is missing," she told her sister. "He wants me to help find her."

"Because of your gift." But her tone was softer, less defensive. Remy knew her sister wasn't as tough as she liked people to think. And Jessie had a real soft spot in her heart for kids.

"Because she found me," Jonas said, facing them. His shoulders were straight, his posture erect. She could almost see the invisible outline of his military uniform. She didn't know what branch he belonged to, but she had seen his photo displayed on his mother's dresser at the nursing home where she used to work.

"Everyone in Baylorville knows the story," he went on. "Remy fell asleep then woke up, crying and carrying on about a little boy in a well. Me." He hooked his thumb toward his chest. "My mother repeated the story a million times or more. You snapped out of your trance and told the police exactly where to find me."

"I never went into a trance." But she couldn't bring herself to repeat her doubts as she had earlier with Jessie. She knew how much Jonas hated her mother. The very last words they'd said to each other before he drove away had been about Marlene.

"I can't believe that whore is your mother, Rem. I'm sorry. That's a crappy word, but it's the truth. Everybody knows she sleeps around. And to get pregnant by her friend's husband when her friend was also pregnant... that's too much, man. Too much." Then he'd left.

And, now, he was back, asking her to be the very person she didn't want to be.

"That happened a long time ago, Jonas. I was a child."

"The same age my daughter is," Jonas said, meaningfully. "She's lost, like I was. Afraid. If someone like me—an ordinary dad—can sense this, so can you, because you're special. You are, Rem. You always have been. Please, please say you'll help."

She pressed her fingertips to her temples. No one had ever begged her to find a missing child. Her mother's friends had always asked for signs, some sort of supernatural permission to make choices they probably would have made anyway. This was different. Dangerous. The risk of failure was far too great.

"Jonas, you don't understand. Sometimes I have dreams that I can remember when I wake up. And sometimes the images in my dreams make sense to people who want them to mean something. I've never, ever claimed otherwise. And if I told you I saw something in a dream that you thought pertained to your daughter and it turned out to be wrong or it led you on a wild goose chase in the opposite direction, you'd blame me. You'd hate me more than you already do."

He stepped closer, ignoring Jessie completely. "I never hated you, Rem. I couldn't if I wanted to. Your mother? Yes. I'm not sorry Marlene is dead. My only regret is I never told her exactly what I thought of her. But none of what happened between us was your fault."

"He's right, you know," Jessie said. "And, not to detract from the seriousness of Jonas's situation, but you two do realize that technology has made certain advances, right? A DNA test would prove once and for all whether Mom was telling the truth that night."

Jonas's eyebrows came together. "Is there some reason you think Marlene lied?"

Jessie threw Remy a look. Funny, this was yet another subject they'd talked about earlier.

"Jessie and I have come to the conclusion that Mama had—how do the politicians put it?—a questionable association with the truth."

Jonas continued to frown but after a few seconds he shrugged. "Whatever. I don't care about the past. I know I probably should, but my only focus at the moment is finding my daughter. If you can't help me, then…I'll keep looking."

He started to leave but paused to pull something from his pocket. "I know this is a long shot, but…well…this is Birdie," he said, holding out a photograph.

Remy's hand started to shake even before she touched it. Nerves, anticipation, empathy…she didn't know. But the moment she saw the picture, her vision blurred and her heart jolted.

Red hair. She had red hair.

Remy pressed her lips together as hard as she could to keep from crying out.

She very rarely recalled color in her dreams. Images, yes. Movement. Structures. Voices. Dialogue. But never hair color.

Until recently.

"Uh-oh," Jessie put an arm around Remy's shoulders in support.

"What?" Jonas asked, his gaze never leaving Remy.

Jessie let her chin drop so her head touched Remy's. "I don't know for sure," she told Jonas, "but I'm guessing Remy has seen this little girl in her dreams. Right, Rem?"

Remy kept her gaze on the photo. "Two nights ago."

Jessie patted her back. "I'm sorry, Remy. I know you wanted to put this dream thing behind you, but, well, you know what they say about the best-laid plans."

JONAS HAD NO IDEA WHAT Jessie was talking about and he didn't care. A jolt of electricity passed through him, jump-starting the tiny bit of remaining hope he'd been nursing. "You've seen her? You saw Birdie in one of your dreams?" Jonas reached for Remy's arm. "When? What happened? Was she okay?"

Despite her bad ankle, Jessie managed to shove her sister behind her and deflect Jonas's hand. "No way. No touching her. Step back and take a deep breath. She's not a circus sideshow act. If you can't control yourself, my cowboy fiancé has a rope and he's not afraid to use it."

Jonas didn't appreciate being bossed around by Jessie Bouchard, but he wasn't a fool. He needed Remy's help, and if that meant going through her twin, so be it. He'd dealt with Jessie in the past and he could do it again.

"So? What now? How do we do this?"

Jessie looked at her sister. "Rem?"

"I need to sit down."

She dashed inside as though she might be sick. Did thinking about her dreams make her sick? Or had she seen something too horrible to recall? He was terrified to ask. He wished he could remember more from high school, but Remy always had downplayed her supposed gift. "It's a scam," she once told him. "A parlor trick that Mama dreamed up to increase her business. You don't believe any of this, do you?"

He hadn't then, but here he was, fifteen years later, asking for help from the one person who had every right to hate him. He'd treated her badly because of something that wasn't her fault. Too bad he'd been so damn confused and hurt he'd lashed out at the wrong person. Unfortunately, the one person he should have lashed out at—his father—was dead and buried.

"Are you going in?" Jessie asked.

Did he have any choice? He wished like hell he could walk away. He didn't know if seeing Remy was causing his head to ache or the fact he hadn't a good night's sleep in weeks. It probably didn't help that he'd been living on coffee and fast food. He was a mess, and that meant he wasn't going to be on top of his game when Birdie needed him most.

"She has your picture," Jessie prompted.

"What's your agenda? One minute you're accusing me of incestuous intentions, the next you're encouraging me to follow your sister into the house."

She looked chagrined. "Honestly? I don't know what to think. But I'm sick of not knowing the truth about anything. And, despite what Remy says, I do think you broke her heart and she's never completely gotten over you. So maybe helping you reunite with your daughter— and, presumably, your wife—she'll be able to close that door for good."

His wife. Cheryl was his *ex*-wife, and he didn't give a damn what happened to her once he had Birdie back.

"Jessie," a girl in her early teens called out from the corner of the house near the garage, "are we taking your bike? Or is this Remy's?"

"That one is Rem's, Shiloh. But mine is somewhere in the garage. Hold on. I'll be right there." She turned and looked at him. "The next move is up to you, Jonas. A part of me wants to tell you to take a hike and leave my sister alone, but you probably won't do that, so…" She glanced toward the open door. "Tell her not to do anything I wouldn't do—at least until the DNA results are in."

She grinned and hopped down the steps, the same way she'd come up.

Jonas knew he didn't have a choice. He'd come here for a reason, and a good insurance investigator followed every lead—not just the convenient ones.

He stepped into the foyer of the home he'd last visited fifteen years earlier and looked around. The place had a completely different feel to it. Bigger. More open. Normal, he decided. The last time he'd been there, the rooms had been dwarfed by an abundance of furniture. Huge dark pieces that didn't match each other.

He turned toward the parlor. The spot where Marlene Bouchard had changed his life forever.

Remy was standing beside the simple, white brick fireplace, her gaze still focused on the picture in her hand.

"Okay, Remy, tell me what's going on. First you say

you don't have dreams and I'd be risking my daughter's life to believe you if you did tell me anything. Then you turn white as a sheet and look like you're going to faint the minute you see Birdie's picture. So, yes or no? Have you seen my daughter in your dreams?"

"I don't know."

His headache spiked and he gave in to fatigue and dropped into the room's lone chair, an overstuffed leather armchair. "That's not exactly the answer I was looking for."

"I can't help it. I've been actively trying not to remember my dreams, Jonas. After Mama passed away, I decided she was the only person who actually believed all that dream-girl nonsense and I needed to move on, find out who I really am."

He bit back a swearword that seemed appropriate.

She held up the photo, waving it slightly. "But a few nights ago, I had a tiny, fleeting glimpse of a little girl with bright red hair. Nothing of any significance happened. She sort of popped in and popped out in the background, like a...spirit," she said, obviously choosing the word with care. "I didn't even remember seeing her until you showed me this picture."

He believed her. "Then, you can't say for sure it was Birdie?"

"No. I can't."

Damn. He shouldn't have come here, wasted his time. All because a Christmas card somehow got mixed in with the file he was compiling about Cheryl and her stupid church. The shiny photo greeting featured a dozen or so doctors, nurses and staff members at Shadybrook, the assisted-living center where his mother resided. A familiar face with a sweet smile and long blond hair had stirred up memories and, unfortunately, a worthless hunch.

"Are you still working at Shadybrook?" he asked.

She looked surprised by the question. "No. I'm going to start job hunting on Monday. Why do you ask?"

He shrugged. "I don't know. Maybe that explains why you saw a kid with red hair in your dream. Mom has a bunch of pictures of Birdie around her room."

She seemed to contemplate that possibility. "That makes sense. Except for the fact I haven't spoken with your mother since they moved her to the full-care wing last fall. You came back for that, didn't you?"

He nodded. A quick, cheerless trip that involved more time on an airplane than on the ground, a flurry of paperwork and an all-too-brief, tearful reunion with Birdie.

"But," she said, obviously forcing a smile, "I suppose it's possible. The subconscious is full of trivia that can pop to the surface for no apparent reason."

He had the distinct impression she didn't believe a word she was saying. He knew it was time to leave, but he couldn't make himself move. He felt mired in a web of dread. Similar to how he felt the entire time he was in Iraq and Afghanistan.

He was responsible for every man in his unit. He didn't always know where they were or if they were in trouble, caught in a firefight, trusting the wrong person, ambushed or wounded. The knot in his gut never lessened, and now it was back.

He pressed on a tender spot just above his belt line to ease the discomfort as he looked around, searching for any sort of distraction. "What happened to all the furniture that used to be in here? Were you robbed? I hope you put in a claim with your insurance company."

She smiled. "The chair you're sitting on is the only one I kept."

Was it the same one her mother sat in that night? No, he didn't think so. He could picture Remy sitting beside him on the red velvet, tufted settee. And he'd nearly broken his neck stumbling over an ugly, lumpy footstool with frayed gold tassels around the bottom in his haste to get away after Marlene made that announcement. He'd kicked it violently, sending it flying into a big wooden hutch of some sort.

Despite the depth of his negative feelings later on, when he'd been dating Remy, he'd secretly admired Marlene's style. He'd found the eclectic and slightly bohemian tone a welcome change from the stifling formality of his mother's rigidly proper decor.

Remy walked into the adjoining dining room and returned a moment later with a simple, straight-back chair—more Ikea than estate sale—and placed it a few feet to his left. "When Mama passed, she left Jessie and me this house with all its contents. I decided to let my sisters take whatever they wanted."

"The Bullies? Do you still call them that?"

She seemed surprised that he remembered the nickname she and Jessie had for their three older sisters. Since he was an only child, he'd had a hard time understanding how her siblings could be so mean and spiteful to the much younger twins. But apparently both Jessie and Remy had felt uniformly picked on—hence the descriptive appellation.

"Actually, they call themselves that now. I think they consider it a badge of honor or something. Their children think that's the funniest thing ever."

He smiled. Birdie would have laughed, too. "Do they live around here?"

"Close enough to be a nuisance," she said, but since this was Remy, he was pretty sure she didn't mean it.

Or maybe she'd changed. How the hell would he know? He'd made a rational, logical decision to never see Remy again—for both their sakes, he'd told himself at the time. Young kids thought they had all the answers, right?

"May I ask you a question?" Remy asked.

Jonas nodded.

"How missing is she?"

That question.

"Missing enough to make me qualify for the Worst Father of the Year award," he said, softly. He'd spent his whole life swearing he wouldn't be like his dad, and he wasn't. He was worse.

CHAPTER FOUR

REMY MADE AN IMPATIENT gesture Jonas remembered from before. "I don't believe that for a minute. What I'm asking is how did she go missing? Did she wander away from her mother while you were gone? Was she kidnapped? Does her mother have her somewhere?"

"The last. Her mom took her. And that's one of the reasons I'm so frantic. As unfair as it sounds, Cheryl— my ex—hasn't officially broken the law. Nobody is willing to call this a kidnapping, even though Cheryl took Birdie out of the state without my permission."

"Is she the custodial parent?"

"Temporarily. When we divorced, I agreed to joint custody because I thought that was in Birdie's best interest. But Cheryl has some health issues and I wound up with Birdie ninety percent of the time. Which," he quickly added, "was great. Everything was good until my National Guard unit was called up."

He decided not to tell her the whole, convoluted tale of his failed marriage, instead, sticking to the current facts. "I transferred custody solely to Cheryl while I was out of the country."

"Where did you say you were?"

"Iraq and Afghanistan. We got home six weeks ago.

And from what I've been able to piece together, Cheryl got involved with a religious cult shortly before the holidays. The group calls themselves The GoodFriends of Christ, or GoodFriends, for short. They remained in the Memphis area for a month or so. Then right before school was set to resume, Cheryl hocked what she could, abandoned everything else in the apartment I paid a year's rent in advance for and basically disappeared."

"How did you find out?"

Her questions came like a practiced investigator's.

"I'd made arrangements with friends to check on Birdie every few weeks. They'd stop by with food, toys, books—little things I'd left with them before I was deployed. When they realized Cheryl and Birdie were gone, they called the police."

"When did you last hear from her?"

This was the part his buddy at the Memphis P.D. found the hardest to get his head around. "Cheryl has been emailing me, off and on. Twice she agreed to meet me and bring Birdie but never showed up. Three weeks ago, she let me talk to Birdie using Skype."

"And Birdie was okay?"

He knew his daughter, and even though he hadn't seen Birdie for several months, he recognized the signs of stress—and fear. "She seemed healthy enough but quiet. Reserved. Like she was afraid to say anything. She's smart and very sensitive to her mother's problems. She's always tried to take care of her mom, which is nice, but a kid should be a kid, right?"

She didn't answer. He didn't expect her to.

"Wasn't your wife supposed to clear any move with you before she took your child to another state?"

"Yes, but, you know what government agencies are like right now—overworked and understaffed. I have a family lawyer who has filed all the proper papers, but who's going to invest the time and money to track down a mom when the kid isn't in imminent danger?"

"What about school? It's against the law to keep a child out of school, isn't it?"

"Not if you fill out the paperwork to do homeschooling. But that's actually the scariest part for me, because Cheryl was homeschooled. She hated it and blamed her parents for depriving her of what she felt was a normal upbringing. 'Crazy hippies,' she called them. I really question her state of mind if she's putting Birdie through something she hated."

"Do you have any idea where your daughter is?"

He hunched forward, weaving his fingers together. He didn't know why he was telling her all of this if she wasn't prepared to help, although it actually felt good to have someone to talk to. "No. The homeschool form Cheryl filled out was filed with the State of Florida, but the address she gave was bogus. My friend who works with the Memphis P.D. ran a check on the GoodFriends. He said they haven't held an official revival meeting for nearly two months."

"They've disappeared?" Her eyes looked alarmed.

"Apparently. Do you see now why I need your help? Any lead would help point me in the right direction."

She swallowed. "Or send you off to Timbuktu when they were actually camped right down the street."

"Yeah, I heard you on the porch. You're afraid of some kind of backlash. But the fact is I don't have a lot of options at the moment. I'm not a sit-around-and-wait kind of guy. My dad used to say, 'Do something, even if it's wrong.'" He let out a harsh snort. "Ironic, huh? Given what he did with your mom."

She crossed her legs and sat forward, her foot bouncing in a nervous habit. She used to call it sedentary pacing—a way to free up her subconscious thought process by distracting the rational, thinking part of her brain. "Why are you so sure something is wrong? Maybe she lost her phone. Or the computer she was using died. Or they're camping in a remote part of the state with no cell service."

He shook his head. "If Cheryl was a normal person, maybe. But she's been diagnosed with clinical depression. As long as she takes her pills, she can function pretty normally. But I checked with her doctor. Her prescription hasn't been filled for two months. Yes, she might have gotten another scrip, but what if she isn't taking her meds?

"Or, what if someone has convinced her to stop taking them? There's no way of predicting what might happen. When she's gone off her meds in the past, Cheryl usually landed on her feet—or, at least, under psychiatric care. But this time she has Birdie with her. Who's going to protect my daughter?"

Remy chewed on her bottom lip. "Would Birdie know to call you?"

"If she had access to a phone, yes. Absolutely. I made her memorize my number before I left for Iraq. And every day that passes that I don't hear from her makes me that much more worried."

She seemed concerned, but not completely convinced that he wasn't overreacting to the situation—exactly the way the FBI had treated him. "As a father, I know something's wrong. I feel it in here," he said, tapping the middle of his chest. "I can't explain how or why. I honestly thought you'd be the one person who would understand." He looked her straight in the eyes. "Remember when I asked you how you found me in the well? What did you say?"

"I don't remember."

"I do. You said you closed your eyes and dreamed me."

"I don't remember."

A lie. He could see the truth in her eyes.

"You described the black roots that looked like witches' hands trying to keep me down at the bottom. You said the walls were greasy and cold. And you said if they didn't find me soon, I'd give up hope and die. And you were right. I was ready to give up."

Her hands were folded in her lap, her knuckles white from gripping the material of her skirt.

"You found me when I was lost. Now I need your help again. Couldn't you at least try?"

She jumped to her feet and thrust Birdie's picture at

him. "I don't know." She glanced around like a cornered animal, fearful and ready to bolt. "This morning I woke up, positive my life was going to be different from this point on. This is so not what I meant by different."

She threw up her hands and stalked toward the staircase. "I have to think. You can wait. Or leave your number. Or talk to Jessie… I don't know."

Then she was gone.

Jonas ran a finger along his daughter's photo. He felt drained and defeated, not yet to the point where he could chart a new course. Getting here had taken nearly all the energy he had.

He'd go to Shadybrook, he guessed. See his mother. Mom still had lucid moments. The last time they'd talked, she'd mentioned her good friend Marlene Bouchard as if the two had recently had lunch.

He knew Charlotte had remained close to Marlene over the years, apparently accepting the reason Jonas had given her for breaking up with Remy. "We're too different," he'd said on the plane to Paris.

His heart had been broken into a million pieces and he wasn't sure he'd ever be whole again, but he'd played the part of the loving son for his mother's sake. None of what his father did was her fault. Jonas had sworn to keep the truth about Dad and Marlene a secret. He'd never told another living soul, not even his wife.

Obviously, Remy had shared the information with Jessie. However, given the fact Marlene's revelation affected Jessie, too, he could understand. Technically, both twins were his half sisters.

"You're still here," Jessie said from the doorway.

Jonas hadn't heard her come in. He stood. "Just leaving."

"Where's Remy?"

He threw out his hands in the universal sign of "Who knows?"

"You upset her, didn't you? Man, I knew this was going to happen. Do you have any idea how long she carried a torch for you, Jonas? She was mad at me for telling you that earlier, but it's the truth. Every guy she's ever dated has been a pathetic half-ass clone of you. It's creepy and sad and she deserves more. I once bought a voodoo doll in Jackson Square and put your name on it. I did. I was desperate to do something to end her obsession with you."

He laughed. He couldn't help himself. "Frank as ever. I always liked that about you, Jessie."

She limped to the chair he'd been sitting in. "I liked you, too, Jonas. And, honestly, I wouldn't have even cared about the whole incest thing if you hadn't been such a prick after Mom dropped the I-bomb on you and Rem. You disa-freaking-peared without so much as a by-your-leave, only to surface in the south of France. Do you have any idea how much that hurt my sister?"

"Hey, what happened was no picnic for me."

She made a skeptical sound. "Rem and I went to the library. We saw pictures of where you were. Topless beaches. Beautiful women. Just the thing to appease a pissed-off teenage boy."

And he'd done exactly what Jessie was accusing him

of. He'd gotten drunk every night. Lost his virginity to some nameless older woman at a party where practically nobody spoke English. The perfect balm to finding out he'd come a heartbeat away from screwing his sister. Too bad he'd wound up hating himself almost as much as he hated his dead father.

"Ancient history. I have to go."

She let him get two steps away before she said, "I agree. It is old news. And there's no changing the past unless…"

He looked over his shoulder. "Unless what?"

"Unless the past was a lie."

She'd hinted at this earlier.

"You still want me to take a DNA test."

"Yes, I do. I would volunteer to do it, but I'm leaving as soon as that truck gets loaded. Cade and Shiloh are part of the reason I want to know. If we have another child, I think I'd like to know with absolute certainty who my father is. Was. You know what I mean."

He did. "Why would your mother lie?"

She shrugged. "Because it was Tuesday. Or the sky was blue. Who knows?" She looked toward the stairs and lowered her voice. "Remy still has feelings for you, Jonas. I saw it in her face the moment she spotted you. Can you tell me you've never thought about her over the years?"

Jonas felt his face heat up. He wished he could deny the charge, but he wasn't a liar. He'd made love with Remy a million times…in his dreams. He wanted to forget her, but he'd never been successful in completely exorcising her memory from his mind. Or his love for her from his heart.

"This isn't about me, Jessie. It's not about Remy, either. I need to find my daughter."

Jessie sighed. "I don't know if Remy can help you, but I do know she'll want to try. And that probably means you two will wind up spending some time together."

He got what she was saying.

"I think it's a simple test." She put her finger inside her cheek and made a popping sound. "Fast."

She was right. The truth was important, not only to him and Remy and Jessie but to future generations. Like Birdie. "Okay. I'll do it."

She pulled a cell phone out of her pocket. "I spotted a sign across from the rental place yesterday. I'll find the number and see if they're open on Saturday."

She was busy poking away at her phone when Jonas sensed another presence in the room. Remy stood at the foot of the stairs. She had a bemused smile on her face. "Jessie got her way, huh?"

"No surprise there, right?" Jonas said lightly, recalling how shocked he'd been when he returned from Europe and learned that Jessie and Remy had moved to Nashville. He'd known that was Jessie's dream, but Remy had adamantly refused to join her sister. He and Remy had their whole future mapped out. They'd planned to move into the city, attend Tulane and share an apartment when they could afford it. But, of course, that didn't happen. Couldn't happen.

Or could it have been a choice they were robbed of? "I've agreed to get tested. Will you do it, too?"

"Yes. Science. I trust science."

An odd response, but he was pretty sure he understood what she meant. She was tired of taking someone else's word for anything and relying on information that couldn't be proved.

He walked to her. "Jessie told me how upset you were because I went to Europe with Mom."

She shrugged. "My feelings were hurt. After Mama told us about having an affair with your daddy, I cried for a couple of days and called your house a million times. Finally, Jessie went over and knocked on the door. A cleaning lady told her you and your mother were traveling around the world."

"Not the whole world. We flew to Paris. Took a train to Italy. Rented a little dinky place on the Mediterranean. Mom called it her last-ditch effort to have me all to herself before I went off to college. She'd been planning it for a year. A surprise graduation gift. After what your mother told us, I would have gone to the moon if someone had handed me a free ticket."

"All Jessie and I could afford was Nashville."

Yeah, he'd been irked when he returned from Europe and found the twins had moved. Although it wasn't fair necessarily, he'd always assumed Jessie coerced Remy into moving with her and was pissed with her for that. He'd worried about Remy—a small-town girl in the big city. He'd even made a couple of trips north to watch the sisters perform in the smoky gloom of the trashy, downscale bars they worked. He'd had to stop because he started to feel like a degenerate stalker. After all, she was hot, sexy and desirable, and he was her half brother.

Although the sadness in her tone now was unmistakable, he got the impression she wasn't still mad at him, so he told her the rest. "In hindsight, I think the trip was as much for her mental health as my life experience."

Remy looked thoughtful. "You're lucky to have those memories. Especially now."

Now that his mother was almost as lost to him as Birdie was. "Remy, I apologize for coming on so strong before. I had no right to demand your help. I'm sorry."

"It's okay. You're under a lot of stress."

She didn't know the half of it. The feeling of hopelessness, of turning into the same kind of failure as a father as his dad had been. Never there when his son needed him.

"I wish I could tell you that knowing you saw a girl with red hair in one of your dreams didn't give me hope, but I can't. It's the closest thing to a lead I've had in weeks." He took a chance. "Do you think you might pick up on something—subconsciously—if I told you about Birdie?"

She didn't look thrilled by the idea. "I have no idea, but I am curious about your daughter. We're old friends—I'd like to know about your life, if you want to tell me."

Her smile was so Remy. The Remy he'd loved forever.

"Would you like a cup of coffee?" she asked.

"No," he said. "Not here. No offense, but I have bad memories of this house—lack of furniture or not. Let's go get tested then I'll buy you a cup of coffee and tell you all about my amazing, highly gifted daughter."

Remy smiled. "You've got a deal."

"WHY YOU LITTLE SHIT," the man hollered, grabbing Birdie's elbow so hard she dropped the match, causing it to fall into the folds of her ugly dress. "What the hell do you think you're doing, Miss Firebug? Where'd you get those matches?"

He pulled her to her feet violently and started hitting at her lap to put out the tiny flame that had started. The material of the ugly dress was cheap and old—a hand-me-up. Or down. Birdie could never remember which.

"I—I—found 'em, mister." He was one of the drivers. Not a father. Or even a brother, like Brother Thom. He hung around, watching the GoodFriends. Birdie had seen him before. He was the one who stared too much at her mom.

"And what you think you're gonna do here? Start a bonfire? Send some kind of smoke signals to somebody?"

Birdie felt her face turn hot. She was a terrible liar. Her skin always gave her away, but maybe he'd think she was red in the face because of the smoke. She'd gotten a few sticks to burn, for a minute or two. Not enough to send a signal to her dad, though.

He cuffed the side of her head, making her stumble toward the fire. She'd stolen the matches from the cook tent where her mother was mixing corn bread. Or trying to. Mostly, she was crying. The sadness in her head was getting worse, but nobody seemed to care except for Birdie. That was why it was so important to get word to her father. He'd know what to do. He'd rescue them.

"You're a homely little thing, aren't you? And not too bright, either. Thom ain't gonna be happy when I tell him about this fire. You're gonna be in deep shit, missy."

"I just wanted to practice, mister. Survivin' skills. We all gotta know 'em, right? I was just practicing."

"Survival skills," he repeated. His mean-looking eyes got smaller and his lip curled back so she could see a few of his brown teeth. "Well, you aren't gonna survive long if you start your clothes on fire." He laughed at his joke then gave her a shove. "Get lost, kid. And don't ever try this again or I will tell Thom. And your ass will be grass."

Birdie had no idea what that meant but she didn't stop to think about it. She ran as fast as she could toward the cooking tent, straight for her mother. She wrapped her arms tightly around Mommy's legs and cried, her fear and hopelessness soaking the material of her mother's equally ugly dress.

CHAPTER FIVE

"I'LL GRAB MY PURSE from the kitchen. Excuse me."

Remy felt strange around Jonas—too formal for everything they'd shared in the past. Awkward and out of step, too. He was a stranger—even though he still looked the same. Well, no. That wasn't true. He looked older. And desperate. But still too handsome for words.

"Damn," she muttered softly, as she entered the kitchen where Jessie, Cade and Shiloh were standing together talking. *Talking about me.* You didn't need to be a mind reader to know that.

"Is the testing place open?" she asked her sister.

"Yes. Do you want Cade to drive you?"

Remy rolled her eyes. "Stop it, Jessie. Just plain stop. A person who crashes cars for a living has no business— nada, zip, none—questioning my decision to ride in a car with an old friend. Across town. In broad daylight." She looked at Shiloh. "Am I right?"

The twelve-year-old nodded. "Sorry, Jessie, but she's got you there. And he's got a real sweet ride. Huh, Dad?"

"Oh, no, I'm not getting pulled into this one." Cade gave Remy a quick hug then headed toward the door. "We are going to be on the road by noon, agreed?"

Jessie heaved a vast sigh of capitulation. "Yes."

"Perfect. Remy, if you're not back before we take off, I'll see you in South Dakota for an official barn warming. If not before."

Remy waved. "Sounds great. Thanks for everything, Cade. Take good care of my sister."

He touched the brim of the cowboy hat he'd donned as soon as he stepped outside. "Come on, Shiloh. We've got work to do."

Remy hugged the young girl she'd grown to love. "I'll miss you, kiddo. Maybe they'll let you come to spend a week this summer."

"Cool," Shiloh said. "I like it here."

Jessie and Remy faced each other. "The test only takes a few seconds. You'll be back before we leave."

Remy motioned her closer. "In case we're not, let's hug goodbye now."

Jessie muttered a low curse. "I hate goodbyes. You know that."

Remy did. Beneath her sister's rough-and-tough exterior beat the heart of a real softy. Cade knew and respected that, too, which was the only reason Remy felt comfortable letting her sister return to the north without her.

"Then, how 'bout we call each other at a set time every day?"

Jessie laughed. "Yeah, like what you did when I spent all that time in the hospital. Did I ever tell you how much that meant? It was lonely and boring between treatments and your daily calls made it better. I didn't feel so cut off from the family." She squeezed Remy so hard she let out a peep. "I love you, Rem. And tell Jonas I hope he finds his daughter ASAP. I mean that. But," she said, a mischievous glint in her eyes, "if he hurts you again, I will track him down and fry one or both of his balls in hot oil."

She boasted the threat in a voice loud enough anyone in the house could hear.

Remy laughed. She couldn't help it. "You are such a big talker."

"I could do it. I know I could."

They looked at each and grinned because they both knew differently. But Remy was willing to let the threat stand because what the underlying message said was "I love you, and I want you to be as happy as I am."

"I'll call you soon. Bye."

Remy was still smiling when she rejoined Jonas in the entry.

"Do you find it amusing that your twin is plotting my demise?"

"Eavesdropping?"

"She practically shouted it."

"Yeah, well, if this test turns out positive, then she's your sister, too. Are you prepared for that reality?"

He didn't move.

"What?"

"I—I'm suddenly paralyzed with fear."

She couldn't tell if he was kidding or not, so she grabbed his arm and tugged him along. "Oh, she's not so bad. Really. She grows on you. I've known her for almost thirty-three years and—"

He leaned around her to open the door—still the gentleman his mother raised him to be, she noticed. "I wasn't talking about Jessie. I've been in limbo—no, purgatory—since I got back from Iraq. You are the first positive step forward I've taken in three months. What if…?"

The part of her that loved him as only a girl with her first crush can ached—yearned—to comfort him. The woman who was determined to change her life and stop being everybody's caregiver squeezed his upper arm. His massive, muscular, manly biceps.

She cleared her throat and let her hand fall to her side. "Let's not assume anything, Jonas. All anyone—including you—can do is try. Okay?"

He swallowed hard and nodded. "Let's go."

"I hear you are a sweet ride. I mean, I hear you *have* a sweet ride." She was so flustered, she nearly tumbled down the steps into his arms. He caught her but kept the contact to a minimum. Thank goodness. Because, technically, until proven otherwise, he was her half brother.

"WELL, THERE," REMY SAID, forty-five minutes later. She made a point of brushing her hands together as if to show the end of a difficult job. "That's done."

The test had, in fact, been quick and painless. Sitting in the waiting room, thinking about what the results might mean to each of them was the grueling part. Jonas had clammed up and refused to talk about his daughter because other people were present, so Remy had resorted to bringing him up to speed on everything that had happened to her family over the past decade and a half.

If he'd been bored, he'd done a good job of hiding his feelings. Something, she realized, he'd always been good at.

"I don't know about you, but I need beignets."

Jonas snickered. "Fried dough and powdered sugar always was your cure-all, wasn't it?"

He remembered. She tried to keep her response casual, even though she was melting inside. He remembered. "I figure if something works, why change it?"

"Well, you won't get me into N'Awlins on a Saturday. Too many tourists. But Catfish Haven still has the best pie in town. Would that do ya?"

She nodded, surprised to hear him name a local diner that had become popular several years after they broke up. If the current owners had been operating it back then, the small, riverside café would have been her and Jonas's favorite spot.

"Wouldn't Jonas love this place?" she'd thought the first time she went there. She'd immediately scolded herself—the way Jessie would have for being a sentimental dope.

He clicked his remote to unlock the snazzy, still new-smelling car and opened the door for her. "I like your car," she said.

"Thanks. I bought it before I left on deployment. Probably sounds stupid, but I wanted to know it was waiting for me when I came home. I kept a photo of the car right beside the one of Birdie. I even made arrangements with a friend to put the thing on blocks and store it until Birdie turned seventeen, if I didn't make it back."

She slid across the fine leather seat and pulled in her legs. The interior was a creamy ivory with gleaming wood accents. Rich and luxurious. She glanced over her shoulder and smiled. As soon as he was seated, she said, "My first thought was this is way too elegant for a teenager, but then I noticed the small backseat. Smart dad."

She'd been thinking about her older sisters' ongoing fears about their teens' budding sexuality when she made the remark, but the serious look on Jonas's face told her he'd read her comment differently.

"Yeah, we came pretty close to breaking all the laws of man, society and God in the backseat of my mom's old Thunderbird, didn't we?"

His tone sounded haunted.

"We were kids, Jonas. Kids make out in the backseats of cars. It's like a job requirement. A rite of passage."

He put the key in the ignition and touched his foot to the gas, making the engine roar impressively. As it idled a moment, he said, "Well, all I can say is it's a good thing we didn't start dating until we were seniors."

She'd thought the same thing many times, although a part of her secretly regretted not doing that most evil of deeds. She honestly did even though she knew how terribly wrong it was.

"You were shy."

"You were too beautiful. All the guys were intimidated

by you. I've heard that sometimes the most beautiful girls sit home for prom because nobody dares to ask them out."

She felt her cheeks heat up. She knew she was attractive, but beautiful? Hardly. She preferred to blend in—or, at least, hang out in the background. Jessie was the gorgeous one—bold, flamboyant, stylish. She'd always been comfortable in the spotlight—even before her big break in Hollywood.

"That's very sweet of you to say. I always figured your friends kept their distance because of my, um, *gift*." She made air quotes and said the word with as much scorn as possible to let him know she didn't consider herself gifted in any way.

"I might have avoided you when we were younger—in say, junior high—because my male ego didn't like to be reminded that a girl saved my life, but I never believed any of the things people said about you. That you were spooky or weird or you could put a hex on people you didn't like."

She'd heard every insult imaginable over the years, but she'd learned to laugh them off. "Did you know Serena Sedgwick once offered to pay me a hundred bucks to make Lilly Smiley fail a math test? Apparently the two were in hot competition for some sort of award. Talk about weird."

He put the car in gear and pulled onto the street. "Did you do it?"

He was kidding. She could hear the teasing quality in his voice. She relaxed into the seat and adjusted her sunglasses on her nose. "I thought about it, but, honestly, I didn't want either one of those girls to win the thing. They were stuck-up brainiacs, who talked down to everybody they considered less intelligent…which was probably everybody."

His low, wonderfully masculine chuckle filled the car and settled quite uncomfortably in her low belly. That old attraction—the one Jessie was worried about—blossomed to life like one of those dormant diseases that never truly left your body. Her chicken pox of love had returned as shingles of lust.

She wiggled to alleviate an itch that lacked one single focal point. Jonas probably noticed her squirming but was too polite to comment. Instead, he pointed out the window. "Hey, isn't that your mom's beauty shop? Looks different. New owners?"

"My sister, Rita Jean, and her husband took it over and gave it a face-lift last year when Mama got sick. It looks nice, doesn't it? Fresh and pretty. Mama would have liked the changes."

They exited Baylorville a few minutes later, pulling onto the highway with a powerful but muted roar of the engine. The car definitely suited him.

"I saw my first naked breast in Marlene's House of Beauty," he said, his tone wistful.

She turned in the seat to face him. "I beg your pardon?"

His smirk told her she'd misconstrued his words. He'd probably intended that. "Your mom had more magazines than the library. Including quite a few copies of *National*

Geographic. Do you have any idea how many young boys offered to accompany their moms to the hairdresser simply because of the August 1986 issue?"

Remy laughed. "I don't know. One?"

"Okay. Maybe. But it was a life lesson I've never forgotten."

Neither spoke for a few miles, until Jonas said, "Your mom was quite a bit younger than my mom, wasn't she? How'd she die? Cancer?"

"E. coli. By the time she saw a specialist, the damage to her kidneys was irreversible."

"Was she a candidate for a transplant?"

She nodded. "Yes, but not a great one. She had high blood pressure and diabetes and some chronic arthritis issues she'd never mentioned to any of us. Apparently she had a very high tolerance for pain. Like Jessie."

"So, I guess they weren't able to find a match?"

"Jessie and I were the closest, but I'd picked up a topical infection at work that would have killed Mama like that." She snapped her fingers. "And Jessie had all those blood transfusions and skin grafts after the fire. They told us the antibodies she'd developed would have been lethal in Mama's body. We both felt pretty useless, let me tell you."

"That's too bad."

She sighed. "The worst part was the timing. Jessie was in Japan with her stunt team, doing an extreme-sports competition when Mama's condition worsened. The Bullies were calling and texting her every few hours pushing her to get tested. Jessie didn't want to risk doing something that might weaken her body when everyone on her team was working so hard to win."

"Bummer. Tough call."

She looked at him sharply. "Listen, Mr. Judgmental, everyone came down on Jess for not selflessly dropping everything and rushing to Mama's side, but the fact is Mama ordered her to stay in Japan and finish the competition. Ordered. I was in the hospital room. I heard the whole conversation."

"Sorry. But, I always got the impression Jessie and your mom didn't get along."

She relaxed a tiny bit, her temper passing. "That's true, but, in the end, love trumps old grievances. Jessie came as soon as she could. Some people even accused her of throwing the contest so she could leave Japan, but I think she was so in tune to my pain, she lost focus. I saw the video. It wasn't pretty."

She felt the car begin to slow. Sure enough, she'd been so busy talking she forgot where they were going: Catfish Haven. She'd brought a date here once for breakfast, but he'd balked. "I'm not eating fish for breakfast. That's disgusting." That was the last time they went out, actually.

"I love this place," she said. "How'd you hear about it? Mostly only locals come here."

He looked hurt. "I'm local. I stay in Mom's house whenever I come for a visit. For a while, I'd sign her out of Shadybrook for a week or two, so she could spend more time with her granddaughter. But there came a point when that wasn't doing anybody any good."

She blew out a low whistle. "I know exactly what you mean. Convincing family members of that is another thing."

"Did you interact directly with patients while you worked there?"

"My official title was Activities Director. But I wore a lot of different hats. The job was never boring, I'll tell you that much."

He got out, opened her door and didn't speak again until they were seated at a tiny table with two mismatched chairs and a Red Stripe bottle filled with sweet peas on it. He looked over the small menu that every diner was handed when they walked in the door. The availability of certain choices changed, depending on who caught what and when.

"Sweet tea and a crawfish po'boy, Suzie," Remy told the waitress, who arrived a few seconds later. "I missed breakfast," she added for Jonas's benefit.

"I'll have the same," he said, then turned his attention entirely on Remy.

She fiddled with the thick, hand-stitched cotton napkin. The place might lack decor, but it had its values straight: good food and nice, big napkins for wiping your hands and mouth. Very little went to waste here.

Suzie delivered their drinks, along with a plastic basket filled with a golden mound of onion rings and hush puppies. Remy's favorite. "We didn't—"

"On the house," Suzie said. "We missed you, girl-friend. Where you been?"

"In South Dakota, actually. With Jessie."

Suzie made a horrified face. "At least she brought you home in one piece. Did you see the video of her rolling an SUV?" The waitress, who had been a year or two ahead of the twins in school, shivered. "Holy moly, that girl's got balls of steel."

Remy grinned. "I'll tell her fiancé you said so."

Suzie's eyes went wide and she squealed loudly. "Fiancé? No way. Do you have any idea how many people in the Bouchard Twins Wedding Pool are going to lose their asses if she gets married before you? You've always had better odds. Even after you and—" She looked at Jonas, her eyes widening in recognition. "I'll shut up, now."

Remy reached for an onion ring. "Small towns, what can I say?"

He didn't reply. In fact, he wasn't even looking at her. His attention seemed stalled on her chest. She looked down, wondering if some crumbs had caught in her cleavage or something.

"Oh," she said with a small peep.

He wasn't studying her breasts like some sort of lecher. He'd noticed her necklace. Or more to the point, the small, oval medallion hanging from her necklace.

She wiped her greasy fingers on her napkin and caught the medal in her fingers, holding it out so she could see it, too.

"You still have it."

"I never take it off."

He seemed surprised, maybe a little perplexed. She didn't know why. "You gave this to me the day your mother brought you over to say thank you. You told me it was your father's."

He nodded. "I was tossing it down the well when I fell," he said. "I didn't mention that part because Mom would have asked why."

She waited, hoping he'd tell her why.

"Dad gave it to me a few months earlier in exchange for my not mentioning to Mom that Dad visited a woman in Morgan City."

"A client?" she said, trying to keep her tone neutral.

He gave her a look.

"Dad said she needed his advice about buying a new car. He went into great detail about how she was a divorcée, trying to get her life back together after her lowlife husband took off with all their savings."

"But you didn't believe him."

"I believed him…until he gave me his St. Christopher and made me promise not to say anything to Mom. He said this lady was proud and didn't want people gossiping about her at Marlene's House of Beauty."

He reached across the table and very carefully took the medal in his fingers. "Even at age eight, I knew that was a lie. I knew this woman was the reason my parents fought, and he made me feel guilty, like I was part of this grand deception."

She looked down again, frowning. "Darn. I thought of it as my only link to the father I never got to meet, but now I'm not sure I want to wear it anymore. How come you didn't tell me that when we were dating?"

He let it drop, but his fingers accidentally brushed her

bare skin, and an electrical charge that she remembered all too clearly from their youth passed straight through her chest and down her spine.

He rolled his neck as if to release any built-up tension. "Ironically, I didn't want you to think less of me because my father cheated on my mother—and yours." He gave a harsh, dry laugh, then took a drink of his iced tea.

She was tempted to take off the necklace, but she didn't. The cheap, little medal had been her most cherished possession since she was the age of his daughter. She'd had to change the necklace many times, but she always kept the silver oval close to her heart.

Suzie brought their lunch a minute later.

"Should I know her?" Jonas whispered as the woman walked away. "She looks vaguely familiar."

Her name didn't ring any bells but she'd seemed to know a great deal about Remy. Of course, Remy had returned to Baylorville after her stint in Nashville, whereas Jonas only visited a couple of times a year.

"Probably not. She was ahead of us in school. She and my sister, Pauline, play Bunko together."

"Pauline…Bing, right? I remember her. Does she still live here?"

Remy chomped down on a mammoth bite and chewed quite a long time before answering. He had to force himself not to grin. She'd always been a big eater, which had amused him to no end. And yet, she remained as trim as ever, with perfect, lush curves he didn't seem to be able to keep his eyes off. Accidentally touching her a few minutes earlier had caused a chain reaction of sensations in areas of his brain that hadn't seen action in months.

"Uh-huh. She and hubby number two bought a five-bedroom house across town in that development that nearly went bust when the economy tanked. Mom's early passing helped her out a lot. Oops. That sounded mean. Bing's always been toughest on me and Jess. I put it down to birth order. Jessie calls her a greedy bitch."

He laughed at that.

"So," Remy said between bites. "Tell me about Birdie."

Jonas had no idea where to begin. As corny as it sounded, she was the light, breath, color and joy of his life. "There was a big storm the night she was born. The hospital was using a backup generator. The very second Birdie slid into the doctor's hands, she let out this huge howl and the power came on." He grinned, remembering the moment. "The staff and doctors all called her Wonder Baby."

"Wonder Baby," she repeated. "I like that."

He watched her nibble a golden-brown onion ring. Normally, he could take down a couple of orders by himself, but he hadn't had an appetite since returning stateside. In Iraq, everyone made long lists of the things they were going to eat or drink or do when they got home. He had one thing only on his list: hug Birdie.

"How long were you married?"

"Too long." Despite all that had happened, he'd felt no rancor toward Cheryl and his marriage until this latest stunt occurred. He'd always told people the situation between them was so complex and overloaded with so many nuances that they both were responsible for how things had ended up. "We had a turbulent relationship that ended in divorce in 2007."

"But you shared custody."

"In theory. I was the one with the stable job and steady income. Birdie lived with me most of the time, but I tried to fit Cheryl into her life as much as possible." He always felt like a failure when he talked about the choices he made where his love life was concerned.

He made himself eat—exactly the way he had in the mess hall in Iraq. Over there, he'd needed his brain functioning, his reaction time hair-trigger and enough energy to sustain him no matter what. He needed to stay sharp for Birdie's sake, too.

In between bites, he tried to describe his daughter in a way that would make her real. "We used to have a cat named Marzipan."

"What kind of name is that for a cat?"

"We read it in a book. Birdie liked the sound of it and she made me read that book over and over. When we went to the SPCA to get a cat, she spotted this older, golden tabby with a white tip on his tail and she said, 'There's Marzipan, Daddy. We have to take him home.'"

Remy's smile made him feel like a good father. He didn't want to tell her the rest of the story, because it would burst that particular bubble.

"Is Marzipan waiting at home for you?"

He shook his head. "Cheryl decided she was allergic. She gave the cat to some friends a week after I left. I heard about it a month or so after the fact. I haven't been able to talk to Birdie about it, so I don't know how she feels."

Remy frowned and pushed her plate away. "That sucks. I'm thinking I don't like this woman very much."

Neither did he, although logically he knew a lot of her bad behavior was driven by her illness, and how could he hate her for that? Also, she was his daughter's mother and there wasn't anything he could do about that. See, complex and nuanced.

"What else can I tell you about my daughter? She likes the number six and told me six was going to marry seven, even though Birdie felt eight was a better choice." He pictured her curled up beside him on the couch, explaining her rationale.

"Why?"

"Because six and eight have more in common. They're rounder. Seven is very upright." He thought a moment. "Or uptight. I can't remember."

"She has a wonderful imagination."

"True, but she's very earthy. She likes to tell you when she farts. And hiccups. Oh, my God, she has the loudest hiccups I've ever heard. It's like they're amplified with a microphone."

Her laugh made the tightness in his chest ease a tiny bit. It also made him remember things he had no business remembering. "Is she close to your mother?"

"She was. Birdie loved to come to Grandma's house. But as the Alzheimer's progressed, it became hard for Birdie to understand. It's frustrating and sad."

"I suppose it would be," she said with a sympathetic

look. "Did Birdie have a chance to visit her in Shady-brook?"

"No. There wasn't time, but I knew I was going to be gone for a long time and I wanted Mom to remember Birdie, if possible, so I filmed a bunch of vide—" A thought hit him. "Good grief, why didn't I think of this before? You're a visual person. Dreams are movies in your head, right?"

"I guess that's one way of describing it."

"Well, I have Birdie's whole life on my computer. Including the videos I made before I left for Iraq. They're at the house."

Her body language shifted subtly, broadcasting a less-than-enthused vibe. "Do you have somewhere you need to be?" Or someone she needed to see?

Jessie had claimed that Remy was single, but maybe Jess didn't have all the facts.

Remy pulled her oversize purse onto her lap and extracted a small case containing a tube of lipstick. She used the built-in mirror to touch-up her shiny pink lips. She puckered just so, then looked at him and sighed, but said nothing.

Why the sudden reluctance? Had he said something that offended her? Was she worried about the time commitment? Maybe this was about money. He recalled that she wasn't working and had intended to start looking for a new job. "I'll hire you." The offer was out of his mouth before he could consider it, but it made sense. She could be his personal P.I.

"What?"

"I need your help. I don't expect you to do this for nothing. I'll pay you double what you might earn at Shadybrook." The idea was taking shape in his mind. "Say, two weeks, no matter what happens?"

"You think this is going to take that long?" She frowned. "From what you said, I thought the situation was more urgent than that."

"I'm praying it won't take that long to find Birdie. With your help and a little luck, we might find a new lead in the next day or two. But if you agree to help me, I want your complete focus. Not worrying about your next job. If, God forbid, this takes longer than two weeks, we'll renegotiate then."

"What exactly do you expect me to do to earn this money?"

"Help me figure out where my daughter is. Go over the information I've gathered so far. I'm too close to the case. I need fresh eyes. Someone who isn't emotionally tied to Birdie or Cheryl to tell me what I'm missing."

She nodded as though that made sense.

"And, dreams or no dreams, Rem, you've always been a free-form thinker. That's exactly what I need, someone who doesn't adhere so strictly to linear logic. Two weeks. Will you give me that?"

She swallowed. "I—"

"I promise to write you a glowing recommendation. No matter what happens." He held out his hand to shake. "And I'll throw in a bonus if we find her within a week."

He was giving her a hard sell. Before he went into

insurance investigation, he'd sold policies from cold calls. He knew all the tricks and not giving her time to deliberate might be high pressure but it also usually resulted in a sale.

"Okay," she said. "But I'm not doing this for the money. You can pay me what I would have earned at Shadybrook, but no bonus. That's simply too avaricious sounding, okay?"

She started to offer her hand but pulled back a moment. "And no more talk about dreams. If I see something that has bearing on Birdie, I'll tell you, but I don't want you to count on that, okay?"

"Okay," he lied. She might not believe in her abilities—her gift—but he did.

He shook her hand. Short and sweet. Businesslike. And despite the memories that tugged on his heart-strings—and a few body parts at points lower—he was going to keep their relationship aboveboard. He had no choice. Because no matter what the damn DNA test said, he and Remy Bouchard could never be together.

CHAPTER SIX

REMY STARTED TO GET to her feet, but a loud "Now, hold on a minute" made her stop. Suzie rushed to their table from across the room, moisture dripping from the sweaty pitcher of tea she carried. She lightly pressed her free hand against Remy's shoulder to keep her in her chair. "You can't go without pie. You always have pie, Remy."

Remy knew she wasn't up to the digestive challenge at the moment—the memories that had swamped her from a simple handshake made it hard to think, much less enjoy dessert.

"Two pieces to go," Jonas said before Remy could respond. "Whatever's best today. You pick. We trust your judgment, Suzie."

The waitress seemed pleased by the compliment. "Back in a few. And I'll bring your bill." She dashed away in the opposite direction.

"Dessert police," he said with a bemused smile. "Who knew?"

Remy loved pie, but she suddenly felt hyper, eager to leave. Once Jonas backed away from demanding access to her dreams, she realized she could be of help. If not as a true investigator then as a sounding board. Her mother often said that was her main role in life. That the ladies who came to her beauty parlor wanted someone to listen, as much as they wanted a new hairdo.

"You don't have to know all the answers, Remy," Mama once said. "You only have to know how to listen. I truly believe people know what's right for themselves but they've forgotten how to hear their own voices. That's where bartenders and hairdressers come in."

"Before we go, Jonas, can I ask you a personal question?" The more personal, the better, had been her mother's motto. "Why did you marry Cheryl?"

He crossed his arms and dropped his chin toward his chest. His expression turned so dark she regretted asking.

"Someone once told me that people with certain types of mental illness radiate a light that can be almost blindingly beautiful. Especially to people who are predisposed to be caretakers."

"You consider yourself a caretaker?" She had never thought of him in that way, but she supposed it fit.

"Yes. I was fifteen when Dad committed suicide. Even though he and Mom had been divorced for a couple of years, Mom was devastated. She blamed herself. She couldn't even get out of bed for a month."

Remy had heard bits and pieces of that difficult time when they were together, but he'd never spoken with quite this candor. Of course, a teenage boy probably didn't have the same perspective as a thirty-three-year-old man.

"Despite Dad's philandering, he was a good provider.

He made sure Mom's house was paid off and she had stocks and a retirement portfolio. I was lucky I didn't have to drop out of school and get a job. But, Mom relied on me a lot."

"So, you're saying you were drawn to Cheryl by her neediness and vulnerability?"

"Direct and to the point—you've learned from your sister." He sighed. "I would say yes. But in my defense, Cheryl's emotional issues have changed over the years. Worsened. Every doctor she saw had a different diagnosis and treatment. One claimed it was a hormonal imbalance. Another prescribed light therapy. And don't get me started on the pharmacological aspect. She's tried all kinds." He rattled off a dozen or so names of prescription medicines. Some she'd heard of, some that didn't sound like something that would benefit an emotionally ill person.

"Did she ever do drugs? The recreational kind, I mean."

"Probably. It's hard to say. She'd go for months, holding down a job, behaving normally, convincing everyone that she had her act together. Then, suddenly, everything would change.

"One time she was working as a flower arranger—she did all their funeral sprays—and she simply walked out. She disappeared without a word for ten days. She came home with no purse, no phone, no ID. I can't tell you how many times I had to cancel all our credit cards and put our banks accounts on hold. She'd apologize up and down and sideways, promise to see a doctor, take any meds he prescribed."

Remy looked over her shoulder to see how their pie order was coming. Suddenly, this felt like much too personal information for such a public venue.

Jonas must have felt the same because he sat forward and added in a low voice, "The last psychiatrist I took her to see used regression therapy to uncover that Cheryl was raped by a family member when she was thirteen. I don't know if it's true or not, but she changed after that. I became part of the problem. Another man in a long string of men who only wanted to control her, use her. She was convinced I never loved her. That I wouldn't have remained with her if not for our daughter." He blew out a breath and added, "And the sad part is, she's probably right."

She heard regret and something else—guilt?—in his tone. "People who already feel disenfranchised are particularly drawn to cults, aren't they? What do you know about this group she's joined?"

Before he could answer, Suzie returned with a white paper bag and their bill. "Thanks for coming," she said. "Hope you enjoy your pie. One piece is your favorite," she told Remy with a broad grin.

"Thanks," Remy said, picking up her purse and pushing her chair back. "It was good to see you."

"You, too. Are going to the picnic next Sunday?"

The all-class reunion. She'd completely forgotten about it. "Doubtful. I've got to update my résumé and get it out there so I can start working again. But thanks for asking, Suzie. Give my best to Bobby and the kids."

Jonas tossed two twenties on the table. A nice, healthy tip for Suzie, a hardworking gal with an unemployed husband and two adorable little boys.

"What sort of picnic?" Jonas asked as he escorted her to the car.

"The Baylorville all-class homecoming. Haven't you gotten any of the flyers?"

"Maybe." He unlocked the car. "I've barely looked at the regular mail. Mostly, I've been focusing on trying to find out everything I can about the GoodFriends. There's a file in the backseat. You can look it over on our way back into town."

He opened her door. Always the gentleman. From her vantage point and the bright midday light, she could see a fleck or two of gray in his sideburns. And a faint sag of his broad shoulders. He was a little thin, too, she decided. Back in high school when his mother had been cooking for him, he'd had to diet to make weight for the wrestling team. No more. He was all muscle, nerves and bone.

He handed her their carryout bag then walked around the car and slid behind the wheel.

She glanced in the backseat and decided to hold off looking at his file until later. It deserved her full attention.

"Wow," REMY EXCLAIMED fifteen minutes later when Jonas ushered her through the front door of his mother's home. "You still have white carpet."

He looked down. God, he'd hated the thick, pristine crap that he'd naively blamed for his father's leaving. "Yeah, well, not for long."

"What do you mean? It's in pretty good shape considering it's, like, twenty years old."

He lugged the cardboard file box he took with him everywhere to his mother's big oak desk in the far corner of the room. He hadn't had time to do any sort of modernization or updates to the place, but he'd thought about this house a lot while he was in Iraq. With a little TLC and seed money, he could make it a viable property. Either to sell or move into. Once he had Birdie back and his life on track again, he'd revisit those plans.

"Mom really let the place go the past couple of years. She was such a fanatic about keeping things neat and dirt-free when I was a kid, I was half-afraid to invite friends over. At least we had a big yard to play in."

"Funny. I came here once when I was a kid to drop off something for my mom. I remember standing in this very spot, thinking how great it must be to live in such a clean and pretty place. Our house was like Grand Central Station at rush hour. And I don't think Mama knew what a dust rag was." She nudged the carpet with her toe. "I had dreams about this carpet for weeks afterward."

Dreams. The word brought back the reason she was here. Not that the urgency of his quest was ever far from his thoughts, but he knew from his military experience that a soldier, while always on duty, had to distance himself from the intensity of his mission every so often simply to stay sane.

Lunch had been good. He needed sustenance. And talking about Cheryl had been good, too. Remy required some understanding of his ex-wife's unpredictable and convoluted, entirely self-absorbed thought process so she wouldn't try to think like a normal person where Cheryl was concerned.

"Look around if you like while I put this in the kitchen," he said, grabbing the bag with the dessert from the top of the box. "The bathroom is down the hall on the right if you want to freshen up. I'll show you Birdie's room after you watch a couple of videos." He paused before adding, "There's a lot to see. Probably more than you can take in at a single sitting. Anytime it gets to be too much, say so."

"Okay. I will. Thanks," she said, walking toward a brass-and-glass étagère his mother used to display two or three dozen framed photographs. Mostly of him and the important highlights of his life: graduation, new job, commission in the Guard, wedding, Birdie's birth. The newer shots were more about Birdie, and he was okay with that. He was gratified that his mother was proud to be a grandma.

He returned a few moments later to find Remy holding the shot of him when he received his commission.

"You look very stern and serious in your military uniform."

He hated that photo. He'd been hours away from proposing to Cheryl. Whenever he looked at his expression in that picture, he decided his subconscious must have known something he chose not to hear.

"Oh, my word!" Remy exclaimed a second later. "What a beautiful baby! Look at that red hair. Where did that come from?"

Of course, if I'd listened to that inner voice, I wouldn't have had Birdie. "My dad," he said, the standard answer that he'd given a thousand times to the same question. Only this time, the person asking had a different connection to the answer. He noticed her hand trembled a tiny bit as she set down the frame.

"Sorry. I wasn't thinking. Mom used to claim that Dad had flame-red hair when he was a young man. There are only a couple of photographs of him from his childhood—all black and whites. His parents were dirt-poor farmers in Mississippi. No money for fancy things like cameras and cars. Could explain why Dad was so absorbed by anything with wheels and a decent body."

"Or, in some cases, a decent body was enough," she said, her tone rich with irony. Marlene had been a shapely woman. All of his pals on the wrestling team had voted Marlene Bouchard as the mom they'd most like to wrestle…naked.

He cleared his throat. "Right. Dad was definitely a ladies' man."

She turned slightly, this time an image of his mother in her hand. "Do you think your mother knew it? Before they got a divorce, I mean?"

"I don't know. She might have turned a blind eye to his extracurricular activities because he kept a roof over her head and a thick white carpet underfoot."

"You sound bitter."

He was. But his family history wasn't relevant beyond where it intersected with his daughter and this present moment. "I'll get my laptop set up so you can meet Birdie."

He appreciated the fact that she didn't press. In fact, she followed orders quite well for a civilian. She walked into the big, open living room, running her hand across one of the plump, persimmon cushions of the sofa his mother had ordered off the internet.

The bright color and modern style matched absolutely nothing in the room. "It jumped off the internet and simply arrived at my door one day for only $9.99, shipping and handling," she'd told him.

That had been his first confirmation of his growing suspicion that his mother wasn't quite herself anymore. He'd canceled her credit cards, pulled the plug on her internet service and made sure the rest of her assets were protected.

"From the pictures I've seen so far," Remy told him once she was seated on the couch, "I can tell I'm going to like her. She's always smiling. You seem to have been able to make up for your wife's, um, problems very well."

He grabbed his leather computer bag and walked to the big-screen TV. He was pretty sure he had the right cables stuffed behind the credenza.

"Kids learn fast to adapt. And Cheryl wasn't always out of it. When Birdie was a baby, there was a period when every night I'd come home to gourmet meals. I'd give Birdie her bath and get her ready for bed while

Cheryl cleaned up the kitchen. It was TV-land perfect. And when Birdie got a little older, Cheryl used to act out Mother Goose tales for her. Birdie loved that."

But, on the opposite end of the spectrum, there was the night he came home and found a stranger poking around in the refrigerator. "A friend of Cherry's," the man said. *Cherry?* Jonas had nearly broken his neck racing down the hall to check on his daughter. Luckily, Birdie was safe in her crib, although she'd soaked the sheets and blankets because she was wearing the same diaper Jonas had put on her that morning before he left for work. *Cherry* didn't come home for a week.

"So about the cult," Remy said. "Is Cheryl extremely religious?"

He plugged the USB connection into his laptop and walked to the coffee table, remote control in hand. "Sometimes, depending on her mood. God, Buddha and Jesus have all dropped by on occasion."

"Some people's idea of the Dream Team."

He gave a caustic hoot. He liked that she didn't try to minimize his experiences or offer some lame platitude. He'd heard them all from coworkers at the insurance company and superior officers in the field.

"Before my deployment, I petitioned the state to have Cheryl hospitalized—for her own well-being and for Birdie's sake. A woman I used to work with—she trained me for my first job with the company—was taking an early retirement to care for her grandchildren. She said she would be willing to take in Birdie—for a fee, of course—while I was away.

"I would have paid anything at that point, simply for the peace of mind of knowing my daughter was in a safe, consistent family setting. I knew these people. They were good Christians who raised three great kids, but Cheryl said she could see into their souls. She called them pawns of Satan. She was able to convince the state she was sane and fit."

"At least you tried."

He hit the power button. "Unfortunately, Cheryl decided that I was the enemy out to destroy her for some nebulous reasons I won't repeat. Even after our divorce, we could usually talk about what was best for Birdie, but this deliberate act of betrayal in her book made her paranoid and supersecretive. She even told Birdie I couldn't be trusted anymore."

"Oh, no. Do you think she brainwashed your daughter into believing you're the enemy?"

No. Yes. He couldn't go there. Instead of answering, he opened the laptop and clicked on a random file. Most were labeled by dates. One said: Birthday. It had said "Last birthday" meaning the last one he'd filmed, but the label had taken on an ominous meaning, so he'd changed it. "This was the October she turned six. Obviously, I missed her seventh."

He hit Play.

"We held it at a Chuck E. Cheese's because the weather was as unpredictable as her mother. Cheryl was managing to keep it together at the time. I brought my mom for the weekend. Mom and Birdie both stayed with me." For one tiny window in time, he'd had the family he'd long ago imagined—with only one key element missing. A wife. A wife was the glue that held the ship together when the seas got rough and the wind started to blow. He believed in that ideal because he believed the person who preached the philosophy—Remy.

"Do you remember what you told me about the roles of a husband and wife in marriage?"

She looked up from the slide show. "Don't tell me you actually listened to that drivel. I was a cockeyed optimist who bookmarked three hundred quotes from *Chicken Soup for the Soul*. I knew less about life than a poodle knows about opening a can of dog food."

"I thought you were pretty smart."

"Because both of our home lives were so mixed up. Look at me. No known father of record. A mother with a reputation for hooking up with married men…including your father. And three older sisters, who I'm sure qualified as serial daters." She shook her head. "So, tell me about Birdie's nickname. Why do you call her that?"

"Well," he began, happy to recall one of his favorite memories, "when she was born, the first thing I saw was this long-legged, scrawny, birdlike creature with a shock of bright red hair plastered to her head." He snorted softly. "God, she was beautiful."

Remy smiled broadly as if she could picture exactly what he described.

"Her mother had already made me promise that if we had a girl, we'd name her Brigitte Leann. Brigitte for—" He winced. *"Bridget Jones's Diary.* The movie. Cheryl changed the spelling because she insisted the movie got it wrong."

He could tell Remy was trying hard not to smile.

"Leann was for her mother. They'd had a turbulent, love-hate relationship. I used to wonder if there was a connection between Cheryl's subsequent meltdown and her mother's dying, but Cheryl refused to talk about her childhood. To me, at least. She must have told her court-appointed psychiatrists something, but I don't know."

Remy watched the birthday-party slide show without comment for a good five minutes. When the show ended, she looked at him and said, "Why does Cheryl look vaguely familiar? Is she from around here?"

He pushed to his feet and walked to the étagère. He opened the door of a lower compartment and took out a porcelain frame adorned with roses. The bride and groom smiling at each other in the staged pose looked like strangers. Happy, beautiful strangers.

He passed it to her.

"Oh."

Oh, indeed. Cheryl was the same height, had the same curvy body and the same color of blond hair as Remy. Were their facial features similar? Not exactly, but there had been moments when Jonas first met his future bride that he could swear he caught a glimpse of Remy in her laugh, her coy wink.

Cheryl had nearly lost what slim hold she had on reality when she stumbled across a yearbook photo of him and Remy. Cheryl had instantly recognized the obvious doppelganger aspect between her and his ex-girlfriend.

"You sick bastard," she'd screamed. "You married me under false pretenses. Do you close your eyes when you kiss me so you can pretend you're with her?"

Nothing he said could sway her. Finally, after hours of weeping, tearing of hair and threats of jumping off the nearest bridge, he calmed her with a promise that he would never have anything to do with Remy Bouchard ever again.

"And if I ever find out that you've slept with that bitch, I will kill myself," she'd told him with such stone-cold truth he had no choice but to believe her.

She might be mentally unstable but she was smart and she instinctively knew where to find his weakest point. As the child of a suicide victim, Jonas would do whatever it took—no matter what—to keep his own child from having to experience that pain and spend the balance of her life wondering if she was to blame.

Remy stared at the photograph for a good minute, finally handing it back with a sigh. "Life is strange, isn't it?" She attempted to smile but there was no sparkle of humor in her eyes. "I dated a couple of boys who reminded me of you at the beginning, but they could never quite match the image I'd built up of you in my mind. Eventually, I was able to let that go. But it took a while."

He wanted to ask about those boys. *How many? Who was the first? Did you love him?* The warble of a cell phone saved him from making a complete fool of himself.

Remy bounced off the sofa, producing a phone from

her purse. "Hello? Jess? Oh, my gosh, I forgot all about you. I'm so sorry. Jonas took me to Catfish Haven. What's up? Are you ready to leave?"

She stepped away—not out of earshot, but across the room to the wide picture window that overlooked a lawn that needed mowing. The neighbor boy he'd hired had been on vacation with his family this week. If nothing broke with the case, Jonas would have time to do it himself.

"Don't be silly. I'm fine. We're at his house now, looking at photos of his daughter. What did you think? He ravaged me on his mama's sofa?" She glanced over her shoulder. "As delightful as that sounds, nothing has happened. No laws of nature have been broken."

Jonas shook his head at the obvious innuendo. He realized she was probably worried that they would let the intense emotional circumstances sweep them away, but that wasn't going to happen.

He grabbed a couple of dessert plates and forks from the cupboard and walked to the patio table.

He had everything set out when Remy joined him a few minutes later. "Sorry. I told her she was turning into a hover mother and if she didn't stop, Shiloh wouldn't let her father marry her."

"Did the threat work?"

"For now." She didn't seem too worried about what her sister thought. "What kind of pie did Suzie pick for us?"

"I didn't look, but guests choose first."

She gave him an incredulous look. "You can't be

serious. This is Catfish Haven pie. Regardless of the disquieting oxymoron of its name, they make the best pie on earth. Two pieces, two forks, one plate. That's the rule."

He laughed. How could he not? This was the Remy he'd loved from day one, thought he'd lost forever, and, now, in a strange twist of fate was sitting across from him in his backyard. Despite all the reasons he shouldn't find pleasure in that fact, he was powerless to resist the sweet synchronicity of being in her company.

He walked into the kitchen and returned a second later with a dinner plate. "Happy?"

"I will be when I start eating," she said, taking a seat. She pulled his chair a little closer with her foot and transferred both pieces to the larger plate.

"One bite of what looks to be fresh boysenberry, then one bite of my favorite—cherry cream. The gods have smiled on us today, Jonas Galloway, they surely have."

CHAPTER SEVEN

"It's pie, sweetheart. Eat it."

Birdie shook her head. "No, it isn't. I saw you grinding up those crackers. You can't make pie out of crackers, Mommy. You can't."

Birdie was hungry. Real hungry. She had to eat her cereal without milk in it this morning. And for lunch all the kids got was some peanut butter spread inside some limp, skinny celery stalks that didn't crunch when you bit down on them.

"Brigitte, stop being difficult. We all have to make sacrifices to do the Lord's work. Be thankful we're not living in the desert, eating locust."

Birdie didn't know what a locust was but she doubted if it could be any worse than cracker pie. "When can we go home, Mommy? I don't like it here."

Her mother moved so quickly Birdie didn't have time to put down her plastic fork. It fell to the ground of the cooking tent, turning instantly black with dirt and leaves. But before Birdie could reach for it, her mother had hold of one of Birdie's braids. Mommy pulled on it. Hard.

She brought her face close to Birdie's and whispered, "Never say that again. This is our home. Until it's time for us to start our missionary work. A mission that will

bring the word to the enemies of God. We've been chosen, Birdie. It's an honor to go."

"G-go where, Mommy?"

Her mother dropped Birdie's braid and turned to pull
a fresh plastic fork from a box. She held it up trium-
phantly like it was a prize, her gaze focused off in the
distance. Toward Brother Thom's RV. "Wherever God—
and Brother Thom—send us."

She quickly served a large piece of the grayish,
mushy-looking pie. "Say grace before you eat, dear. We
must be thankful for the good Lord's gifts."

IT WAS NEARLY THREE IN the afternoon by the time
Remy finished watching the videos Jonas had compiled
over the seven and a half years of his adorable daughter's life. He had a good eye for capturing small, perfect
moments that truly told a story about the person he was
filming. He was particularly astute where his daughter
was concerned.

Brigitte Galloway was a normal kid. Average height
but a tad skinny, Remy decided, comparing her to the
many nieces and nephews Remy had rocked, chased
and babysat over the years. Her proud papa was right,
though, Birdie was also special.

Remy couldn't define that exact essence that made the
child so adorable. Was it her gangly legs that churned
with happy abandon, running even before she could walk
without falling? Or possibly the wide, gap-toothed smile
that robbed you of the ability to breathe with its sheer
cuteness. More than likely, the sparkle of intelligence

and curiosity in her big green-gold eyes had a lot to do
with Birdie's appeal.

"Your daughter is a doll. And I love how feisty she is
when the two of you butt heads." Remy had seen all she
could take. Feeling a little bit like a voyeur, she'd tried to
skip ahead through the parts that showed Jonas and his
ex-wife. But it hadn't been easy. She was curious. How
could she not be? This was the man she'd loved with all
her heart, and he'd married someone who could have
been Remy's sister.

He looked up from his mother's older, dinosaur of a
desktop computer, which sat on a boxy oak desk in the
far corner of the room. Terrible feng shui, she'd decided,
since the person at the desk had his back to everyone.
The entire home was in need of a serious makeover.

And Jonas was right about the carpet. It didn't look
bad, but she was quite certain it was the source of the
smell that seemed to have settled in her nostrils. Cat?
Coffee? Or simply a residual mustiness that came with
age?

"Thanks. She is amazing. And you're right about
us butting heads, but I always figured this was a good
thing."

"How so?" She checked her cell phone to make sure
she hadn't missed any calls from her sister. She wondered how far north they would make it today.

"Kids need to feel safe enough to test their boundar-
ies. When you live with someone with mental-health
issues, the parameters change daily, sometimes hourly.

I tried my best to give Birdie unconditional love with room to take risks."

"That's very evolved. Where did you learn to be such a good parent?"

He swung his high-back upholstered chair to face her. "The one positive aspect of Cheryl's condition was it forced me to read everything I could get my hands on about coping with craziness—for want of a better word. Knowledge saved my sanity and, I hope, made our family a little bit more normal for Birdie. It was the best I could do under the circumstances."

"Is Birdie the reason you stayed together as long as you did?"

He leaned forward, resting his elbows on his knees. His sigh sounded sad and reflective. "Even though life was a roller coaster some of the time with Cheryl, there were moments when it was a fun ride. I've never been big on spontaneity. Probably 'cause the one time I acted impulsively, I wound up in a deep, dark well, right?"

"So, having a partner who kept things edgy might have seemed like a good mix."

"Exactly. Until things got out of hand with her disappearances. She wouldn't call, text or email. I once filed a missing person's report with the police, the whole she-bang. They were considering sending out search parties along the river when she strolled in as calmly and carelessly as if she'd been shopping and forgot the time."

"Where was she?"

"I don't know. She told the police one thing. Me, another. My mother something else completely. I moved out, totally prepared to call it quits. But a month later, she called to tell me she was pregnant."

A thought Remy had no business thinking popped into her head, but before she could even scold herself for being so quick to judge, Jonas added, "The first words out of my mouth were, 'Whose baby is it?'" He made a face. "Not the best way to start a reconciliation. Cheryl insisted she'd been faithful. But, given what happened with my dad, I suppose you could say I'm not the most trusting person in the world."

"Did you ever…"

"Get a paternity test?" he finished for her. "Yes. Even though I knew the minute I held Birdie that she was mine. I didn't want some stranger from Cheryl's past to show up one day and make claims that I'd be forced to disprove."

"You're a smart man, Jonas. And a good dad. I'm proud of you."

He seemed bemused by her comment, but before he could say anything, his phone rang. He looked at the caller ID. "Oh, crap. I have to take this. And I need privacy. Would you mind?" He looked apologetic.

"No problem. I'll be outside, soaking up some sun in that beautiful yard."

He flipped open his phone. "Thanks," he mouthed before his expression turned stormy. "Goddamn it, Greg, what's taking so long? How can a caravan of freaking motor homes suddenly disappear off the face of the earth?"

Remy hurried out the sliding door from the kitchen

to the covered patio. She made a slow circumnavigation of the perimeter, pausing to admire the brilliant color of a bird of paradise.

When the heat started to get to her, she moved to a padded chaise and sat, letting her head rest against the cushion. For the past hour or so, Remy had felt a memory hovering at the edge of her conscious mind. As she became more familiar with Birdie through her father's pictures and videos, Remy realized she'd had a second dream.

Last night.

She closed her eyes and the image came rushing back to her.

The child's hand was icy cold, pale and very small. Fragile-looking, like an old woman's.

Remy had held the hands of many elderly patients as they prepared for their journeys onward and beyond. But the little girl who had appeared with no warning was young, pretty and very much alive. Only her eyes were dead.

Remy swung her new companion's hand, back and forth as they walked—the way Remy and Jessie had when they were children. They'd sung made-up songs and chattered the way children who felt safe in their skin often did.

The girl was like a puppet whose strings had come loose. Remy's heart twisted in her chest. *Poor little kid,* she thought. This isn't right.

She stopped moving and looked around. They appeared to be in a shadowy jungle of naked trees with exposed roots and a miles-tall canopy of some dubious color that blocked the sun like gauze. A skinny silo of smoke drifted upward from a dying fire. The ring of rocks encircling the smoldering embers was haphazardly placed, small and irregularly sized, as though a child had arranged them.

"Did you build this fire?" she asked the youngster.

The girl's dull red-orange braids bobbed ever so slightly against the bodice of her old-fashioned dress—the sort a friend of Tom Sawyer's might wear. Her skinny legs were bare and her shoes didn't match.

"Are you a ghost?"

"Not yet," the child answered, then she turned and walked away, disappearing into the maze of dead-looking trees.

"Wait," Remy pleaded, her own feet welded to the earth apparently. "Come back. Do I know you? Can I help you? Please..."

But her calls and questions went unanswered.

She opened her eyes and looked around. She felt chilled even though the day was hot and humid. Her pulse still raced a little. She didn't know what it meant, but the overall sense she had was that Birdie was close to giving up.

The dream was legit, but was the child Birdie? If it was, how had Remy come to see this kid hours before she ever saw a photo of her? Was it possible Miss Charlotte had a picture of Birdie in her apartment at Shadybrook and Remy's mind somehow squirreled away the image?

She rubbed her knuckle across the pain in her temple. *Right,* she thought, *and I fabricate a dream about the kid on the very eve of her father's reappearance in my life. Sure. Why not?*

Jonas popped his head out the door. "Done. You wanna go? You look wiped out."

She stood. "Yeah. I am. I didn't sleep well last night. But, would you mind swinging by Shadybrook on the way? I'd like to say a quick hello to your mother."

"Seriously? You're not sick to death of my family?"

"No. I'm good. Plus, I can ask the director if she's picked up any extra funding recently." She smiled at him. "For after my temporary job is up."

"No problem. I was going to stop and see Mom this evening."

He locked the house behind them—a gesture that seemed out of place in Baylorville. Probably a result of living in a big city, she thought. Although when she and Jessie had lived in Nashville, their friends knew the twins' apartment would be open if they needed a place to crash for an hour between shifts. Mama had prided herself on always offering an open door, which probably accounted for why there were always so many women hanging around Mama's kitchen—including, on occasion, Jonas's mother.

"Do you remember coming to our house with your mother when you were a kid?"

"No." He leaned forward to start the car but paused to look her way. The sunlight, filtered in a dappled effect by the giant magnolia in front of his mother's home, made the skin of his bare arm seem to glow in a warm, peachy color that made her hungry again.

Not for food.

She forced her gaze out the window. The fields behind his home had long since been built upon. New streets and smaller, less interesting houses had cropped up like watermelons in late July. The empty well he'd fallen into was probably somebody's basement, she thought with a shiver.

"Are you okay? Did you see something? Was it Birdie?"

"No. I don't get messages," she said, angrily. In all truth, she was mad at herself. For thinking things she had no business thinking. "I told you, I'm not a psychic. I do not receive sudden, trancelike revelations from above. I was thinking about something else and I shivered. That's all."

He turned on the car. "Sorry. I guess I'm still pissed off about getting blown off by the Memphis P.D. My friend is swamped with work and he's gone above and beyond checking databases. He'd even called in a few favors from friends in other counties, but there's no trace of these people, and that's really got me worried."

"Why?"

"This sort of traveling gospel show relies on contributions. They usually have a couple advance teams that plaster the target area with posters and give away a bunch of free admissions to drum up interest. If the GoodFriends have pulled out of the revival business, then that might mean they have to find some other source of revenue."

"Drugs?"

"I have no idea. I'd like to think they simply disbanded and went legit but that would mean people like Cheryl would resurface at home. And there's been no sign of that."

They drove in silence for a few blocks then Jonas asked her, "Why did you ask about coming to your house when I was little? I'm positive the first time we met was after I was rescued."

"Jessie and I were talking about how chaotic it was in our house growing up. Mama had lots of friends. Male and female. There was always a pitcher of sweet tea spiked with a little something—wine or moonshine, I don't know. Jessie stole a glass one time and said it tasted like rubbing alcohol."

"I'm not surprised," he said.

"That our mamas were imbibing in the afternoon?"

"That you didn't taste the cocktail. You always were the straight arrow. A good girl. You wouldn't even kiss me good-night till we'd been dating for two weeks."

She bolted upright. "Stop the car and let me out. That's the meanest thing you've ever said to me. You have your nerve, Jonas Galloway. Asking for my help, then insulting me before…before…" Some of her bluster left when he burst out laughing.

"You're mad because I called you a good girl? That was a compliment."

She crossed her arms. "It was not. You're still mad at

me because I wouldn't put out that night after the spring formal."

He looked at her, mouth gaping, then pulled to the side of the street between a broken-down Jeep and a brand-new Hummer. The juxtaposition would have amused her if she wasn't still fuming.

"I know exactly what night you're talking about. I remember it like it was yesterday. I can tell you what color your dress was and what kind of perfume you were wearing. I even remember the color of your fingernail polish. But the reason I remember isn't because you said no."

"You called me a prick tease."

"Okay, yes. I was frustrated. Blame it on my hormones. You were gorgeous. Sexy. God, I walked around semihard the whole night. My stupid male ego was convinced you were going to put out, even though you told me—oh, I don't know, a million times—that you weren't going all the way until after you graduated from high school."

"That's because Rita Jean got knocked up halfway through her senior year, and Mama said she ruined her life."

He turned to look at her. "Did it?"

She shook her head. "I don't think so anymore. That child is my eldest niece. She's gorgeous, brilliant and has three or four colleges courting her to play basketball for them. Rita's the most stable one of us all."

"Well, there you go. Our mamas didn't know everything, after all."

The comment gave her pause. "But they were friends. Remember when Mama sat us down for the big revelation? She made you promise not to tell your mother because she didn't want anything to come between them."

"Yeah. So what? We already discussed this."

He was right. This was old news. Mama was dead; Miss Charlotte's memory was fading like cheap wallpaper. Maybe she should let the whole thing go, but...

"When you and your mother left for Europe so suddenly, I wondered if it was because Miss Charlotte didn't want us to talk. You know, compare notes. Mama refused to say another word, but that was Mama. I couldn't help but think that maybe your mother knew more than she let on."

"You think our mothers colluded to break us up?"

"No, not necessarily. But, come on, your dad was no angel. And your mother was a smart woman. She couldn't have been completely in the dark."

Jonas wasn't sure where she was going with this misstep down memory lane, but his head was starting to pound from talking about his father. Their father.

He put the car in gear. "Mom made a lot of excuses for him. Maybe she loved him. Or wanted to believe for the sake of their marriage vows. The whole 'for better or for worse' thing, you know?"

Remy didn't answer.

"I don't know, Remy. Mom was never the most independent woman on the planet. And her family cut her off when she married Dad. Maybe she was afraid. Fear

can make you do a lot of things you don't want to do."
Or make you not do something you do want to do.

"You're right. This is old news. We've taken the DNA test, so until we get the results it's all speculation, isn't it? We need to be talking about what steps have to be taken to find Birdie. Do you have a plan?"

"I wish I had a plan. It kills me that I don't. I guess that's why I'm here, hoping you'll sort of jump-start the process, which is definitely stalled. Do you have any ideas?"

"Not really. But when you mentioned Cheryl's medications, it occurred to me there might be a way to trace her through her prescriptions. Especially if she used any of the larger chain pharmacies."

He parked in a spot marked "visitors" in front of the small, homey-looking, one-story brick building that was his mother's current residence. "That's a good idea. I'll give my friend a call."

She climbed out. "I'm going to say hello to my friends. I'll meet you inside."

He watched her stroll toward the building. He called his buddy but had to leave a message.

He felt bad for assuming the worst where Cheryl was concerned. Just because she didn't fill her existing prescription didn't mean she hadn't found another means of staying on her meds.

Remy was standing at the front desk, exchanging hugs with the nurses and staff when he entered the building.

"Jonas," Patsy, the head nurse, exclaimed. "We didn't know you knew our Remy. What a small world."

"How's my mom today?"

"Fantastic. I was just telling Remy, Miss Charlotte—" all of the residents were either Miss So-and-so or Mister Whatever "—seems on top of her game today. A young gal from that new fitness center in town has been stopping in once a week to teach… What's it called, Bev?"

"Zumba," a woman filling little cups with pills called out.

"Modified, of course. But I think the music and movement, even limited, is great for our residents."

A buzzing sound made Patsy clutch a walkie-talkie at her waist. "On my way," she said into it a moment later. "Remy, come talk to me next week. We've really missed you. Especially the residents. We'll see what we can work out."

"Great. I'll give you a call."

Remy headed toward the wing where the full-care folks resided. His mother's door was wide-open, of course. She never remembered to close it—even when she wasn't dressed. An oversight that would have shocked her beyond dismay if she were aware of the social gaffe.

"Hello," Remy called, knocking as she entered. "Miss Charlotte? Are you home? It's me, Remy Bouchard, and your son, Jonas. We're here to see you."

"Mom?"

They looked around the one-bedroom studio.

Jonas checked the bath. "She's not here."

"Is today her regularly scheduled beauty-parlor visit?" She walked to a large calendar the residents used to help keep track of appointments.

Her finger landed on a big red mark that Jonas couldn't read but assumed said hair appointment. He didn't care that his mother was gone—he would see her later. But the mix-up seemed symbolic of everything he'd tried to accomplish in the past few weeks—and failed.

"Shit," he swore. "Why is this so damn hard? I used to be able to make things happen. I taught Afghan soldiers how to fight. Uncovered dozens of complex insurance scams. I don't wait around for information to drop out of the sky or from someone's dream. And, yet, here I am. Twiddling my thumbs. And, frankly, it sucks."

Remy appeared more sympathetic than alarmed by his outburst. But the last thing he wanted was her feeling sorry for him. Sympathy meant something bad had happened. He refused to think about that.

He ran a hand through his hair. "I just want my daughter back."

As he turned to leave, his phone rang. He unhooked the little clip on his belt loop and flipped it open without looking at the display. He figured it was his pal from Memphis calling back. "Jonas Galloway," he barked, his tone sharp.

"Daddy?"

CHAPTER EIGHT

BIRDIE'S HAND WAS SHAKING so bad she could barely
hold the phone. It was Brother Thom's phone—he'd left it
on the picnic table after the prayer meeting he'd ordered
all of the GoodFriends to attend. Her mother had stood in
the very front row, directly across from Thom, her hand
holding Birdie's so hard Birdie nearly cried.

But Mommy had let go partway through when Brother
Thom said something about the missionaries who were
bound for glory. Birdie didn't know where Glory was.
She hoped it was a long way from here.

When Mommy made a funny crying sound and ran
off before Thom was done preaching, Birdie got a bad
feeling in her tummy. She stayed where she was, not sure
if she should follow after her mother or not.

Brother Thom ended his prayer pretty quick after that.
Birdie dropped her chin and put her hands together like
she'd been taught, but she'd kept one eye on Thom, too.
She'd noticed his phone, and when everybody else was
praying for redemption, she prayed that he would walk
away and leave the phone.

And he did.

God was listening.

She'd sat at the picnic table, ignoring the scratchy seat on the backs of her legs. Slivers were nothing compared to getting the chance to call her daddy. Being fast, she'd reached out and grabbed the small black phone. She pushed the number buttons in the order her daddy showed her then pushed the button marked Send.

She'd slipped to the ground under the table as soon as she heard the ringing sound. Her heart was beating hard. She wanted to talk to him so bad she was afraid she'd start crying if he didn't answer.

Then she heard his voice. His name. He was there. Somewhere. Real.

"D-daddy." Her nose started to run and a sob got caught in her chest, making it hard to speak. "Daddy, you have to come and get me and Mommy. Right away. I don't like it here, Daddy."

Daddy asked her a question and she tried hard to think past her fear so she could answer him. But before she could finish telling him, a face suddenly appeared to one side of the table.

"Why you obnoxious little brat," Brother Thom yelled. He looked madder than she'd ever seen him. His hand stabbed at her face. She closed her eyes and tried to roll away but he caught her.

His fingers clamped down hard on her hand—the one holding the phone. She let out a shriek of pain.

"Gimme that," he said, his voice mean and hateful. He pried the phone from her fingers.

"Daddy…" She fell on the ground, crying. She saw the

look in Brother's Thom's eyes. He hated her. She didn't know why, but he did. She was so scared all she could do was lay there and cry. Like a baby.

"BIRDIE," JONAS CRIED, his hand trembling. "I'm here, little girl. Oh, my God, it's so good to hear your voice. I miss you so much. Where are you, baby? Can you tell me so I can come get you?"

He looked at Remy who made a motion to slow down.

Of course. He needed to let Birdie talk. Some shred of rational thought told him to hit the speakerphone button.

"Daddy, you have to come and get me and Mommy right away. I don't like it here, Daddy."

He squeezed his eyes closed to keep all the pent-up emotion he felt from spilling out. "I'm sorry, baby. I'll come right this minute, but I don't know where you are, sweetheart. Can you tell me where you are?"

There was a pause. "There's lots of trees. And water that comes up around their roots. It's brown and Mommy says there are snakes and alligators in the water. And bugs that suck your blood and make you die. I don't like this place, Daddy." Her voice broke and she started to cry.

"Oh, honey, I'm so sorry. I wish I could come pick you up right this minute but I need to know a little more about where you are. Is there a building? Or street signs?"

"Why you obnoxious little brat," a voice shouted. "Give me that."

A man's voice. An angry man's voice.

"Birdie? Birdie?" Jonas shouted.

He could hear her crying in the background. And she let out a shriek as if she'd been struck. Jonas felt a blast of adrenaline explode in his veins. "If you lay a hand on my daughter, you bastard, I will kill you," he shouted. "Do you hear me? Let her go. She's an innocent child. Let—"

He stopped ranting the moment he felt Remy's hand on his shoulder. He looked at the phone. The line was dead. His screen showed his daughter's happy, Tooth-Fairy's-a-coming grin.

"Oh, God, Remy. She needs me and I'm standing here as useless as my father. What do I do?"

She took the phone. "What did the caller ID say?"

Why hadn't he thought of that? He watched her press the appropriate buttons. Her frown told him the news wasn't good. "Restricted," she said, showing him the display. "Let me try redialing." She shook her head. "It says 'invalid number.'"

She set the phone on a nearby table and stepped closer to give him a hug. "I'm sorry. At least you know she hasn't forgotten how to reach you. You taught her well."

Birdie. I'm so sorry, baby. I never should have left you. This wouldn't have happened if I'd stayed home. Not that he had any choice in the matter, but his guilt was eating him alive. Images of what might be happening to his brave little girl at this very moment nearly brought him to his knees.

"I'm so sorry, Jonas." Remy patted his back. "Don't give up hope. We're going to find her, Jonas. We will. I promise."

Remy's kindness and support, her declaration—regardless of how empty it might be—eased the fist-hold on his heart somewhat. He took a step back, forcing her to remain at arm's length. He was a freaking soldier, for God's sake. He knew how to plan and mobilize. He didn't wallow.

"I need to go. I'll drop you off, then call my friend. Maybe there's a way to trace the call." He didn't believe that. They'd only been on the line a few seconds. But that call was the first authentic lead they'd had in weeks. And, above all, it proved that his daughter wanted to come home. She was being kept somewhere against her will. Surely that constituted kidnapping in somebody's book.

They closed the door to his mother's room and hurried down the hall to the side exit. There was no way Jonas was going to make small talk at the front desk. "Do you think he'll hurt her for making that call?" he asked.

"She's a little girl. Only an absolute monster would hurt her," Remy answered.

He hoped she was right.

"Do you think your friend who works in law enforcement could retrieve that cell-phone number?"

"I'll call him, but if this Brother Thom guy is determined to stay on the down low, he probably bought a disposable phone. If he was worried that Birdie told me something, he could be pulling up stakes and moving as we speak."

Once they were seated in his car, she said, "We need a plan. And a map. A big one."

"What are you thinking?"

"I'll explain when we get to my house. Step on it."

He did as she asked and a few minutes later pulled into the driveway where the moving van had been parked that morning. A small sedan in need of washing was the only vehicle present.

He got out and slammed the door. "Do you have anything to drink?" he asked, following after her.

"I might. Do you plan to get drunk?"

"I might. Do you have any idea how bad it feels to know you're virtually powerless to help the one person you love more than life?"

"I might."

He followed her into the house through to the kitchen. He'd always like this room. He associated it with the smell of chicory and coffee and he took a deep breath without meaning to.

Remy didn't notice because she was reaching for an odd-shaped bottle from the shelf beside the refrigerator. "Cade brought this. It's got a hint of chocolate."

"It's not that kind of sickly sweet crap you made me buy you in high school, is it?"

She laughed. "No. My taste buds have matured a little bit." She poured two small shots then handed him the bottle.

Kraken. He'd never heard of it. He took a sniff. "Strong. You drink it straight?"

She grinned saucily. "Yes, but you can add water or ice if you need it." Under her breath, she might have added the word "Wuss," before taking a sip.

"Ah." She suddenly blinked. "What time is it?" She spun around to look at the digital clock on the built-in microwave above the stove. "Oh, good. It's nearly five. Mama always said you weren't a lush if you could hold off drinking till four-thirty—on weekdays, at least."

"Why four-thirty?"

"That was the latest appointment she'd take at the beauty parlor. No evening hours at Marlene's House of Beauty. Clients could come to the house, of course, but they knew they ran the risk of arriving after she'd poured her first cocktail."

Why did I always assume her life was peachy cool and normal compared to mine? Probably because she had siblings. He'd hated being an only child, and he hated it that his daughter was growing up alone, too. If Birdie came home in one piece and wasn't completely, utterly psychologically messed up from this experience, he'd try to do something about that sad state of affairs.

If the man who yelled at her did anything...

He grabbed the drink and downed it in one gulp. The liquor burned his esophagus, making him choke. "Holy smokes, Remy. This is strong."

"I warned you. Want a refill? With water back this time?"

"One will do, thanks."

She finished off hers with a ladylike chugging. He was impressed. "You've changed."

"I would hope so."

She put away the bottle then turned to look at him. "Have a seat. I'll be right back. There might still be an atlas around here, unless someone took it, in which case, we'll use the internet. You can start by thinking about the call and writing down any sounds you heard in the background."

"I only heard her voice."

She handed him a pen. "No. That's what you were listening to, but your mind heard everything else. It's a trick I learned from lucid dreaming and that's what you hired me for, right? Close your eyes and think, Jonas. You can do this."

He sat at the round oak table, grabbed a piece of paper and clicked the pen she'd given him a couple of times. Stalling. He hadn't heard anything. Just his daughter's sad voice and terrified cries.

His heart rate started to increase but he ordered himself to breathe. Slow and steady, as if he were at target practice. Focus.

Where were you calling from, Birdie?

Outside. His gut told him that. She'd probably found a phone sitting around after someone had walked off without it. Long enough for his smart, desperate child to take advantage.

As his brain confirmed the location, he heard other noises, as Remy said he would. The wind, steady and strong, not gusty. And bird noises.

What kind of bird noises? Think.

He tried to imitate the sounds. Who-who-ee. And a screech that made him think of his and Birdie's last trip to the zoo. In the monkey house, where long-tail birds scolded visitors and monkeys alike.

"She's someplace semitropical, I think," he said, opening his eyes. He wasn't surprised to find Remy sitting across from him even though he hadn't heard her return. "Between the bird noises and her mention of gators, I think we can eliminate about ninety percent of the country."

She smiled encouragingly. "It's a start. And that jibes with your ex-wife's intention to provide homeschooling in Florida, right? That's good, Jonas."

"But Florida's a big state."

She opened a large, slightly mangled road atlas. "True, but one thing we do know for certain is your daughter hasn't been brainwashed. She wants to leave."

She thumbed forward to a two-page spread showing the Panhandle on one page and the main part of the state on the other. "We also know she's observant and brave enough to take advantage of an opportunity when she sees one. And, like I said, even under extreme pressure, she remembered your number."

"She memorized it when she was three."

She looked intrigued by that fact. "Three is young. You must have had a pretty good reason for pushing that. Do I dare ask why?"

He didn't answer right away.

"If it's too personal…"

"I think we're past any worry about privacy, Rem. You saw the whole soap opera of my life on screen today. I'll tell you anything you want to know if it'll help get Birdie home."

"Okay. Why did you make your three-year-old memorize your phone number?"

"Cheryl never liked coming to Mom's. She said it smelled funny and bothered her allergies, so, usually, Birdie and I would come together. But the Thanksgiving after Birdie's third birthday, we agreed to celebrate here as a whole family. Long story short, Cheryl decided I didn't love her. I'd never loved her." Thanks to his senior class album and all the photos of him and Remy— Cheryl's much more vivacious and beautiful clone. "She even accused me of having an affair."

He looked at Remy pointedly. "I wasn't."

"Never would have occurred to me to ask. You're the most faithful person I've ever known."

They both knew why. His unfaithful father, who ruined both their lives.

"She made a bunch of wild threats, including taking her own life if she ever found out I cheated on her." *With you.*

"You believed her."

"I believed that she was capable of anything and self-centered enough to jump off a bridge with our daughter watching. I wanted Birdie to have the means to reach me if something happened."

"Very smart. And, luckily, she hasn't needed to use the information before now, right?"

He flipped a few pages ahead in the atlas and pointed to New Orleans.

"My National Guard unit got called up when Katrina hit. I worked practically around the clock, seven days a week for two months. None of us could get home. Phone lines were messed up. We had crappy cell service. It was chaotic and stressful, even without having an emotionally unstable wife who convinces herself her husband is using this disaster as a way to hook up with…a woman."

"Why would she think that?"

He looked at the short distance from New Orleans to Baylorville but couldn't bring himself to admit the ugly truth.

"Did Cheryl try to commit suicide?"

"She took a bunch of pills. Fortunately, Birdie was spending the night with a neighbor, but she came down with the flu suddenly and started throwing up. The woman took her home and found Cheryl. She called an ambulance. The E.R. pumped her stomach. I got an emergency pass to fly home because my wife was being held on a seventy-two-hour suicide watch and my daughter was alone."

She walked to the sink to pour herself a glass of water. "I don't know what to say, Jonas. I'm sorry."

He looked at his watch. "I better go."

"I was wondering how we were going to do this," she said. "I didn't think you had a mobile sleep lab with you, but it occurred to me that you might want to stay here and watch me sleep in case I had a dream that might be pertinent to your case."

He could tell she was teasing, but the thought had crossed his mind.

"Not necessary. You'll call me if you see her. Won't you?"

Remy was touched that he trusted her, but it killed her to see him so defeated, so broken.

"I'll try to dream tonight, Jonas. I can't promise you anything, but maybe we'll get lucky." *Maybe Birdie will come back and tell me if the fire pit was a clue that held some significance to where she was.*

"Call me anytime. I'm used to working on four or five hours of sleep. If we can get some idea of where she is, I'll be out of here like a bat out of hell."

She believed that, too. "Will you do one thing for me?"

"What's that?"

"Take me with you."

"No. That's insane. If the cops decide this is a kidnapping, they won't even want me involved in this investigation. Trust me, police don't like civilians poking their noses in."

She crossed her arms and shrugged. "Maybe I'll wander downtown and let some handsome tourist buy me a hurricane," she said, naming the most alcoholic abomination she could think of. She'd tried one once and had been disgustingly sick so she'd never had one again. She drummed her fingers on one cheek, theatrically. "Yes, it's true that an excess of alcohol can interfere with the brain's usual nighttime activities such as dreaming, but…" She let the implication hang.

"We're arguing about going to a place you may or may not dream about." He let out a snarky hoot. "Is it just me? Or does that strike you as nuts?"

"Are you suggesting I'm crazy?"

"Absolutely not. I know crazy. But you are slightly cracked."

She couldn't say for certain whose scowl gave way to a smile first, but a second later they were both laughing. And a second after that, kissing.

She wanted to blame the Kraken—or the intensity of the situation—but she wasn't a liar. She'd been thinking about kissing him from the moment he showed up on her doorstep.

He broke it off, first. "Damn. I promised myself I wasn't going to do that."

"Me, too," she said, touching her fingers to her lips. She'd kissed a dozen boys and men over the years but not a single one had left the sort of impression on her mouth as Jonas Galloway.

He sighed weightily. "Jessie was right. The lust between us is like our invisible pet elephant—it takes up all this space and we waste a mountain of energy trying to ignore it."

"Well said. I couldn't agree more. The damn thing went on every date I ever had, too, after we broke up. Voyeuristic beast," she muttered under her breath. "You think three in one bed is crowded, you should try it with an invisible elephant."

She realized that was probably TMI—too much information—as Shiloh would have said, but if he could hold up his mistakes to the light, so could she. "As you've probably deduced, I've never been married. I was lamenting that fact this morning with Jessie. No long-term steady beau, as Mama would have said. My social life never really found its footing after you left town." She smiled sheepishly. "Not that that's your fault or anything. Merely a coincidence."

"I'm sorry?"

His reply was halfhearted at best.

"One day at the hospital when Mama was still doing fairly well, the Bullies and I were sitting in the waiting room, talking. One of them—I can't recall which— declared that if it weren't for Jessie, they'd be almost positive I was switched at birth."

"That's mean."

"Actually, I think they meant it as a compliment."

They both smiled.

"I'm going, now," Jonas said, waiting politely for Remy to lead the way to the door. She noticed that he left plenty of room between them.

"I'll see you when I see you," she said, remembering too late the phrase was one they'd used every time they parted—except the last time.

He paused and reached out to touch his finger to her nose. "Not if I see you first."

He remembered.

She stayed at the door until he had backed his car out of the driveway and driven away. Her brain was mush, her insides as mixed up as the agitation cycle on her washing machine. Her first impulse was to call someone. Jessie or one of the Bullies. But she didn't.

Instead, she dashed upstairs to change clothes. She had six gallons of the boldest and craziest colors of paint known to man—or woman—and she wasn't afraid to use them. Her personal-image remodeling might be on hold, but she could still redo her home.

CHAPTER NINE

"TURQUOISE? I MEAN, really. Turquoise?"

Remy laughed at the exasperation in her sister's voice. "It's only one wall, Jessie. Mama would have loved it."

"Our Mother of the White Walls, you mean? Yeah, right."

Remy squeezed the phone between her ear and shoulder as she finished cleaning her brush. Jessie was right, of course, and Remy had known she'd get flack from all of her sisters when she group emailed a photo of her finished product, but she didn't care. She'd needed the distraction after spending nearly a whole day with Jonas Galloway.

"Where are you guys? Still on the road?"

"Nope. Shiloh found us a dog-friendly motel and we are hunkered down for the night." She gave an amused chuckle. "The boys—Cade and Beau—are bonding. I'm looking out the window right now. It's a hoot to watch Cade walking the dog, waiting for him to do his job. He—Cade, that is—says ranch dogs can do their business without any help from him, but of course, we're not on the ranch. Yet."

"Where's Shiloh?"

"Playing pool in the lobby with a couple of girls her age. So far, so good. What's happening with Jonas?"

Remy turned off the water. "He got a call this afternoon from his daughter." She lowered her voice. "You should have seen him, Jess. It broke my heart. He loves her so much and there isn't a damn thing he can do at the moment. It's horrible."

There was a pause, then Jessie said, "Okay. I don't know if Jonas has a private investigator working on this or not, but Cade told me about a guy who is supposed to be really good. I can give you his number if you want it."

Remy walked to the table where she'd left the map and lined paper she and Jonas had used. "Sure. Why not? The worst he can tell me is no. But, at this point, I think he'd jump at any help he can get. He hired me, didn't he?"

"Hired you?"

Remy winced. She hadn't intended on sharing that bit of information. "In theory. I agreed to let him match what I would have made at Shadybrook for two weeks. Mostly to keep things more businesslike." So she didn't feel as though she was using his situation as a way to spend time with him. Talk about opportunistic. Was she really that low?

Instead of commenting on Remy's admission, Jessie rattled off a phone number. "Cade's coming back, and, honestly, I'm trying not to look like a nosy, micromanaging sister. He likes you and all, but he wants us to focus on us."

Remy smiled. "Good for Cade. Tell him I understand completely, and I'm fine. Really, I am. Jonas and I are adults. He hasn't made a pass at me." Surely one harmless kiss didn't count—even if it did stir up all sorts of crazy memories on her part. "He only has one thing on his mind—finding his daughter."

"Yeah. That's what Cade said. He tried to imagine someone keeping him from Shiloh. That's why he made some calls. That number I gave you belongs to a private investigator in Tampa, Florida. Supposedly he's the best."

"Thanks, Jess. Tell Cade, too. I'll let Jonas know tomorrow."

"Will do. Oh, here come my boys. Call me if anything breaks. Bye."

Remy hung up, then stretched. Her shoulders were sore from painting. She'd draw a bath, take a nice soak, then go to bed. With any luck, she'd dream. About the little girl with red hair and a big smile. Not about the girl's daddy.

Unfortunately, Remy knew all too well that dreams came from a person's subconscious. Her reaction to the one, harmless kiss made it abundantly clear that she had never completely gotten over Jonas.

A fact she feared might interfere with her best intentions.

BIRDIE WOKE UP BUT SHE kept her eyes closed, hoping that if she tried hard enough she could go back to the nice, safe place of her dreams. A big meadow with a pretty blue sky and white clouds. A nice lady with yellow hair had been holding her hand. The lady had pointed upward. "That cloud looks like a donkey. See his two long ears?"

Birdie had laughed. "Or a really big bunny."

"Maybe. Or a stork. Those ears could be wings."

"Is it true that a stork brings new babies? I want a brother or a sister, but Mommy says I can't have one because Daddy doesn't love us anymore."

The lady dropped to her knees on the tall grass and put her hands on Birdie's arms. "Oh, sweetheart, that isn't true. Your daddy loves you very much. And storks don't bring babies. Ask your daddy when you see him. He'll tell you where babies come from."

Birdie liked this lady. She made Birdie feel safe. And she liked knowing she'd see her daddy again soon. Talking to him had been worth what happened when Brother Thom found her and dragged her out from under the picnic table. He only hit her once before her mother saw them and came rushing to Birdie's rescue.

Brother Thom looked ready to hit her, too, but his friend—the man who caught Birdie with the matches—stopped him. "Temper, temper, Brother Thom. Remember, thou shalt not be accused of child abuse," the friend warned.

Mommy had hurried Birdie away and made her tell exactly what happened. "Oh, Birdie, please. You've got to stop looking back. Your father had his chance and he left us. God found us and now we are doing His work. We're never going back to our old life."

Birdie had cried herself to sleep. Her mother had tried to wake her up to eat, but Birdie wouldn't open her eyes. She liked her dreams better than the world her mother picked for them. Maybe she'd just stay asleep forever. Safe and sound with the dream lady.

"I'M SORRY, JONAS. I had a lot of dreams. Some really crazy stuff, but I'm not sure which—if any—pertains to Birdie."

Jonas closed his eyes, glad he'd called instead of going over to Remy's as he'd planned. He'd been awake since before dawn, following dead-end after dead-end on the internet, trying to find any hint to the current whereabouts of the GoodFriends.

"Except maybe the one with the alligator. Birdie mentioned that yesterday, and alligators symbolize treachery and deceit. Some people think they're a sign of needing to take a completely new approach to a problem. You know, like, if you keep on your current path, you might lose a leg." Her laugh sounded forced.

"Have you ever dreamed of alligators before?"

"No. Never." She paused a moment, then added, "I also bumped into the devil in a different dream. He looked like an ordinary man, but he was leading a donkey and they blocked the road so I couldn't get past."

He shook his head. "Does that mean something?"

"It might. Donkeys are stubborn. If you're able to lead one, you obviously have the power to influence people. The fact that I could tell he was the devil and not the friendly salesman he appeared to be, gives me hope that I'll be able to stay clearheaded and on task."

"So, which one am I? The donkey or the devil?'

She didn't answer right away. "Actually, you were in a different dream, and that's all I'm going to say about that. Have you decided about the P.I.?"

Jonas was glad to get off the topic of dreams if she didn't have anything specific to say about Birdie. He'd dreamed, too. Hot and steamy dreams that made him want the impossible.

"Actually, I checked out his website last night. I filled in a contact sheet and left a phone message this morning. His bio seems legit, and he claims to return calls within two hours. We'll see," he said, checking his watch. An hour and ten minutes to go.

"Good. I might have met him in my dreams last night, too. Not the man himself, but a symbol of him."

"Are you trying to confuse me?"

She laughed. "No, but that's the thing about dreams. They're not an exact science. In fact, they're probably the exact opposite of science."

"This is what I hired you for," he said, more to himself than her. "What was his symbol? A parrot? A baboon? A goat?"

"Stop it. You can make fun on your own dime. Oh, wait, this is your dime. Okay. Make fun all you want, but in most dream-interpretation circles, a stationmaster or gatekeeper is still a stationmaster or gatekeeper. You and I were climbing this long, winding staircase, and at the top we met a man who handed us two tickets. I don't know where we were going or what sort of transportation we were supposed to take because the dream changed, but I do remember that. And I was left with the impression that this man will be of help."

He looked at his cell phone. He'd called her from his mom's line so that he didn't miss the P.I. Time would tell.

"What happened when your dream changed?"

She didn't answer right away. Long enough for him to get suspicious. "It's not pertinent."

He would have argued the point but his phone jingled. He picked it up, noting the area code. "It's him. I'll call you back."

He hung up without waiting for her goodbye and pressed the receive button on his phone. His heart rate quickened, but he forced himself not to get his hopes up. "Jonas Galloway. Hello?"

"Mr. Galloway, this is Leonard Franey in Tampa. I just got off the phone with an old friend of mine by the name of Shane Reynard. The good news, sir, is you've got the right connections. The bad news is you need my help."

"Did you read my email?"

"Yes, sir, I did. And one of the reasons I'm interested in taking your case is because this happened while you were in service to our country. As a veteran myself, I made the decision a long time ago to give priority to fellow vets."

"Thank you. I appreciate that."

"No thanks necessary. Let's get this ball rolling. How soon can you be here?"

"Florida?"

"Yes, sir. I gave the name of this two-bit charlatan to two of my best researchers and I'm not liking what they've come up with—and that's after less than an hour on the phone and the web. I won't go into details on the phone because there are some aspects of this case that would be best addressed in person. Is that a problem?"

"No. I could grab a plane and rent a car or I could probably drive in it ten or twelve hours," he said.

"I suggest you drive. That will give me time to narrow down the focus of our search. And, best-case scenario, you'll have your own car here when we find your daughter."

Jonas's breath caught in his throat. The man's confidence could be bullshit, but Jonas chose to believe otherwise. They'd found the gatekeeper, just like Remy predicted.

They talked for another ten minutes. Jonas gave him all the pertinent information he had regarding Birdie, Cheryl and the names of the authorities involved in his daughter's case to date. He also agreed to email several photos of his ex-wife and daughter, along with the most recent video he had. The same one he'd shown Remy. "Would you have any objection to me bringing along a friend?" Jonas asked. "She has good instincts and I trust her."

"You can bring along the Pope if you want. Makes me

no never mind. Just plan on staying in the background. I don't like civilians underfoot any more than the cops do."

Jonas smiled, remembering his response to Remy the night before. Why had he changed his mind about taking her along? As bizarre as it sounded, he'd had a dream—beyond the hot and steamy ones—where he'd heard his daughter's laughter. He'd raced down a poorly marked trail, losing his way more than once, until he stumbled into a meadow. There, not forty feet ahead of him, sat Birdie and Remy playing cards. Old Maid. His daughter's favorite game. They appeared safe and happy and when Remy looked at him he'd felt a peacefulness that had been missing from his life for months, maybe years.

"Got it. We'll be on the road inside an hour. Thanks again, Leonard. I can't tell you what a shot in the arm this is. I look forward to meeting you."

"Drive safe, soldier."

He opened his laptop and sent everything the P.I. had asked for, then faxed copies of the reports he'd filled out with the Memphis P.D. He was on his way to his room to pack, when he remembered he hadn't called Remy back.

She picked up on the first ring. "What did he say?"

"He said, 'I am the gatekeeper. Come to Florida.'"

She made a sound of exasperation. "Stop making fun of me. Wait. He wants you to come to Florida? Really?"

Jonas pulled the suitcase he'd never completely unpacked off the chair and tossed it on the bed. "I told him I'd be on the road in an hour."

"He's going to help. That's wonderful, Jonas. I'm so glad."

"I want you to come with me, Remy. This is the first break I've had in a month. And it wouldn't have happened if not for you."

She didn't say anything for a minute. "I'd like to come, Jonas. But I have to be honest. I'm afraid. Being with you has stirred up a lot of feelings I've spent a long time trying to deny. DNA test or no DNA test, I'm not sure spending more time with you is a good idea—especially considering your focus has to be on your daughter."

Being with Remy was risky on more levels than she knew. But that same voice that told him Birdie was in trouble insisted Remy was the key to getting his daughter back.

"I know what you mean, Remy. I do. But you've breathed new life into this investigation. That's why I promise you I will keep things aboveboard. No more kisses. No more trips down memory lane. This is all about Birdie, and I can't do it without you. You saw the gatekeeper. And devil for who he really was. Please say you'll come."

"Mama used to say the worst thing you can do when something is troubling you is to overthink it. When are you picking me up?"

"Is half an hour too soon?"

"I'll be ready."

CHAPTER TEN

REMY TOSSED SOME CLOTHES into her oversize carpet bag—the one she'd only unpacked a few days earlier—and was debating which shoes to take when her phone rang. Thinking it was Jonas calling back, she didn't look at the caller ID. "Yeah, yeah, I'm almost ready."

"Pardon? Remy? This is Gloria over at Shadybrook."

Gloria? For a second, she tried to place the name as someone in personnel, but then it hit her: charge nurse for the full-care wing. "Oh, hi, Gloria, what can I do for you?"

"I was wondering—hoping, actually—that you could come over. Mrs. Galloway is extremely agitated this morning. She keeps asking for you. I honestly don't know why. We called her son, but his line was busy. Do you know if he's still in town?"

"Yes, but I believe he has business out of town and was planning to leave this morning. Should I give Mrs. Galloway a call?"

"You could try, but you know how some of the residents get with the phone. It might be even better if you could come and see her."

"I'll be there as quickly as I can, Gloria."

As soon as she hung up, she sent Jonas a text message: Meet me at Shadybrook.

Then she called a cab.

"Aren't you a little young to be moving in?" Raul Lopez, the cabdriver who picked her up, asked when she pulled her overstuffed bag onto her lap and gave him her destination.

"Depends on who you ask," she quipped.

Raul was a veteran cabbie, who probably knew more about the history—written and wishfully forgotten—of her hometown than anyone. "Mr. Lopez," she said, sitting forward to rest one arm on the front seat. "Do you remember my mama?"

"Of course. Marlene was the nicest woman in town. She did my late wife's hair, free of charge, a few days before she passed away. Came to the hospice. Told us, 'Every woman wants to look her best in her casket and I simply don't trust those undertakers to do this right.'"

Remy had no memory of that but she wasn't surprised. She'd heard similar stories at her mother's funeral. "I'm glad of that. She was kind and generous, but you'll agree she had another sort of reputation, too."

He chuckled, not unkindly. "Marlene did enjoy people. Men and women. For different reasons, mind you."

She looked ahead. Shadybrook was only a few blocks away. "Do you remember hearing about her association with Charlotte Galloway's husband? I believe his name was Merrill."

The man thought a few seconds, then slowly shook his head. "Nope. That doesn't ring a bell. I knew of the man, of course, but can't say as I ever drove him in my cab. He was a car dealer, after all. But, truthfully, I can't picture the two of them together."

"Why not?"

"Miss Charlotte was your mama's friend. Your mama would never have stabbed her friend in the heart. Never."

Remy's hand was shaking as she paid the man. She tipped him well, despite the fact she was sorry she'd ever opened her mouth. She'd asked; he answered. Did he tell her some fabulous, life-altering revelation? No, she realized, as she walked toward the brick building. No, he told her a truth she'd always known.

But if Jonas's father was not one of her mother's lovers, then why had Mama told them he was? "Why?"

"Why what?" a voice asked, startling her.

"Jonas." She'd been so wrapped up in her thoughts she hadn't even looked around.

"Yes, it's me. Right where I'm supposed to be to meet you. May I take that bag for you?"

She relaxed her white-knuckle grip on the handle and held it out. "Thank you. Have you been inside?"

He nodded. "The nurse told me Mom woke up agitated, muttering about something she couldn't make out. She wouldn't eat breakfast and she tried to walk out the front door about an hour ago, insisting she needed to go see you."

"Me? Why me?"

He made a "who knows?" gesture. "I'll put this in the

car and meet you inside. The nurse thought maybe you should talk to her alone to start out."

"Is this holding you up? I know you wanted to get on the road."

"It's a ten-hour drive. We're not going to get there before Mr. Franey leaves for the day, so no worries. Take your time."

She might have appreciated his flexibility more if she wasn't dreading this meeting.

"Miss Charlotte? It's me, Remy Bouchard. I haven't seen you in so long. How are you?"

The woman was sitting in a floral-print chair closest to the window that opened onto Shadybrook's rose garden. She looked the same as the last time Remy had visited her—except for the nervous wringing of her hands and the pinched expression on her face. "Remy, child. You're here. I told your mother you'd come."

Remy glanced around, half-expecting to see her mother's ghost wandering past. "Are you feeling okay, Miss Charlotte?" she asked, pulling up an embroidered footstool to sit on. "You look a little upset."

"Well, who wouldn't be? Kids these days. They don't listen. They go off and do whatever they want—even if it's not in their best interest." She looked out the window, her hand worrying her chin, back and forth. "I nearly lost him once, you know. Marlene understood. She lost someone once, too."

Remy had heard many elderly people in her care suddenly talk about events in their lives that left indelible impressions but meant nothing to the person listening.

But she knew that wasn't the case now. Charlotte had come close to losing her son when he was child. Who had her mother lost?

"They were too young. They had their whole lives ahead of them. A mother can't sit back and watch her boy make a terrible mistake, can she?"

She's talking about Jonas and me.

Charlotte looked down. "I did a terrible thing. I used my friend's secret against her. She never wanted her girls to know the truth about that preacher man. He left town before he knew she was pregnant. Rolled up his tent and moved on. Never came back."

Jessie, our father was a preacher, not Jonas's dad.

"I'm sure Mama understood, Miss Charlotte. She wasn't one to hold a grudge." She waited half a heartbeat to find the courage to ask, "You don't happen to remember his name, do you? The preacher man? The one she loved?"

The woman's eyes closed and her head lolled back against the chair. Her body seemed to deflate like a blow-up doll with a slow leak. Remy checked her pulse. Slow and steady. The temporary short-circuit had passed, along with Remy's link to her real father's identity.

She put her hands on her knees and pushed to her feet. She felt a little wobbly, too, as though they'd traveled through the same time warp together. A movement at the corner of her eye alerted her to Jonas's presence. His warm, strong fingers on her elbow helped anchor her to the present. She looked at him and tried to smile. "I think we might have wasted our money on that test."

Miss Charlotte suddenly straightened. She looked at them both but with no spark of recognition. "Thomas Goodson. Good. Son," she said, repeating the two words distinctly. "Marlene thought that meant she'd have a boy, but she had twin girls, instead."

Remy left the room without saying goodbye to Charlotte. She took the side door—the same one she and Jonas had used the day before. She walked to the middle of the rose garden and stopped dead in her tracks.

Thomas Goodson.

She had a name. Thirty-two years after the fact. Maybe not the right name. The woman who gave it to her could barely remember her own name most days.

"Are you okay?"

She took a deep breath of rose-scented air and released it. "I don't know. I think so."

"Do you believe her?"

She debated a moment but, in the end, answered truthfully, "Yes. Do you?"

"I'm reserving judgment until the test results come back."

So like him.

"Are you still up for going to Florida with me? I'd certainly understand if you changed your mind. I mean, now, instead of blaming your mother for ruining our lives, we get to blame my mother. Could this get any weirder?"

She flew to his side and shushed him with one finger

pressed to his lips. "Never say that. Mama always said only a fool invites Fate to show you how crazy life can get."

The look in his eyes made her heart go all fluttery. She knew this was big. Important. Life-changing, for heaven's sake. She might truly know the name of her father for the first time her in life. She needed to call Jessie. Get online. Try to find the man. What if he was still alive? Mama had died young. Her father might still be walking this earth and she could see him.

"Remy? You didn't answer me. Do you want me to take you home? I would understand."

What to do? She glanced toward where his car was parked in an unloading zone. The sun was angled so that the bright purple paint on the funny frame his daughter made for him caught her eye. Birdie.

Go. She felt the answer in the same way she knew which dreams held meaning and which didn't.

"Can I drive?"

His laugh was all guy. "Absolutely. If I'm dead, drunk or otherwise incapacitated."

"Fine," she said, marching toward the door with a bit of Scarlett O'Hara flair. "But I get to pick the music."

Was she making a mistake by going with him? Maybe. Probably. Especially where her heart was concerned. But, she reminded herself, there was one other element in her dreams last night. One she hadn't mentioned to Jonas when they talked.

When she bumped into the devil, he'd invited her to

come with him. "Your father's been looking for you. You want to meet him, don't you? He's just up the road a bit."

She wasn't a fool. She didn't believe him, but now she wondered if *just up the road a bit* was exactly where she was supposed to be.

"ANOTHER DEAD-END. No pun intended."

Jonas looked up from the computer on his lap. They'd stopped for the night in Gainesville. He could easily have made Tampa, but his passenger specifically had asked—no, begged—for a bed. "Jonas, if you don't want me to spend my entire night driving in my sleep, you have to stop soon. I need to eat and move around a little bit. And I want to check my email."

She'd already decided, out loud, that she wouldn't mention the name Thomas Goodson to her sister until she had more information.

"Nothing? No Thomas Goodson?" he asked Remy, who was sitting on the bed next to his.

They'd discussed the necessity for two rooms and she'd agreed that the added cost was silly. "We're adults. We're not teenagers, anymore," she said. "Just give me clean sheets and free Wi-Fi."

She turned her laptop so he could see. The only word clearly visible was *Obituary*. He swallowed. "You found him?"

Her shoulders lifted and fell. "I found a Thomas Goodson. There are thousands." She returned the screen her way. "This one is the right age, thereabouts, and he was a minister. But the obit doesn't say anything about him ever being an itinerant preacher or living in Louisiana."

"How long ago did he die?"

"Ten years ago."

"Hmm. So, you're still not going to call Jessie?"

Her lips pursed thoughtfully. "I don't know."

He closed his computer and turned on his side to face her, his elbow cocked to support his head. "Call her. She's going to be pissed if you don't."

"Since when do you care how Jessie feels about anything?"

"She did me a very nice favor by putting me in touch with Leonard Franey. I owe her one."

She let out a deep sigh. "I hate it when you're right." She pushed her laptop to the drab striped bedspread and reached for her phone. "I didn't want to get her hopes up. Plus, it would have been really great to tell her I'd found him. After all these years… Wow, right?"

He rose and grabbed his windbreaker. "I'm gonna buy us some water to have in the car tomorrow. I'll be back in a few."

A lame excuse but he didn't want to eavesdrop on her conversation, plus he needed the break. She'd been great. Cheerful, optimistic, even funny when she'd relate some outrageous story about her wild and wacky family.

Having her with him all day had saved him from going out of his head with worry. She'd kept his mind off all the worst-case scenarios that kept popping into his head. He didn't know how she did it. Especially after his mother delivered her cryptic, potentially earth-shattering revelation that morning.

He had to get away from Remy for a few minutes because he needed to come to grips with the truth. He still loved Remy Bouchard. Always had. Admitting his feelings didn't change the fact that he could never act on those feelings. He couldn't fall down on his knees and beg her forgiveness for everything he and, apparently, his mother had done. He could only keep his distance and continue to exploit Remy's gift, her goodness.

"Shit," he swore, walking straight into the cool, evening breeze. He was the lowest of the low. Even offering to pay her had been a lame attempt to disguise the fact that he was using her. But what choice did he have? He had to find Birdie. Remy was part of this now. He couldn't turn around, take her home and say goodbye. Not yet.

He bought a six-pack of water at the convenience store. While waiting to pay, his gaze fell on the condom display behind the counter. Temptation was an ugly, powerful force. He looked over his shoulder, half-expecting to see the devil grinning smugly. But, no, he was the only customer.

"Gimme a package of those, too," he said, nodding behind the clerk.

He cursed his weakness all the way to the room. He almost threw away the vibrantly hued box. Finally, he convinced himself that he had the willpower to resist the temptation Remy presented simply by being herself, but on the impossibly remote chance he lost his mind and his self-control, then wasn't it better to be prepared?

The compromise made perfect sense—until he opened the door of their motel room and he saw her.

Crying.

"Uh-oh. What happened?"

He set the bag near the closet and hurried across the room, shedding his jacket. "Remy? What's wrong? Tell me. Is it Jessie? Did Mr. Franey call?"

She made a feathery motion with her fingers as if trying to blow away her tears, but her bottom lip continued to quiver—the same way Birdie's did when she was trying not to cry. "It's nothing. I'm f-fine. Well, I was until I heard Jessie's voice. Then I sort of fell apart."

He sat and put one arm around her. "I'm sorry. How did she take the news?"

She let her head fall against his shoulder. "She laughed, actually. She said it made perfect sense. A used-car salesman versus a preacher, they both were trying to sell you something."

He let out a soft huff. "Well, that's one way of looking at what happened."

She grabbed a tissue from a box beside the bed and blew her nose, then she looked at him and asked, "Will you do me a favor?"

"Of course. Anything."

"Sleep with me."

His arm dropped like an anchor. "What?"

She pointed from his bed to hers. "Nothing sexual. I just feel very alone at the moment. If Jessie were here,

I'd crawl in bed with her. But she isn't here. And…and she has someone and I don't."

He could tell the tears were beginning to build again. He understood. Probably better than she could possibly imagine. He hugged her again. In support. "Sure. No problem." He looked at the plastic bag in the corner. "Nothing sexual."

CHAPTER ELEVEN

"Thanks for coming, Jonas. It's a pleasure to meet you, Remy. Have a seat."

Jonas held out one of the matching brown leather chairs for Remy then sat beside her. The two chairs faced the largest desk Jonas had ever seen. The top could have been used as a landing strip…if you could find the bottom of it through the massive stacks of papers. In stark opposition, the man behind the desk was compact—five-six, at best, bald and austerely dressed completely in black.

"Thank you for taking this case. Have your investigators found anything, Mr. Franey?"

"Call me Leonard. And, yes, Jonas, we've got a plethora of facts for you. I've had my secretary copy you on everything. She'll hand you a flash drive on your way out. I'd like you both to look over the information after you leave here. Sometimes a victim's loved ones can catch small points that lead to big breaks."

Victim? Jonas looked at Remy, whose eyes had gone wide with alarm.

"So, Jonas, now that you're here, I'd like you to tell me everything you know about the GoodFriends. How and when did you learn that your ex-wife had joined the group?"

"Cheryl hooked up with them while I was out of the country. Apparently the leader of the group—I believe he calls himself Brother Thom—was interviewed on local TV. Cheryl told one of our friends she thought he was the sexiest preacher she'd ever seen."

Leonard nodded. "I watched the video clip included in the background information you sent me. You did a very thorough job, by the way. If you're ever in the market for a job…"

He didn't finish the sentence, but Jonas was pleased by the praise. "You called my ex-wife a victim. If she joined this group willingly—and she made it clear to our friends that this was her intent—how does that make her anything but self-serving and maybe naive?"

Leonard sat forward, his hands clasped in front of him on a pile of papers. "While you and I can clearly see that this sort of religious group is a sham, there are many people who are seduced by a charismatic leader or minister who convinces them to do things that would immediately raise a red flag to the average person. Being gullible shouldn't make you easy prey, but it often does."

Jonas relaxed slightly. "Okay. I'll buy that. I was afraid you meant a physical sort of violation. Bondage, rape, abuse."

Leonard picked up a piece of paper and said, "I'm not ruling out anything at the moment."

"Pardon?" Remy asked. "What do you mean?"

"A friend of mine in the FBI faxed me this. It's a copy of an interview he had last summer with a woman who claimed she barely escaped from the GoodFriends with her life. We haven't had a chance to verify any of her charges. The police dropped the whole thing because, like your ex-wife, the woman has a history of mental instability."

Jonas reached for the folder Leonard handed him. He quickly scanned the transcript. The woman was deemed "hysterical" by the interviewer. She also came across as traumatized and desperately afraid of Brother Thom.

"Isolating people is a good way to establish control over them," Franey said. "On their website, the Good-Friends promote a separatist lifestyle called InFaith living for the most faithful followers. Some of the photos from a couple years back show quite a gypsy caravan. For some reason, the group's numbers have severely declined."

Jonas closed the folder, intending to read it thoroughly later. "I've been checking the site daily and have yet to see any updates. There's still a donation button, and I sent them five bucks when I first got back. The charge has never shown up on my credit card."

Leonard shuffled through the pieces of paper on his desk, finally pulling one sheet free of the others. "My staff has been following the money trail, and, unfortunately, it's as if the well has dried up. Whatever was working for the GoodFriends in the past, isn't happening at all now. The church appears to be broke."

"Do you have any idea where they are?" Remy asked.

The P.I. turned to a very large, very sleek and modern-looking computer. A wave of his hand seemed to bring the thing to life. By stretching close to Remy, Jonas could see an image that might have come from a satellite. "He's dumped his regular cell phone. Since you documented a recent call from your daughter, we assume he's using the prepaid sort, although we have no record of him purchasing one. In fact, his credit cards are all maxed out and frozen. My contact at the IRS says they've seen nothing from either the pastor or the church in two years."

He glanced at Remy. "So, the answer to your question is a slightly qualified no. People who have found success in a certain area tend to return to that area when they're in trouble. I would bet you anything he's still in the South."

Jonas thought so, too. "Unfortunately, the group has held revival meetings in every state from Louisiana to Florida, and as far north as Tennessee."

Leonard looked at him. "That's where the new toys come in. Facial recognition software, for one. And, don't kid yourself, Big Brother is watching. Brother Thom might be keeping a low profile for now, but he'll have to surface some time. Every big tent evangelist I've ever met has a bit of the stage performer in him. These guys get off on the adulation. I promise you, Brother Thom's ego isn't going to let him stay in the backwoods and boonies forever. He will resurface. And soon. I feel it."

Jonas was heartened by the man's confidence. He looked at Remy and smiled. She smiled back but not quite as enthusiastically as he would have imagined.

"Do you have some kind of contract or agreement I need to sign so you can get paid for your services?" Jonas asked.

"Normally, yes. But I've taken this job pro bono as a favor to a friend."

"A friend? Who?"

Leonard didn't answer. Instead, he looked at Remy and studied her a few seconds. "You look very familiar, Remy. Have you appeared on Shane's television show?"

"You mean, Shane Reynard? The producer of *Sentinel Passtime*?" she asked. She didn't know Shane well, but Jessie had worked with him when she did stunts for the show that was loosely based on Cade's hometown of Sentinel Pass. "No. I take care of old people. My twin sister, Jessie, has done some work on the show. She's also a free runner with Team Shockwave."

Leonard snapped his fingers. "Jess deLeon. Of course. One of my favorites. I heard she was injured."

The two chatted a few minutes longer before Jonas cleared his throat. "Is there anything else I should be doing right now to find my daughter? Can you put me to work or point me in the right direction? I'm going a bit crazy here."

Leonard rubbed his chin pensively before answering. "I haven't seen anything to indicate your daughter is in any immediate danger. Long-term, of course, the brainwashing and cult mentality could have a detrimental effect. And given your ex-wife's mental-health issues, you have a right to be concerned, but I'd say for the moment, why not let me do my job?"

Jonas looked at Remy, who gave him a nod of agreement.

"I've sent one of my associates to talk to the woman who says she escaped from the group. She's staying with family in Tallahassee and works a swing shift. He probably won't have anything for me until tomorrow, but I promise to call the minute I hear something. Where are you staying?"

"A resort on St. Pete's Beach," Remy said.

"Good choice. I know how stressful waiting can be, but, truthfully, everything that can be done at the moment is being handled. I promise you that. And we will find your daughter." He looked less stern and more fatherly when he stood and reached across the desk to shake Jonas's hand. "Birdie is going to need you at your best when she comes home. There's no way of knowing how traumatic this has been. Luckily, she's very young and her mother has been with her, but the most effective use of your time may be to take a walk on the beach, have a glass of wine and get some rest. Let Florida work its magic and let me do my job. Okay?"

Jonas shook the man's hand. He felt hopeful for the first time in much too long, but he honestly didn't know if he could relax until Birdie was in his arms. Still, the man did make a valid point. Jonas wasn't going to be any good if he fell apart the minute she was back.

Remy got up, too, but when she shook Leonard's hand, she said, "This is probably going to sound a little woo-

woo, but in my dream last night I saw a big brown-and-silver motor home parked near a bunch of run-down buildings. Nobody was around and I didn't see Birdie, but I felt…creeped out. Like people were watching me from behind the rusted, sagging window screens."

The hair on Jonas's arms stood up. "You didn't tell me you had a dream."

She looked embarrassed. "It could be nothing. Like I said, I didn't see Birdie. I probably shouldn't have mentioned it."

Leonard leaned back abruptly and pawed through one of the piles on his desk withdrawing an eight-by-ten piece of paper. "Did the motor home look like this?"

"Yes. I remember the wavy emblem on the side. I wondered if it was supposed to represent heaven."

"I had a granny who had the sight. Others might scoff at dreams, but not me," Leonard said. "Anytime you see something, Remy—big or small—you let me know."

"I will. Take care. I hope you find her soon." She glanced at Jonas as if she might add something else, but walked toward the door, instead.

"Thank you, Leonard. I'll have my phone on me at all times. Call me if you hear anything."

They exited the office, which occupied an entire corner of an upscale strip mall. It was nearly noon, but Jonas's stomach was a ball of knots. The thought of food did nothing for him. "How about we check into the hotel and take a walk on the beach? Maybe grab a bite later."

"Good idea."

Despite the focus on relaxing, the fear of not knowing where his daughter was, combined with the stress of worrying that he wasn't doing more, had produced a blinding pain in his head.

When they reached the car, he made an impulsive decision and handed her the keys. "Would you mind driving? My head is killing me."

"Seriously?"

Now that he'd admitted the problem out loud, the signs he knew all too well started multiplying. "Stress migraine. I have some pills the army doc gave me. Can you pop the trunk?"

His hand was shaking by the time he tapped two horse tablets into his palm. He took them then gulped down a couple of mouthfuls of water. Room temperature, since they'd left the plastic bag on the floor of the backseat instead of putting it in the cooler in the trunk.

The bag.

He looked at Remy but she was busy pulling a pair of oversize sunglasses out of her purse. She had to have seen his other purchase. A foolish, idiotic buy. He'd apologize to her for sending the wrong message as soon as his head stopped pounding.

He lowered himself into the car and put on his seat belt.

"I'll be fine by the time we get to the hotel," he said, watching her adjust the power seat and mirrors to her satisfaction. She also turned off the AC and opened the windows while she programmed the hotel's address into his built-in navigational system. She'd mastered the unit he'd never even used until this trip.

Typical, he thought. Everybody always underestimates the blonde. He closed his eyes and willed himself to let go and relax. But he couldn't stop thinking about the motor home she claimed to have seen.

"Why didn't you tell me about your dream?"

"It wasn't exactly a dream. I slept like the dead last night," she said, her tone wistful. He understood completely. He'd felt the same.

"While I was showering, I tried to revisit the place in my mind where I first met Birdie. She wasn't there, but that gave me a chance to look around."

And she saw a motor home identical to the one their disappearing preacher drove. He didn't know if he believed that or not. Maybe she simply had a very fertile imagination.

Did it matter? Not really, he decided. He shifted his thoughts to Leonard. The guy was the real deal. Jonas trusted him. He didn't know which of the two approaches—the mystical or hard science—would be the one to find Birdie, but he honestly didn't care. As long as one of them did.

He was nearly asleep, the drugs doing their magic on his brain chemistry, when she said, "Do you remember that night in high school when we slept together?"

"I must have been the dumbest high school kid in the world. I convinced myself that spending the night together chastely would prove we really loved each other—unlike all our dopey friends who called it love but only wanted to have sex. That was without a doubt the most grueling night of my life." His breath caught. "At the time."

"Don't think you were alone, my friend. Girls have hormones, too. You have no idea how much I wanted to do it."

He opened one eye to look at her. "Why didn't you say so? I was being good because you were being good."

"I was being good because Jessie bet me twenty bucks I couldn't spend the whole night in the same bed with you without having sex. I had to prove her wrong."

"I've changed my mind. I do hate your sister." Then he turned his head to take advantage of the sudden cessation of pain and stopped thinking. Destination: oblivion.

Remy studied Jonas in repose. He looked tired and defeated, but still as handsome as the boy she hadn't slept with all those years ago.

A short toot let her know the light had changed. She waved and stepped on the gas. His car was an absolute dream to drive. She loved the new-car smell, the responsiveness and, above all, the lovely English voice on the speaker that told her when to turn.

Tampa was a big, bustling, busy city, but once she was on the freeway and headed in the right direction, she could let her mind roam a bit. Like past the image of a box of condoms in the sack with the water bottles.

He'd bought them last night, even though he'd made it abundantly clear that he wasn't interested in having sex with her. Granted they were still awaiting the results of the DNA test, but his mother's confession seemed to clearly reject the possibility that her mother had had an affair with Jonas's dad.

Did that explain the condoms?

She didn't ask because he was in such obvious pain, but she planned to find out tonight. They'd booked one room again and had direct orders from the P.I. to relax. Did relaxation therapy include sex? she wondered.

If it did, how did she feel about the idea? She wanted him. That was a no-brainer, but sex without a commitment—emotional or verbal—was so Mama. Could she risk the inevitable hurt? How many trips did she and Jessie make to the market for boxes of tissues after Mama's current Mr. Perfect went back to his wife? Too many.

Remy didn't believe Jonas would do that—reunite with Cheryl. But the woman had some sort of hold on him. Remy could sense it. Guilt? Grief? She couldn't say, but Jonas was an emotional quagmire—plus, as Leonard pointed out, he was the father of a little girl who had been dragged through something scary and potentially devastating.

She glanced at him once more, then touched the Bluetooth receiver she'd put in her ear the moment she got behind the wheel. She had only one number programmed: Jessie.

"Hey, Rem," Jessie answered. "I was just going to call you. Did you meet with the P.I. already?"

"Uh-huh. He's top-notch. And a big fan of Jess deLeon."

Jessie let out a small sigh. "I hope he won't be too

disappointed if Jess deLeon quietly disappears from sight."

Remy gaped in silent surprise. "Seriously? You've decided to stop doing Parkour and free-running?"

"My body has. I just got back from the orthopedist. He wants to operate later this summer. He says it will take at least six months before I can start limited physical therapy. I'll be able to lead a—" she coughed meaningfully "—normal life, but extreme sports are history."

"Oh, Jessie. I'm so sorry. You must be completely bummed."

Jessie didn't answer right away. When she did, she made a strange sound. A giggle? "Thanks, Rem. I probably should be more upset than I am, but, honestly, I'm too happy to worry about it. Not happy about the surgery, but happy every other way. Love will do that to you."

If you're lucky.

"I'm glad. Really glad."

Jessie babbled on a few minutes, telling Remy about her first meeting of the Wine, Women and Words Book Club the night before. Cade's sister, Kat, was a founding member and she'd dragged the road-weary Jessie to the meeting. "Luckily, Cade and I rented the book on tape while we were on the road and listened to it all the way home. Very cool. I didn't feel dumb at all."

"You're not dumb."

"I know, but I'm not a brainiac like you, either. It was fun. I think I finally understand why Mama always had all those ladies hanging around. They were her support group. You and I had each other, and the Bullies were sort of off by themselves. Mama needed those ladies, didn't she?"

The insight made Remy smile. *Just like I need you and now you're not only going to be miles and miles away but you're going to be married.* The thought made her mouth go dry.

She reached behind the seat for a bottle of water. Her fingers grazed a small box first. The one she'd spotted earlier.

"Jessie, is there any reason I couldn't have sex with Jonas?"

She asked the question softly, but the man in question was a few inches to her right. Fortunately, his smooth, even breathing didn't change pitch.

"Are you asking me for permission?"

"We don't have the test back, but that seems to be a moot point if you believe his mother."

"And we do believe her, don't we?"

Yes.

"Well, Rem, I certainly can't say as I blame you. He's still a great-looking guy, and you've always had a thing for him. But…"

"But, what?"

Jessie sighed. "Well, I'll come right out and say it. He's as emotionally unattainable as any of the men Mama used to date. He married a crazy woman. He's got a kid who will probably need some serious counseling, the poor dear. And if what his mother said was true, then Miss Charlotte is to blame for breaking you two up, not Mama. That's a lot of heavy old baggage, Remy.

Short of having a flashing warning light over his head, you couldn't ask for more red flags." The navigation system warned that her exit approached.

"I have to go, Jess. I'm glad things are falling into place for you. I mean that."

"Thanks, sweetie. Oh, wait, I almost forgot. I asked Cade to look into finding our Bible-thumping daddy. He emailed you everything he found. It's a lot. It's kinda freaky, actually. I'm not sure how I feel about the idea that this guy is our dad. Call me after you've had a chance to look it over, okay?"

Remy put her blinker on. "I will. Is he still alive?"

"Oh, hell, no. Dead as a doornail. Which is probably a good thing. You'll see. Drive safe. You're gonna love the Tradewinds. Order a golden margarita for me. Bye."

Remy ended the call and hit the brake with a tad more force than necessary. Her slumbering passenger shifted position, slowly rousing. "Are we there, yet?" he asked with a yawn.

"Just about."

"Reminds me of Mexico," he said, stretching to look around.

She'd never been south of the border, but the scent of the ocean combined with all the palm trees and flowering plants, along with the high-rise hotels that displayed an interesting blend of architecture—part resort, part Disney World—made her wonder if she was still in the United States.

Following the directions, she pulled to a stop beneath their hotel's wide portcullis. Two doormen hurried to greet them. Remy was happy to hand over the keys. At the moment, the idea of a frosty cocktail sounded very inviting—even if it was several hours before her mother's rule about what was socially acceptable.

She had a decision to make. Did she give in, accept the fact that she was her mother's daughter and seduce Jonas? Or not?

BIRDIE LIKED ANTS.

Most people hated them. Her mother dumped a bucket of soapy water on top of this very anthill not ten minutes earlier, flooding them, probably killing hundreds of ants, but they weren't all dead.

She poked her stick at the opening to let more of the water flow off. A few dead bodies were carried away by the wave, but the survivors ignored her, intently getting to work.

Her daddy had a word for people who carried on even when things got bad. She couldn't remember it, and that made her sad. Run-away-and-cry sad, but she didn't dare.

Brother Thom had warned her. "I'm watching you, girl. If you ever touch another phone or do anything bad, I will put the fear of God in you."

Which proved he wasn't as smart as Mommy said. Birdie was already afraid of God. It was pretty clear He didn't like her. When He sent her daddy off to war, it was like dumping dirty water on her and her mother. Poor Mommy was like one of the wet ants, running around, lost, trying to find a place to fit in.

She looked at the stick in her hand and without stopping to think she jabbed it into the hole of the anthill as hard as she could. Then she jumped to her feet and stomped in the soft mud furiously. She wanted them to die. She hated the ants. She hated God and her mother and Brother Thom and the GoodFriends. She hated everything and everybody. She wanted to go home. Now.

CHAPTER TWELVE

"THIS HAS GOT TO BE wrong on so many levels," Jonas said five hours after checking into the hotel.

The economy room Remy had reserved, the clerk at the registration desk told them, would not have been available until the regular check-in time of three-thirty, so Jonas had handed over his gold card and traded up for a ground-floor suite with a charming lanai and a great view of the beach.

The lush, tropical grounds of the hotel made Remy squeal with delight. The trek to their room included crossing an arched bridge under which passed two very large, very elegant swans. "Look, Jonas, look," she'd cried. "Wouldn't Birdie love this place?"

The innocent question had thrown a damper on her joy, but she seemed to recover some of her good spirits after she investigated every inch of their room. "This might well be the nicest place I've ever stayed," she told him, using her phone to take a picture of the living area with its bright floral-print cushions and white wicker furniture. "I could see this style in Mama's house."

He couldn't, but he kept his opinion to himself.

After changing into shorts and flip-flops, they grabbed a quick bite at the hotel's beach bar, then went exploring. Remy was right, Birdie would have loved this place. From the giant waterslide on the beach to the kids-only pool and paddleboats that navigated the waterways where big, colorful koi swam, along with the swans.

He'd invited Remy to join him for a jog on the beach, but she'd laughed off his suggestion. "No, thank you. I'm going to sit here on my lovely padded chaise, sip this delicious margarita and catch up on email."

When he spotted the swimsuit she pulled out of her bag, he'd been tempted to join her poolside, but his libido vetoed the idea. A run had been the smart choice. Plus, he'd worked off a little extra stress by swimming to the buoy and back. That hadn't left time for anything besides showering and dressing for dinner.

He took another bite of his meal. "As God is my witness, this is the best sea bass I've ever eaten. Rem, you have to try this."

She put up her hands. "And risk burning in environmental hell? I don't think so. My chicken is fine, thank you very much." She stabbed a piece, twirled it in the creamy white sauce rife with capers, and said with a distinct air of superiority, "And it's organic, sustainably raised, free range." She chewed it thoughtfully. "In fact, I'm pretty sure this chicken practiced yoga."

He threw back his head and laughed. It felt good to pretend for a few precious moments that his life was normal. Here he was an ordinary guy out on a date with a gorgeous, smart, witty woman at a fabulous restaurant on a beautiful moonlit night.

Almost.

He took a sip of wine. They'd ordered two glasses, rather than a bottle. In case Leonard called. Not because Jonas didn't trust himself to let down his guard where Remy was concerned.

"Cade emailed me while you were running," she said, her tone casual.

Why, he wondered, did he get the feeling she had something weighty to tell him? He took another bite but the flavor wasn't quite as good.

"He did an extensive search using the name your mother gave us. He's a smart guy. Instead of looking at all the Thomas Goodsons in the world, he went to the Baylorville community archives and found that, yes, indeed, a minister named Thomas Goodson lived in town from 1974 through 1976. Remember the Covenant Church? That little white building on the west side of town? It burned down ten or so years ago."

"Vaguely."

"Apparently, he was married. One child."

Jonas wiped his mouth on his napkin and pushed his plate to one side. "Where did he go after he left Baylorville?"

She shrugged. "I don't know. Cade thinks the obit I found is of the same guy. The seminary school he graduated from and the date he graduated is the same."

He touched her hand. "I'm sorry, Remy. That bites. But the fact he was a preacher probably explains why your mother kept his name a secret. He was a man of God. He might have been human and had an affair with one of his parishioners, but at least he wasn't a serial philanderer, like my dad."

Neither spoke for a minute or so, then she sighed. "This revelation makes me feel sorta upside down."

"I bet. Is there anything I can do?"

"You could take me for a walk on the beach."

He'd already signed the bill to their room, so leaving was simple; they stepped off the patio and onto the warm white sand of the beach. Remy paused to remove her sandals then she took his hand and followed.

The beach had quieted a great deal since his run. The outline of dozens of wooden cabanas were visible in the lights from the silvery moon and stars. The steady whoosh of the waves invited him to return to the water's edge, but they stayed on the dry sand, which retained some of the heat from the day.

The air temperature was mild, but the breeze—more powerful than he'd expected—felt both balmy and exhilarating. Every nerve in his body tingled, alive and aware of this moment in time.

"Have you ever wondered what our lives would have been like if we hadn't fallen in love in high school?" she asked, her tone somber. "Our mothers wouldn't have felt the need to fabricate a lie. Maybe my mother might have broken down and told Jessie and me who our father was before he died." Her tone was wistful, sad.

"I'm really sorry for all of this."

"It wasn't your fault."

"My mother—"

"Our mothers collaborated to deceive us, Jonas. And

at this point, there's really no one left to blame. I only meant that our lives might have been entirely different if we'd gone to college and bumped into each other at a reunion five years later."

"Does that really happen?"

"Sure. Remember Suzie? Our waitress at Catfish Haven? She married some guy from Chicago, lived up north for ten years, and had two kids before he ran off with his secretary. After their divorce, she came home for the all-school reunion and ran into a guy she dated in high school. They'd broken up over something trivial. They started dating and got married as soon as her divorce was final."

"Wow. Of course, they didn't spend all those years apart thinking they were related."

She knocked her head against his shoulder. "Well, there's that, and," she added with a rueful chuckle, "her current hubby is no great prize, either. But she claims he's the love of her life."

The love of her life.

He tightened his grip on her hand. "Remy, I need to tell you something. I've been back in Baylorville a thousand times since graduation. Even after my divorce, I could have come and found you, asked you out. The idea that we were related was partly why I never attempted to talk to you, but there was another reason, too."

"What?"

"Remember when you asked me why I married Cheryl and I showed you her picture? Well, you're not the only one who saw a certain resemblance. One day we were visiting Mom, and Cheryl ran across our high school yearbook. She saw the pictures of you and me together."

"She was jealous?"

"Oh, more than jealous. She flew into a rage. She yelled and swore and broke things. Luckily, Mom had taken Birdie to visit friends."

He was glad Birdie didn't have to see that outburst. There had never been anything like it before or since then, at least in his presence.

"You became a sort of demon obsession for Cheryl. She couldn't let it go. There came a point where, if Mom needed my help, I'd lie and tell my wife I was going out of town on business rather than get into an argument over my *real* reason for visiting Baylorville." He'd told himself he was lying for Birdie's sake. So she didn't have to witness the arguments, threats and name-calling that accompanied one of Cheryl's paranoid outbursts. But maybe his need to avoid confrontation ran deeper—all the way back to his childhood.

"I'm so sorry."

He dropped his head to his chest, ashamed and slightly sick. "I lied. I was desperate. I told her we broke up because you cheated on me, and that's why I hated you. I was attracted to blondes but I would cross the street rather than have to face you again." He'd felt like the most despicable liar and fraud on the planet, but his lies had worked.

"I knew our marriage was doomed. But Cheryl figured out a way to use my worst nightmare against me.

And as much as it kills me to admit this, she still has power over me—through Birdie. It's pure manipulation. Unfair and awful, but effective."

"She told you if you had an affair with me, she would commit suicide and her death would be your fault—just like your dad's," she said in a pained voice.

"Pretty much. Only, Cheryl's threat was more specific. She didn't care about other women. She just cared if I cheated with you."

He didn't confirm her astute guess. He couldn't. But hadn't he always, at least in part, blamed himself for his father's death?

"How come you didn't tell her about your dad and my mom? Wouldn't the threat of committing incest have made her less anxious?"

He shook his head. "Maybe. I don't know. I couldn't risk that she wouldn't tell my mother. Besides, that was our secret, Rem. Yours and mine. I never told anybody. I wouldn't do that."

They walked a good distance before she spoke. "I saw the condoms in the grocery bag, Jonas. Does that mean you don't believe her threat anymore? You don't care? Or you want to make love with me as long as we keep things on the down low so your ex-wife never finds out?"

He wished like hell he knew the answer to any of those questions. "I want you, Remy. Always have. But my life is a freaking mess. I don't want to do anything to hurt you or Birdie. And as much as I hate to say this, I'd never forgive myself if Cheryl followed through on her threat because she found out you and I had been together." He grabbed her hand and pulled her close enough to see her eyes. "Not because I give shit about what happens to her, but because I don't want my daughter to spend the rest of her life wondering why her mommy didn't love her enough to stick around."

"Then we'd better make damn sure nobody ever finds out what we did—what we're going to do—here tonight."

He looked at her—a blonde angel in a white dress standing in front of him in the warm sand, the ocean breeze caressing them like the lovers they had no business being. He swallowed against the thickness in his throat. "You don't mean that, Remy. I know you. I know that secrets eat you up inside. You deserve a whole helluva lot more than a one-night stand."

"You can look at it that way. Or you could say the universe has given us a tiny window of time—a gift to make up for how badly we were wronged." She sounded so convincing but he wasn't sure he believed her. And he sure as hell couldn't make any promises beyond tonight.

"Can't we pretend we're two adults—two strangers—who find each other attractive and want to have sex together?"

Sex? Would that be enough? Could he make love with her, then leave? The way her father did nine months before she and her sister were born? "Do you really want this, Remy?"

"I'm not my mother's daughter for nothing," she replied wryly. "Yes, I do."

"You can't be there when we find Birdie. Cheryl will know something's happened between us. She'll know."

She reached out to stroke the side of his face tenderly. "I'll take the bus back to Baylorville the minute you tell me to go."

Maybe it was the romance of the night, maybe she was right about Fate's role in their lives. Whatever excuse seemed to fit best, he was ready to grasp it.

He reached into his pocket and pulled out the key card to their room. "Hi, there, stranger. My name is Jonas. Have we met before?"

"Absolutely not. Are you new in town? Me, too. How about I join you in your room and we get to know each other?"

He took her arm. "Right this way, Miss...?"

"Bouchard. Remy Bouchard. Of the Baylorville Bouchards. Perhaps you've heard of us."

"Nope. Absolutely not. But I'm dying to know everything about you."

A ONE-NIGHT STAND. *Oh, lord, Jess, what am I doing?*

Doubts nibbled on Remy's self-confidence like minnows at her toes when her mother used to take the family to the lake. But she kicked them away. She was an adult. This was her chance to grab what she wanted with no apologies and damn few regrets—exactly the way her mother had lived her life.

Mama would be proud of her.

"So, Ms. Remy Bouchard of Baylorville, Louisiana, what do you do for a living?"

They'd reached the walkway where sand met sidewalk. A conveniently placed bench allowed her the chance to relace her sandals. "Well, I'm between jobs at the moment. In addition to my teaching degree, I have a minor in human services. I thought I might make a good headhunter—using my ability of reading people to find the right person for the right job."

"That makes sense. How come you're not working for some big company?"

She shuddered. "Do you have any idea what a jungle business can be? Too many people want too much without really doing the work." She looked up and caught him staring at the neckline of her dress. She was glad now she'd brought her white dress. Not only did it pack well, it was made of a soft jersey that clung to her rounded parts in a very flattering way. "So, I took a job in geriatric care, instead."

"You opted out of the jungle in favor of a more serene environment."

She stood. "Serene? Is that code for boring? Because if that's what you think, then you've never spent any time with old people. The ones who still have their wits about them are some of the most interesting people I've ever met."

"I didn't mean to sound judgmental. I was picturing the work as less competitive, not a snooze-fest."

"Oh. Well, you wouldn't be the first to accuse me of hiding out from life. My older sisters constantly email me articles about how to meet eligible men. Unfortunately, the dating pool at ShadyBrook is seniors only." She grinned. "Not that the place isn't rife with romance, but I'm not part of it."

He pointed to his eyes. "Those old men need glasses."

She pretended to blink coquettishly. "Why, don't you say the sweetest things," she said, laying on the drawl. "I do believe you have intentions of the lascivious kind in mind."

They'd reached the door of their room and in the shadow of a huge, flowering bush, he turned, trapping her between his arms. "If you mean that in a good way, then, yes, I do. Most lascivious indeed."

To prove it, he kissed her, full on the mouth in that ravishing way she once loved—still loved. She wrapped her arms around his neck and returned the kiss with all the passion she'd stored up over the years.

A sudden and loud applause from the nearby bar where Remy procured her delicious cocktail that afternoon made her shrink back in embarrassment. "That's not for us—the band's starting up," he told her. "Come, my love. Let's check out the privacy of our room."

Not an appropriate endearment for a one-night stand, but she didn't scold him. Even if this affair—for want of a better word—could go no further, she planned to make the most of her opportunity.

"That's a pretty serious frown on your face. You're not facing a firing squad, I promise. And if you want to call this off, just say the word."

She took the key card from his fingers and ran it through the electronic lock. "The only word I plan to say is 'Yes, yes, yes,'" she said, putting a little *When Harry Met Sally* urgency in her tone.

He followed her into the room. She sat on the bed to remove her shoes. She hiked up her hemline a few inches and crossed one leg over the other. "So where's that bag with the condoms?"

He looked at the ceiling, a bemused grin on his face. "If you had any idea how close I came to throwing them away…" He walked to his suitcase and unzipped it. "I know how this looks, but I really didn't plan…"

Remy laughed to let him off the hook. "Don't worry. I'm not appalled. And if it makes you feel any better, I have some in my cosmetics bag."

His jaw dropped. "No way."

"Way. Jess and I made a pact when we moved to Nashville that we'd always carry ECs—emergency condoms."

He tossed the box on the bed, shaking his head. "You two always did speak your own language."

She walked to him and casually brushed back a lock of his hair. Then leaned in and kissed him. Slow and methodically, so she'd be able to remember every moment later on.

He pulled her closer, linking his hands across the base of her tailbone. "Do you know what I remember most about kissing you? Your crooked tooth."

She pulled back slightly to run her tongue across her eyetooth, which sat slightly off center. "Why?"

"Because even though you looked perfect to everyone else, you had one tiny little flaw that only I knew about."

His confession warmed her. Well, actually, it did more than warm. Or maybe that spark of heat ignited when he tightened his arms around her and buried his face between her breasts.

She rubbed her cheek across the top of his head and closed her eyes with a sigh. There was no denying how right this felt—even after so many years of believing it was wrong.

"I put on a few pounds since high school," she warned, reaching behind her to unzip the fitted bodice of her dress.

"I lost ten pounds in Iraq."

"Braggart."

"No. I simply meant we're not the same people we were fifteen years ago. Living in this crazy world has changed us. I'm not expecting you to be the same Remy, and I don't want you to be disappointed, because I sure as hell am not eighteen."

She slipped out of her dress, letting it drop to the floor. She'd packed her nicest undies and matching bra. She felt pretty, sexy and so nervous she thought she might throw up. Until she looked in his eyes and saw Jonas. The old Jonas. The boy she'd loved forever.

The lines around his eyes softened; his smile was boyish and filled with glee—as if he'd rubbed a lamp and she was his genie about to grant his most heartfelt wish.

She unsnapped her front-closing bra and tossed it aside. She knew she looked pretty good. Not as fit and trim as Jessie, but she'd always had more curves than her twin. *Does my tan line look too obvious?* she wondered, glancing down.

Jonas stepped closer and caught her chin in his fingers, urging her face upward. "You are the most beautiful woman in the world, Remy Bouchard. I can't believe you're here. With me. I swear, I must be dreaming. Maybe those pain pills I took had a hallucinogenic agent in them."

She placed his hand on her breast, molding his fingers to her warm flesh. "You're not hallucinating, Jonas. I'm real. I'm here. And we're going to live this dream together."

He undressed with speed and surprising grace, despite her mostly inept attempts to help. She was so past any ability to fake coolness. She was excited, happy, giddy and a bit scared. Not of what would happen later. No, she was afraid she'd built this up in her mind to something so big, so perfect no man could possibly meet her expectations.

As if reading her mind, he said, "I need to warn you, Remy. I haven't been with a woman in a long time. And, even though I've made love to you a million or so times in my mind, there's a good chance I'll blow it this time."

She plastered herself against his naked body, wrapping her arms tight across his back. "No," she said, rubbing her cheek flat against the finely toned muscles of his chest. "This is too right to go wrong. There's no performance review, I promise. Just love me, Jonas. Now. Please."

That one plea proved a trigger. He swept her into his arms and turned to lower her carefully to the bed. He kissed her from each extremity inward, fingertips to breasts, toes to her aching, heated core. She limited her attention to his skin, licking the wonderful curve of his collarbone, nipping and teasing each taut little nipple. She loved the taste of him, salty and slightly spicy. She couldn't explain it, but her memory said, "Yes. This is your Jonas."

"Kiss me," he demanded, his voice low and rough.

She opened her mouth to him the same moment his fingers found her central core. He swallowed her moan of need and desire. They let their tongues wrangle, revealing the old friends they were, remembering and at the same time forging new memories.

"Now, please, Jonas. Now," she whispered, ready—oh, so ready—to climb to the next plane of pleasure.

It took him a moment to locate and open the condom he'd tossed on the bed. But she used the time to touch the part of him that would soon be inside her. She'd never been quite this bold in high school. A few tentative caresses in the backseat of his car. Enough to form an image in her mind. An image that didn't do justice to the body she now held and stroked.

"Damn, that feels good," he said with a gravelly groan. "Your touch is so you. But any more and I'm not going to get us where we need to go."

She dropped back to the pillow and watched as he prepared. This was it. The moment she'd waited half her life for. When he slipped between her legs, she closed her eyes to savor every wonderful sensation. They fit together like two halves of a whole.

And when he moved, that missing piece—the part that never seemed quite right with some other man—fell into place. Or rather, rose to the occasion, pulsing with life and heat and a power that took her straight out of her mind and into a level of awareness she never knew existed.

Oh. Of course. This is it.

And when Jonas joined her in that unique and wonderful space a moment later, collapsing into her arms with a cry of something male and real, it was all she could do to keep from saying the one thing that would ruin everything. *I love you, Jonas.*

CHAPTER THIRTEEN

JONAS WAS STILL AWAKE a good hour after he and Remy made love a second time. She was nestled comfortably in his arms, but he couldn't relax. Never in his life had he felt more conflicted. When he was with Remy, he got so lost in the moment that a bomb could have gone off next door and he wouldn't have known it. Losing control that way was never a good thing.

He'd read somewhere that children of divorce could spend the better part of their life trying to put things together again, either in their work or in their personal relationships. He was pretty sure he was guilty of that on both fronts. His professional life was all about recreating a puzzle to find the truth. In his personal life, he spent more years, months, weeks and days than he could count trying to keep the people in his life from spinning out of control.

Now, he'd made the biggest reconnection of his life. The girl who not only got away, but was driven away by a lie. That both their mothers were to blame for this lie did little to ease his anger and hurt. He'd loved Remy with every ounce of his teenage body and mind.

And now she was here. In this bed. Beside him.

She was still beautiful, still sweet, but with a new and surprising dose of her sister's mouth and backbone.

He could imagine what their first time would have been like if they'd "gone all the way" in high school. Fast, for sure. Sweaty and cramped considering the lack of space in the back of his car. Nervous and worried about being found out or getting pregnant. An embarrassment of youthful trial and error ending with a big bang for him and an "Isthatallthereis?" for her.

But the one thing that hadn't changed was how he felt about her. He still loved her. He probably always would.

A fact that made this night all the more poignant. It was their one and only. Birdie would need him when she got back, and who knew what would happen with Cheryl? Any way he peered into the dark crystal ball of the future, he couldn't see even a hint of personal fulfillment.

He rolled over and sat up, the covers bunching around his waist. He'd done as the P.I. instructed—he'd taken the night off and recharged his batteries. With Remy's help. Had he used her? Again? He didn't want to think about that.

He started to stand but a warm hand laid flat against the middle of his back stopped him. "No. Stay."

He turned and nuzzled her cheek, soaking up the scent of her. His love. "I need to go over those files Leonard sent. There might be a clue or two I missed. The man has resources a small-time insurance investigator like me can only dream about."

Dream. The word made him shiver. "Go back to sleep," he whispered.

He pulled on his sweatpants and grabbed his computer bag. As quietly as possible, he heated up a cup of instant coffee in the microwave, then set up an impromptu desk at the glass-top table in the living area. His plan was to cross-reference his facts—and assumptions—about the GoodFriends with Leonard's findings. Anything that didn't jibe was a red flag worthy of a follow-up call.

He stumbled across the first such situation a few minutes later. "How did I miss that?" he muttered under his breath.

He re-read the police report from the first interview with the woman who escaped from the GoodFriends. A name he'd never seen in this context seemed to jump off the page straight into his brain.

No. It wasn't possible, he thought. A bizarre coincidence, maybe? But he'd been in the insurance business too long to believe in coincidences of this magnitude.

He made several notes then continued reading, but his inner investigator hummed with curiosity and he couldn't let go of the idea that what he'd circled wasn't a mistake. Remy's laptop was resting on the sofa a few feet away. He debated the ethics of snooping without permission for about a minute. He'd broken half a dozen laws and more than a few moral codes since this investigation began. What was one more? Besides, Remy would be the first to offer any help if he asked her. Which he couldn't do because he needed her to dream.

So, what you're saying, his conscience griped, *is*

you've figured out how to use her two ways—three, if you count sex.

He snatched the computer and opened it, praying the files weren't password protected. They weren't. He clicked on her email icon and a minute later had his hands on the file Jessie's future husband had sent.

He skimmed the page until he found what he wanted. A date of birth. A date that matched the one on the GoodFriends's website.

"Interesting." But he didn't see how the fact that Brother Thom changed his name had any bearing on his case. Unless he could find out why a guy who followed in his late father's well-established footsteps would want— or, perhaps, need—to distance himself so irrevocably.

He returned to his laptop. He'd give the name to Leonard in the morning to do a thorough background search. In the meantime, he decided to check his company's database to see if anything popped up. A recent claim? Any sort of anomaly associated with either of the guy's names.

He typed in the URL for his company's mainframe computer in Memphis and, when prompted, supplied a password he wasn't authorized to have. He prayed the code hadn't changed since the last time he hacked his way in.

Ten seconds never seemed so long, but finally the menu he was looking for popped up on the screen. His company had an extensive record of criminals and repeat offenders—people who had made a habit of trying to cheat insurance companies out of money that wasn't due them. In addition to that list, there was a collateral file. Names of everyone who ever settled a claim or accepted a check for a death benefit.

He quickly set up the parameters of his search and hit Enter. The results were instantaneous. He sat back as if hit solidly in the chest by an iron fist. The coffee he'd drank a few minutes earlier nearly made a return trip up his throat.

In the past eighteen years, Jonas's company had written six checks to the good reverend. Six deaths. A sad coincidence? Not very damn likely.

Brother Thom was more than just an opportunistic evangelist who traded on people's faith, fears and generosity to make a living. Somehow he'd contrived a way to supplement his income by convincing members of his congregation to take out insurance policies that named Brother Thom as the sole beneficiary.

Jonas had no problem seeing how such a heinous crime could take place. A respected and revered spiritual guide, the man had easy access to the disenfranchised, the easily swayed. Society's lost and most vulnerable members who didn't have close friends or family to look after them.

Once indoctrinated into the cult, the chosen soul would be convinced to leave all their worldly possessions—including a life-insurance policy the church would pay for—to help the good work continue after he or she was gone. The chosen would be an honored guest of the cult for a year—until the policy was vested. After that, all Brother Thom had to do was figure out a way for that member to die—an accident, suicide, a health condition in keeping with the person's age or physical problems.

Jonas didn't have access to cause of death. But he knew his suspicions had merit. Brother Thom was a murderer at the very least, and possibly, a serial killer.

I wonder if the bastard calls each death "divine intervention."

Jonas surveyed what he'd found. Circumstantial evidence spread over several states. Murder would be difficult to prove without exhuming a body. If there were any bodies left. The man was probably smart enough to pay for his victims' cremations.

Jonas tried not to let his imagination probe too far into Brother Thom's psyche. The man might have gotten caught up in an easy way to make money. Wrong. Vile. Reprehensible. That didn't mean he was serial killer, per se. The kind who thrived on human sacrifice. Who got off on murder. It was one thing to be broke and make a really horrible choice; it was another to lust for blood.

Jonas didn't see any way of convincing a D.A. in one of the cases to go hunting for foul play. Nor did he care at the moment. His main concern was whether or not Brother Thom was poised to cash in on Cheryl's accidental death.

He quickly typed in his ex-wife's name. Nothing. There was no record of a life-insurance policy being issued in Cheryl's name. Unfortunately, that didn't mean she wasn't a target. There were hundreds, possibly thousands, of insurance companies worldwide that sold life-insurance polices. That this asshole used Jonas's company more than once seemed sloppy. Although, Jonas had to admit, no red flag had surfaced to date. The guy was undoubtedly counting on a big company being too large to notice a few relatively small payouts.

He didn't have a printer handy, so he picked up his pen and quickly made a list of the payouts his company had made to Brother Thom, starting at the first check he'd received twenty years earlier. Forty thousand dollars for the loss of his father, Reverend Thomas Goodson, Sr.

Jonas stared at the name with a heavy heart. If Jonas's mother was right, he was looking at the name of Remy's birth father. Which meant the man behind this cult, Brother Thom, aka Thomas Goodson, Jr., was Remy's real half brother.

Bizarre. Incredible. Freaking messed up, no matter how you tried to spin it.

He had no idea how to break this news to her.

He started to turn off his computer but paused, his gaze falling on the date of Brother Thom's last claim. Four years earlier. He did a quick calculation. The woman who escaped from the GoodFriends claimed her life had been in danger. She'd just celebrated her first anniversary with the group. If she'd been Brother Thom's next victim, that might explain the group's current lack of funds.

A thought hit him. Cheryl wasn't the only one who joined the cult a few months after Jonas left the country. He frantically typed in another name: Brigitte Leann Galloway.

The search result flashed on the screen. Pain as swift and intense as a bullet strike ricocheted through his body. "No. God, no."

He pawed through the papers he'd printed from the GoodFriends's website until he found a head shot of Brother Thom. "You hurt her, you bastard, and I will kill you. You have my word."

Before he could decide what to do—or even get his head back in the game and out of the deep pit of terror—his phone rang. It wasn't quite 5:00 a.m. "Hello."

He hadn't had time to check the caller I.D. but he knew who it was.

"It's Leonard Franey. I think I've found your cult. By *found*, I mean a general location based on recent credit-card sales to one of the core members. One Reuben G. Baker."

"Where?"

He didn't answer right away.

"You've found something, haven't you?" Leonard deflected the conversation to Jonas.

"Yes. I'll tell you after you bring me up to date. Did your associate talk to the woman who ran away from the cult?"

Jonas looked toward the kitchenette and wasn't surprised to see Remy standing there in the pretty yellow cover-up she'd worn on the beach. Her hair was a sexy, messy tumble and she rubbed the sleep out of her eyes like a child.

"I'll make coffee," she whispered.

"He did. She confirmed—"

"Excuse me, Leonard. Remy just came into the room. I'm going to put you on speakerphone."

"Sure. No problem. Good morning, Remy."

"Hi, Leonard," she called out. "You're an early bird."

"Very true. Now, as I was saying, the gal who got away was very happy to talk about these people. She was madly in love with the good reverend—even had a kid with him. Apparently the boy died in an accident. I haven't been able to track down a police report, but she pointed the finger at the whole lot. Even accounting for bias, she gave us a lot of inside information that seems valid.

"For instance, she said the operation has been going downhill. Lower attendance means fewer donations. The faithful have been dropping like flies, so to speak."

"What do you mean?" Jonas asked sharply. Dead flies? And what kind of accident was to blame for a young child's death?

"Attrition. Infighting. Petty politics that caused a serious division. Apparently, they bought a big hunk of swampland for more than it was worth and when the economy tanked, they couldn't afford to pay the taxes, much less make the necessary improvements to provide for a growing community."

"So, people dropped out."

"Right. And, the remaining followers went back to traveling again, doing the one-night or weekend tent revivals to raise money. They never stay in one place very long. A day or two at most, usually long enough fill up their vehicles with gas and hit the road again."

"How many are with him, now?"

"When she left the group, they were down to three men, counting Brother Thom, and six women—all mothers with young children. The other men appear to be drivers. There's the reverend's high-end motor home, along with a truck and fifth-wheel combination. They pitch a couple of tents when they stop.

"The drivers park the campers then head off and do advance work for the gospel meetings. You know, put up flyers and hand out free tickets."

Jonas didn't want to bring up his unproven theory— not with Remy listening, so he kept his questions general. "Which vehicle do Cheryl and Birdie travel in?" The farther away from Brother Thom, the better.

"I can't say. It would appear the social dynamics are in a constant state of flux. Some nights Brother Thom invites one lady to stay with him, some nights another. I don't know where your ex-wife falls in the hierarchy."

Jonas looked at Remy who reappeared, a mug in her hand. She motioned to it, asking if he wanted one. He shook his head.

"We do have one piece of good news," Franey said. "One of my researchers found a video posted by someone with a screen name of JCSBaby. Apparently this person is a loyal fan of the GoodFriends. I've sent you the link. There's a little girl who looks like your daughter dancing with the other children. We think it was taken about two months ago."

Remy moved to where Jonas was sitting. A few seconds later, the laptop screen was filled with a circle of children holding hands as they danced to a fiddle playing off camera.

"That's her," he cried, pointing to Birdie. "Thank God. Look. She's smiling." He let out a long, shaky breath. "Thank you, Leonard."

But Jonas knew something Leonard didn't. He had to tell Leonard his fears and suspicions—even if that meant Remy would receive the news secondhand.

"I went through the transcripts you gave me, Leonard. Before I tell you what I've found, let me add that my theory is completely unsubstantiated at the moment. But, I've been doing this sort of work a long time and my gut thinks we have a major problem. If you see any flaws in my assessment, I would truly like to know, because this changes everything—particularly the speed in which we need to act to find Birdie."

Remy took the chair across from him. Her expressive face showed fear and concern. He hated to think what she was going to feel when she heard what he was about to say.

He took a deep breath and plunged in, outlining exactly what he'd uncovered and how he came to his conclusion. "I don't have all the files, obviously. The details of these cases aren't accessible outside the office. I can only see the name of the deceased and the date of the payout. No cause of death, age or medical history. If we were talking one or two claims, I wouldn't be that suspicious, but six, Leonard. Six death benefits to one person. In my company alone."

The P.I. let out a low whistle. "That's one serious and ugly can of worms you just opened."

Jonas agreed. And the worst was yet to come. "I've tracked this back twenty years, Leonard. The first payout Brother Thom received was from the death of his father, one Reverend Thomas Goodson, Sr."

Remy inhaled sharply. "My father?" she exclaimed.

Jonas quickly brought the P.I. up to speed and what they knew—or thought they knew—about Remy's family history.

"But that would make Brother Thom…" Leonard said, letting the obvious stand like a big striped elephant.

"Thomas Goodson, Jr., legally changed his name to Brother Thom shortly after his father passed away."

He looked at Remy. Her eyes were round, her expression horrified. He wanted to wrap his arms around her and make all of the bad news go away.

"Check the last entry that I emailed you, Leonard. He's taken out a policy on my daughter."

"How is that possible?"

"Ask my ex-wife. Something I intend to do the minute I see her. So, I need a location. Where are the Good-Friends? And how soon can we get the cops there?"

Franey hesitated. "If you're right about him being a killer, the last thing you want is for law enforcement to show up and push him into a corner. He might pull a Jim Jones and take everybody out."

Remy made a whimpering sound and rushed from the room. Jonas wanted to break something, but he had to admit, Leonard was right.

"What do you suggest?"

"What I want to suggest is against the law. Only a complete and utter fool would walk into this sort of thing without backup. But if we could narrow our search grid, a small group of highly trained Special Forces types might be able to get in, retrieve your daughter and get out without a fight. Best-case scenario."

"Maybe I didn't make it clear when we met. I'm not the sit-back-and-wait sort of guy. By the time you put together a commando force, my little girl could be dead. Tell me where you think he is. I just got back from the Middle East. I can handle this myself."

There was a long pause. "I was afraid you were going to say that. Unfortunately, I have a relatively copacetic relationship with law enforcement predicated on me not getting civilians shot and maybe killed."

Jonas made a fist. "Is there any reason to believe this guy is armed?"

"No, but one of his drivers has a record. I don't remember the details, but I can find out."

"I'd rather you find me a location."

"I know where they are," a voice said.

Jonas turned to see Remy standing in the doorway. "I saw something in my dream. I could be wrong, but...I could be right."

Jonas didn't hesitate. "Leonard, I appreciate your help, and I'd doubly appreciate it if you didn't get me arrested before I can save my child."

"If anyone asks, I advised you to sit back and wait for a call from your ex-wife, correct?"

"Correct."

"Then I will wish you well and safe travels. Don't forget your mosquito repellent."

The line went dead.

Jonas looked at Remy. "Where are we going? You lead, I'll follow."

CHAPTER FOURTEEN

REMY PACKED WHILE JONAS took his laptop to the hotel's business office to print off the information Leonard had forwarded, including a topographic map of the land the GoodFriends owned. There were even a few photos. Photos that matched the images Remy had seen in her dream.

She crammed her cosmetics bag into her satchel. Jonas hadn't asked her to pack his things, too, but she looked around the room and made an executive decision. The sooner they were on the road, the sooner they'd find Birdie. And, even if Jonas hadn't come up with a reason to fear for his daughter's life, Remy did.

Her final dream of the night had been more of a nightmare. She'd been in a long hallway marked by dozens of doors, all closed. She'd been vacuuming, using her mother's older model that was difficult to push and impossible to maneuver in tight places. She could feel an overwhelming sense of urgency—if she didn't finish her work, something terrible was going to happen.

She woke, heart racing and armpits tingling.

The vacuum was symbolic of feelings of emptiness. It also signified the loss of control, of literally being sucked up by a problem.

She looked at herself in the mirror. Her eyes looked haunted. So had Birdie's. She'd seen the little girl in an earlier dream, before the vacuum. Birdie had taken Remy's hand and led her into a clearing where a collection of buildings sat. Remy had been to this place before, but this was the first time she noticed the abandoned train track, built up above the marsh with knee-high weeds growing between the rails. The weathered gray framework of an old building—a loading dock of some kind—bore a faded sign, half-destroyed by shotgun pellets.

Big Stump, the sign read.

Remy felt a thrill of excitement. She knew where to find Birdie, but at the same time, she could feel the child's despair run through her veins as if they shared the same blood. She reached out a hand to touch the little girl's head, only to have someone grab her from behind and spin her around. "Who are you?" a stranger shouted. "Why are you here?"

Remy tried to warn Birdie to run, but no words would come out of her mouth. It was as if the man with hazel eyes as dead as glass had cast a spell on her.

And the next thing she knew, she was vacuuming. An endless hallway leading straight to hell, she feared.

"Hey," a voice said behind her. "Are you okay?"

She turned. "Yeah, I'm fine. I was remembering my dreams. They were...vivid."

Jonas held up a sheaf of papers. "Leonard was more than generous. A map and photos. Sounds like this place was an old town at one time."

"A cotton depot," she said, dashing in the opposite direction. "We have to hurry, Jonas. I have a bad feeling about this. Are you sure you don't want to call your friend in law enforcement?"

"I already did. I gave him a heads up in case this goes south, plus I needed someone to know where we were and why. I also forwarded him the stuff I sent Leonard. One thing about insurance agents, we live for redundancy."

She watched him stuff the papers into his computer bag, then give the room a quick once-over. She could tell he was in his element here, focused and intense while moving forward with a plan. He joined her by the door. "So, the plan is you and I are going to find the Good-Friends's compound—this Big Stump place. Then, I'm going to drop you off at the closest police station, where you'll go in and raise holy hell if I don't come back for you in an agreed upon time, right?"

That was the plan she'd let him devise. She hadn't actually agreed to it because she knew it wasn't going to happen that way. In her dream, she was there looking straight into the eyes of her half brother. He didn't look like a murderer, but how could you tell? If he was a murderer, she might never get another chance to talk to him outside a jail cell. So, whether Jonas liked it or not, she was going to see this through.

"The GoodFriends might not even be home when we come calling, Jonas. Let's worry about what happens next once we find the place." She opened the door and stepped into the mild Florida morning. "Are you coming or not?"

"YOU HAVE ARRIVED AT YOUR destination," the onboard navigator declared with authority.

"Liar," Remy snarled, leaning forward in her seat to look at the locked gate preventing them from traveling the remaining half-mile or so to Big Stump.

"For a religious group they're not too friendly," Jonas said.

She pointed at a large Foreclosure Notice posted a few feet away. "Maybe they're not the ones who put up the gate."

They sat in brooding silence, the car purring quietly while they studied the thick jumble of skinny pines mixed with dense underbrush that blocked their view beyond a few feet to either side.

"Maybe they locked the gate on their way out," Remy suggested, fumbling with her seat belt. Understandably, she seemed nervous and on edge.

Jonas understood. The trip to this remote hunk of land had been long periods of tense silence punctuated by a repeated argument that neither seemed willing to give on. She wanted to accompany him to confront Brother Thom. He wanted her to stay on the outside. For her own safety.

"You heard Leonard. Confronting this guy straight on would be suicide."

"Based on your assumption that he's a killer. Yes, I

got that. And I could see how the man might react hostilely if you showed up dressed in a uniform. But I am his half sister looking for a little closure. It's the perfect ploy to get inside, Jonas. Tell me why my plan doesn't make more sense than yours, Rambo?"

"Because if Cheryl sees us together, all hell will break loose. And there's no freaking way in the world that I'm letting you walk in there alone. None."

The stalemate. The same impasse they'd reached a hundred miles back. He put the car in gear, intending to drive to the nearest town and drop her off at a coffee shop, but before he could put his foot on the pedal, Remy cried, "Wait. Someone's coming."

Jonas pulled the car ahead and lowered his window, prepared to ask for directions from the tall, broad-shouldered man who jumped out of the half-ton pickup and raced toward the gate. Jonas could tell the man looked upset. So did the woman in the passenger seat. She kept blowing her nose and turning to pat the head of the young boy in the seat behind her.

The man undid the padlock and gave the gate a forceful push to send it arcing across the road. He barely glanced their way before he jumped back into his vehicle.

"He must be one of the drivers Leonard mentioned."

The loud diesel engine roared past them, hauling the fifth-wheel camper behind it like it wasn't there.

"He sure left in a hurry," Remy said. "Did he look upset to you?"

"Very. And he left the gate open."

Jonas made an impulsive decision. In combat, when the situation changed, you adapted your mission to fit the circumstances. He put the car in Reverse. "Okay, we're doing it your way. If Cheryl outs me, we—"

"We tell them the truth. That you hired me to help you find Birdie."

The Cheryl he knew wouldn't believe that for a minute, but he didn't say so. Something in the GoodFriends's dynamic had changed. He could smell it. The members who just left had "sinking-ship" written all over their faces.

He drove slowly, his mind racking up worst-case scenarios every inch of the way. "There's an extra set of keys in the glove box. Take them. If something happens to me, I want you to promise you'll get in the car and the get the hell out of here."

Remy looked at him a full minute before doing as he asked. "I appreciate your caution. It's part of your nature. But everything is going to work out better than you think."

"Did you see that in your dream?"

"No."

"Then, until we know otherwise, we are going to approach this guy with extreme caution. Got it?"

She made a huffing sound but, he noticed, she stowed his extra set of keys in her bag, right beside her phone. And, he'd already checked, they had reception here. He could call for reinforcements if he needed them.

A cloud of red dirt billowing behind them reminded

him of the desert. At least, here, he didn't have to worry about hidden explosives.

They'd left the windows open, allowing the scent of pine forest and swamp to fill the car. The lack of a breeze and dense humidity had him sweating before they rounded the first curve.

He glanced over his shoulder at Remy. Her white, eyelet blouse and aquamarine capri pants gave her a modern Southern-belle look—right down to her plat- form sandals. She looked the part of a long-lost relative seeking answers to a family mystery. With luck, they'd get one foot solidly inside the door of the GoodFriends's compound before all hell broke loose.

"We're close," he said softly. "People ahead."

As they negotiated one final turn in the road, the tab- leau changed. A clearing that at one time might have held a dozen or more buildings but now held only two—an old store and a partly caved-in brick gas station sat juxta- posed to the covered train dock Remy had described.

Kitty-corner to the ramshackle, one-story wood-clad market sat the motor home Jonas recognized from Leon- ard's intel—even without being able to see the wavy, New Age symbol on its side.

A few feet away—beneath a sprawling magnolia tree—was a white, portable canopy. The kind you saw at every flea market and outdoor event in the country. Two women—one carrying a baby in her arms and the other herding two toddlers froze and stared at them as Jonas parked near the gas station.

"Do you see Cheryl?" Remy whispered softly.

"No."

Not a single red-haired child was in sight, either.

He got out. "Hello. Sorry to bother you. Is Brother Thom around?"

The younger of the two mothers—a petite brunette with a skittish look about her—pointed toward the main building. A second later, the women hustled the children toward the motor home and disappeared inside.

The mammoth vehicle was pointed outward with curtains pulled tight across the front windshield. Were his ex-wife and daughter inside? He knew it would do no good to pound on the door and demand an answer. The women would only feel threatened.

That left them no option but to approach Brother Thom, the man Jonas suspected of being a serial killer.

As if on cue, the man emerged from the doorway of the old store and stepped onto the crumbling concrete sidewalk. He was taller than Jonas had pictured. Six-two, at least. And thin. His scraggly beard, shoulder-length hair—lank, medium brown, worn parted down the middle and tucked behind his ears—gave him a sort of religious-icon look. Or, possibly, a cross between Jesus and Liam Neeson.

"It's Sunday," the man said, his voice loud enough to reach the rear pews of his nonexistent church. "Since when do bankers work on Sunday?"

The Foreclosure sign, Jonas thought.

"We're not bankers," Remy said, starting toward the building. "My name is Remy Bouchard. This is my friend, Jonas. I'm here on a personal matter, uh, Brother Thom." She stumbled over the last and her cheeks blossomed with color.

The preacher cocked his head and looked at her. "Well, I hate to sound inhospitable, but now isn't the best time. Our little fellowship is in the process of dismantling. I don't see how as I could be of any help to anyone at the moment."

He started to leave, but Remy rushed forward. Jonas made a grab for her arm but missed.

"Wait. Please. I have to know. Are you Thomas Goodson, Jr.?"

His eyes narrowed and he let out a small, harsh laugh. "There's a name I haven't heard for a while. If there's a long-overdue bill attached to your question, then the answer is no. Otherwise…unfortunately, yes."

She stopped a few feet from him, her arms clutching her purse like a shield. "In that case, I need to tell you I have reason to believe you're my half brother."

The man looked from her to Jonas, as if seeking a second opinion.

"I live Baylorville, Louisiana. It's near New Or—"

"I know where it is." Brother Thom's suspicious look didn't lessen. "We lived there when I was a kid. Who did you say you are?"

"My last name is Bouchard. My mother, Marlene Bouchard, owned a beauty parlor in town. She put *Unknown* as the father on my birth certificate. And my sister's," she added. "I have a twin named Jessie."

His face showed a reaction to that comment, but Jonas

couldn't interpret it. "What makes you think my daddy's the one?"

"A friend of Mama's—Jonas's mother, actually—gave me his name. Mama passed away last year, so I don't have any way to confirm this unless you'll talk to me. It might not be true. Jonas's mother has been diagnosed with Alzheimer's. I don't want anything from you. Just the truth. Please. Can't we talk?"

The man heaved a great sigh and looked upward, shaking his head. "You ridiculous old fool," he muttered. "Look at the legacy you left me. No wonder God has abandoned me."

Jonas heard the despair in the man's voice and stepped closer to Remy. People who had nothing left to lose were often the most dangerous. Did that make him a serial killer? Jonas didn't know, but his gut said the good brother was more than simply a washed-up preacher.

"Oh, fine," Goodson said, shaking his head. "Come in. I'll give you the answers you seek. But, believe me when I tell you God has a way of throwing a monkey wrench or two into the mix. You might wish your friend's mother had never opened her mouth."

He pivoted and marched inside. Remy started to follow, but Jonas stopped her. "Do you mind? I think I should go first. Does the name Jeffrey Dahmer ring any bells?"

"I don't know why you're so quick to believe the worst about a person, Jonas, but this man is not a killer," she told him.

Jonas didn't argue the point. Instead, he opened the

rickety screen and cautiously led the way inside, his senses on high alert. He didn't want to admit that the warning bells he'd expected to hear inside his head weren't chiming in the least.

The old store, apparently, had been converted into a place of worship. Twenty or so folding chairs lined up before a long narrow table covered with a white linen cloth. The pulpit, Jonas assumed.

Several of the chairs were scattered about and open packing boxes took the place of parishioners. Brother Thom stood beside the table where a black leather-bound Bible rested, his shoulders slumped, hands loose by his sides.

"Where are all of your followers?" Jonas asked.

Goodson turned. He made a grand encompassing gesture. "What you see is what there is, such as it is. I await my promised grace, because you don't get much more humble than this."

Remy spoke. "We saw your website. It doesn't say anything about this place."

The man gave a half-smile. "This was going to be our permanent home. We were all tired of traveling. We reached a lot of people through our revivals, but the toll on the body can't be ignored. When the chance to buy a whole town came up, the GoodFriends voted. We planned to launch a new website when we were further along. That didn't happen. Building costs were exorbitant. We lost some of our funding…"

Because your intended victim ran away?

Jonas didn't ask because Remy stepped closer to the

man, dragging a chair with her. She waited until Brother Thom sat, then joined him. She looked at Jonas questioningly but he preferred to stay on his feet. He walked to stand behind her.

"Could you tell me a little about yourself, your family? Jonas and I read your father's obituary online, so I know he's been dead a long time. Is your mother still alive?"

Thom shook his head. "She was ill when we lived in Baylorville. Passed on not long after we left Louisiana. Liver cancer," he said, flatly. "Never took a drop of alcohol in her life."

"I'm so sorry. You were very young. Was it just you and your father?"

"Yes. I had a twin brother, James, who died in childbirth. My mother wasn't a warm person. Father claimed she never got over that loss."

Jonas checked his watch, his ears listening for the sound of children. He knew this interview was important to Remy but he couldn't lose sight of his mission while the two compared genealogies. "The women we saw when we came in…that's all the followers you have left?"

"Sadly, my flock has scattered. The women you saw are waiting for my driver to return. They'll go home to their families…reluctantly. It's never easy to give up on your dreams."

The word jolted Jonas. He looked at Remy, who seemed to read his impatience. "Thom, in addition to looking for information on Thomas Goodson, we're here for another reason, too. Jonas believes his ex-wife and daughter are members of your—"

"Cult," Jonas said bluntly.

"Church," Remy corrected with a glare.

Brother Thom looked between them. "Cult. Don't worry, Remy, I've heard that misnomer before. The people who joined the GoodFriends did so of their own accord. They have always been free to come and go as they wished. Some, like the three mothers you saw outside, have nowhere else to go. Banding together for a joint purpose does not make us a cult."

Before Jonas could debate the point, Remy interrupted. "Three? There were only two women outside. Jonas's ex-wife and daughter were not present."

"What are their names?"

"Cheryl and Brigitte Galloway."

Brother Thom's face changed. At first, Jonas thought he saw fear, but then the man started to laugh, making it impossible to tell whether or not he was faking his reaction. "Crazy Cheryl is your ex? That's…rich. Maybe God is listening to my prayers." He seemed to take note of Jonas's body language because he quickly added, "I'm sorry. Forgive me. That was terribly rude. It's been a hellacious week, but, still, that's no excuse, is it?

"The fact is I have been praying about this problem for weeks. Cheryl stopped taking her meds, insisting, instead, that I cure her. With my powers," he added, wiggling his fingers as if to prove the digits were simply ordinary fingers. "We've all tried to reach her, but none of us is clinically trained to handle this sort of mental-health issue. Surely you know what I'm talking about."

Jonas knew exactly what the man was saying, but he wasn't going to admit to it until he saw Cheryl and made certain she and Birdie were safe. "Where are they?"

"I have no idea. Things have been a little hectic around here. My most trusted friend and right-hand man told me this morning he was leaving…and taking the woman I believed was my soul mate with him." His admission sounded hollow with pain.

Jonas and Remy looked at each other. The truck and fifth-wheel they'd watch leave, Jonas assumed.

"Cheryl was here for that, I think." His brow wrinkled. "But, quite honestly, I don't remember seeing your daughter. She's pretty hard to miss with her bright-colored hair."

"Could your driver have taken her?"

"You mean, Ziggy? No. I sent him after supplies."

"And he's not back yet?"

Thom looked resigned. "He's an ex-tweaker. Drugs are a powerful demon. Zig does the best he can. He'll be back. He knows he has a home here. But he definitely didn't take Birdie." He reached for a small, cheap phone and fiddled with it a moment. "I'll show you how I know. This is a picture I took last night around the fire. It's time-stamped."

Jonas checked out the image and passed it to Remy. His daughter was sitting on Cheryl's lap, front and center. Everyone smiled for the camera but Birdie. "She doesn't look happy."

"No. She hates it here. Always has. She looks at me as though I'm the Antichrist." His gaze shifted from Remy to Jonas. "Sort of the way you're looking at me now. Is there something else you think I've done?"

"Try murder."

The man's eyes opened wide. "*Murder?* Me? You may well be as delusional as your ex-wife."

Jonas started to move past Remy's chair but she stopped him. "Jonas works for an insurance company, Thom. According to his files, you've been the recipient of several life-insurance policies."

"Six," Jonas volunteered.

"Oh," Thom said, sitting back in his chair. He held up one hand to count, his lips murmuring a name for each finger. "You're right. The GoodFriends have lost six of our brethren. By God's design, of course. Not mine."

A flat denial didn't prove anything to Jonas. He planned to dig deeper into the man's file once he was safely home with Birdie. He was about to say so when the man looked at Remy, his head cocked thoughtfully.

"You're a very brave young woman. You came here to meet me regardless of the fact that your friend thinks I'm some kind of serial killer. I'm impressed. But I hope you'll believe me, Remy, when I tell you that five of the souls who passed on to God's great beyond were beloved elders of our congregation.

"Catherine was eighty-six. She went to sleep one night and didn't wake up in the morning. Judd was a veteran of the Second World War. He'd lived with a piece of shrapnel lodged in his spine for nearly sixty years. His release came as a gift. Do you want the other names?"

"You said five," Jonas answered. "What about the sixth?"

Brother Thom reached for his Bible. "Tommy." He rubbed the binding of the book against his cheek, his gaze unfocused. "You're right, Jonas. I killed him. How did you guess? I paid one of my followers to say he was at fault. I convinced myself that was in the best interest of the GoodFriends." He looked at Jonas, his anguish clearly visible. "I endorsed the check your company issued over to Tommy's mother immediately. She still ran away, got high, stole a car and told the police that I was running a cult that preyed on women and children. I spent half our building fund defending my so-called reputation. But, after a while, I decided why bother? Nothing—not even prayer—has lessened the guilt I feel from backing over my own son."

Jonas knew the man was telling the truth. The hollow emptiness in his voice was matched by the look of pure agony in his eyes.

"Is that why you don't drive?" Remy asked.

"Yes. I can't. My hands begin to shake and I suffer what I assume is a panic attack every time I try to get behind the wheel." He looked at Jonas. "My personal cross to bear."

"Tell me where my daughter is."

Goodson shrugged. "Birdie stays as far away from me as possible."

"Why?"

"Children see what adults often miss. I figure she can see the truth—that I am dead inside, my soul withered and corroded."

"She called me on a cell phone a few days ago. I heard you shout at her."

Thom shook his head. "I don't recall that. It could have been Ziggy. Or the man who just left. Tempers have run high around here lately. It's not easy to watch everything you've worked for slide into a great abyss lined with the open hands of greedy bankers."

The exterior door suddenly slammed, making Remy jump. Footsteps rushed toward them and a woman burst into the room, crying, "Thom, you have to help me. I can't find Birdie. She's lost. My little girl is lost."

CHAPTER FIFTEEN

BIRDIE KNEW SHE WAS GOING to be in trouble when they found her. Big trouble. But she'd watched as David's mother moved all their stuff from Brother Thom's motor home to the other camper that morning. She'd heard the two men arguing, and even if she couldn't follow all their words, she'd sensed Brother Thom's anger and disappointment.

Something bad was going to happen and her mother wouldn't listen. Birdie had tried talking to her last night when they went to bed, but Mom rolled over so her back was to Birdie. A few minutes later, she started making that low, sing-song humming sound that told Birdie her mother was sinking into the dark sad place Birdie feared most of all.

Mommy needed help. The kind her daddy always got for her. Daddy would know what to do. And since Birdie spoke to him on the phone, she'd been thinking about how to reach him. She would walk to town—there was one nearby. She knew, because she'd heard Thom tell someone that Ziggy—the skinny, nervous man Birdie tried to avoid—had taken the other car for supplies.

She wasn't sure where this town was, but she remembered her daddy telling her once that train tracks linked the country together like a big quilt. If she followed the tracks, she'd find a town eventually, she figured.

But she'd been walking a long time and the rails were clogged with weeds, and the boards that separated them were rotten in places and hard to walk on. And the sun was hot. And she was thirsty.

She looked around, trying to decide what to do. Would Mommy be looking for her? She didn't want to make her mother scared. But, no, Birdie decided. When Mommy's head got fuzzy inside and she started making that sound, it usually meant she would stay in bed for days.

So, Birdie could rest for a little while, then start walking again. The tracks were high, so Birdie didn't worry about gators or snakes getting her. She could even walk at night if she had to. Not that she wanted to do that. She wanted to find the town and call her daddy. But, first, she'd hide somewhere safe.

An interesting tree caught her eye. Two trees, actually, that were so close together they sorta grew up connecting with each other, but near the base of their trunks was a hole. Bunnies might have lived there once. Maybe something bigger. It looked empty now. That's all Birdie cared about.

She took off the light jacket she'd tied around her waist and spread it out in the little nook. If she could see the tree hole then so could other people, she figured, so she dragged a broken limb that had fallen to the ground nearby closer to the opening before crawling into her spot.

The tightly woven branches of the dead limb hid her well, she decided. Well enough that she could close her eyes and sleep. For a few minutes.

"WHAT DO YOU MEAN SHE'S gone?" Jonas cried, spinning around to face his ex-wife. "For how long? How could you lose our daughter, Cheryl? What the hell is wrong with you?"

Remy had jumped to her feet the minute the thin blonde woman appeared. Cheryl looked both frantic and bewildered. "Jonas? What are you doing here? How did you find me?"

"I've been looking for you and Birdie ever since I got back from Iraq," he shouted. "What do you think—I'd let you run off with my kid without a care?"

"You left us first," Cheryl cried, coming at him with fists raised. "You shouldn't have gone, Jonas. You knew I wasn't well. This isn't my fault. Birdie wanted to go home, but I told her you'd be mad. I was afraid you'd never let me see her again."

Jonas's handsome face was contorted with contempt and fury. "You got that right, lady."

Cheryl seemed to crumple on the spot. She probably would have fallen if Brother Thom hadn't rushed to her side. "People, please, put your hostility aside until we locate your little girl."

He helped Cheryl to a chair, then went down on one knee so he could look her in the eyes. "Why do you think she's missing, Cheryl? When did you last see her? Have you looked in the motor home? Could she be playing hide-and-seek? You know how she likes to do that."

Cheryl let out a thin wail. "I didn't feel well last night." She put her hands up to cover her ears. "All the yelling and people leaving…it was too much. I took some pills. The ones you wanted me to take. Maybe more than I should have. I don't remember."

"Cheryl," Jonas said sharply, walking closer to where his ex-wife sat. "Where was Birdie when you decided to get stoned on prescription meds?"

Cheryl's face scrunched. "Stop yelling. I didn't mean to sleep so long. She was right beside me when I went to bed. But…but…when I woke up, she wasn't there."

Cheryl clasped one of Thom's hands, as if in prayer, and leaned closer. "I thought she was having breakfast. Or telling David goodbye. I didn't think she might be missing. She's never run away before."

Remy and Jonas looked at each other.

"What makes you think she's run off, Cheryl?" he asked.

"Because she took your paperclip, Jonas."

Jonas shook his head in confusion. "My paperclip? What the hell are you talking about?"

Cheryl shrunk, almost as if she wanted to disappear, but she answered, her tone flat. "I told her we were going to make a new life with Thom and the GoodFriends, so we needed to leave all traces of our old life behind. The last letter you sent had a picture of you attached with a paperclip. She wanted to bring your picture but I wouldn't let her. So…" She looked down. "When I found it one day, clipped to her undershirt right above her heart, I—I took it away. I put it in my Bible. And now it's gone." She let out a thin wail and collapsed.

Thom got to his feet, one hand resting on the sobbing woman's back. He looked at Jonas. "It was a hectic morning. I don't remember seeing Brigitte anywhere. We're on thirty-five acres here. The nearest town is sixteen miles away and it's mostly swamp between here and the road. If she did leave the compound, she could be in big trouble. You're an investigator, what do you suggest?"

Jonas pulled out his phone. "Call 9-1-1, then get the rest of your people together. We'll do a sweep through the buildings and the motor home first. That will save time when then search parties get here."

Brother Thom took the phone and stepped onto the landing to make the call.

"What can I do?" Remy asked.

Cheryl, who had been rocking side to side and wringing her hands, looking every bit the madwoman Jonas had accused her of being, suddenly shot to her feet. "Wait a minute," she exclaimed, pointing a long, bony finger Remy's way. "I know you. You're Jonas's old girlfriend. The psychic." Her eyes went wide with panic. "Oh, my God. You're here because you find dead people, don't you? No. Go away. My Birdie is not dead. She's not dead," Cheryl shrieked, launching herself at Remy.

Jonas caught her from behind, pulling her in the opposite direction. Remy's pulse exploded from the adrenaline coursing through her system. She staggered back a step, sending a tower of boxes tumbling.

Brother Thom rushed in. He handed Jonas his phone. "They're on their way." Then, he took Cheryl by the arm. "Calm yourself, Cheryl. No on believes Brigitte is dead. Remy came here to see me. Come on, now. We need to organize the others."

Remy's heart was pounding. She felt as though the world was spinning out of control and she was somehow to blame.

Jonas hurried to her side. "Are you okay? Sorry about that. Volatility is a side effect of her meds. It usually levels out after she's been on them for a while. That's one of the reasons you're not supposed to arbitrarily start and stop."

She was a little surprised that he bothered to offer an excuse for his ex-wife's actions, but she pushed the thought away. "I'm fine. What can I do?"

"The topo map. I need to see the bigger picture."

She hurried to keep up with him as they crossed the wide, open square. She hadn't noticed earlier but the roadway was littered with quarter-size chunks of brick and rock, probably hauled away from the demolition of other buildings.

The sun had come out and the steamy heat seemed to weigh her down like a damp blanket. Suddenly a cold shiver passed down her spine, making her come to an abrupt stop. Déjà vu? Or something else?

"Jonas, I remember being here in my dream last night. We were looking for something. I walked and walked until I couldn't take another step."

He spun round to face her. "Were you looking for Birdie?"

"I don't know. But I saw my mother. She was sitting on a flat spot where two trees twisted together. They formed a sort of heart shape. She looked beautiful. Rested and happy. I remember starting to cry, and she said, 'Don't fret, child. Hearts heal.'"

"*Hearts heal*. Does the symbolism mean anything?" he asked. "Something that might help us find Birdie?"

She put a hand to her temple. A sudden pain made it hard to think. "I don't know. I need an aspirin."

While Jonas spread the maps they'd printed off the computer on the hood of his car, Remy found a bottle of over-the-counter painkillers in her purse and retrieved a bottle of water from the backseat. She cracked open the lid and sat to swallow the pills.

The black leather was warm, the headrest soft. She closed her eyes a moment to catch her breath. She wouldn't be any help if she couldn't focus, and so much had happened that morning, she wasn't sure she'd ever make sense of it all. The most upsetting part was realizing Jonas had jumped to the worst conclusion possible about her half brother with limited information. He'd reacted impulsively in the past, too…running away to Europe with his mother, cutting off all memories of his father after the man committed suicide, believing her mother's lie without making any effort to prove or disprove it.

Yes, she'd bought that lie, too, and she could even excuse their naivety given their age and inclination to trust anyone in authority. But could she love and respect someone who rushed to judgment without considering all sides of the story?

He'd begged her to help him find his daughter—not because he trusted in lucid dreaming but because he trusted her. But all he really knew of her was the girl he'd once loved—and left without a backward look.

The sound of a siren cut into her thoughts. She knew she needed to stand up, open the trunk and find a more practical pair of shoes so she could join the search, but she didn't move. Sleep pulled her eyes closed tighter.

Where are you, Birdie? Why did you run away?

"To find my daddy," a voice in her head answered.

Of course. Her mother was ill. The GoodFriends were falling apart. The only person she could count on was her father. And how would someone Birdie's age go about finding her father?

Remy pictured Birdie walking to the road to hitch a ride, but immediately crossed the idea off the list of possibilities. Birdie was a smart kid. She'd know better than to get in a car with a stranger.

A phone.

She'd try to find a phone to call him.

And the fastest way to find a phone would be to find a town.

Her eyes blinked open. The loading dock with the faded sign that had led her here was directly across from where Jonas's car was parked. The loading dock that, at one time, served to link this bustling community to the world at large.

She jumped to her feet, holding tight to the open door while her equilibrium settled. Two police cruisers roared into the plaza, sending a dust cloud mushrooming into the still air. Coughing and sputtering, Remy tried to reach Jonas before he jogged away to greet the officers.

"The train tracks, Jonas. If we follow…"

"In a minute, Rem. I have a grid search laid out. Let me talk to these guys. I'll be right back."

Maps over dreams. Grid over hunches. The facts, ma'am, stick to the facts.

Why should she expect anyone else to believe in her if she didn't trust herself?

She popped the lever for the trunk and dug out the pair of sneakers she'd packed on a whim. After grabbing her sun hat and an extra bottle of water, she walked to the elevated loading dock. She paused in the shade of the crumbling structure to survey the chaos unfolding in the plaza. More vehicles with flashing lights had arrived. Men—in and out of uniform—huddled around Jonas, who was barking orders like the good commander he was. Brother Thom was busy shepherding his flock in a contained search of the existing buildings.

No one appeared to notice when she gave a mock salute and stepped to the rusty steel tracks. Right? Or left? She closed her eyes and let an answer form in her thoughts.

Right.

"Right it is," she murmured softly, heading away from the cluster of buildings.

She hadn't walked along a railroad track since she and Jessie were kids. They'd always loved hopping from board to board, lining up rocks and pennies for the slow-moving freight trains to run over.

Unfortunately, she decided a short while later, the spacing of the crumbling ties were not so accommodating to an adult's stride. She was huffing and puffing and cursing under her breath by the time she'd traveled half a mile.

Bending over to catch her breath, she looked between her legs at where she'd come from. The blue sky looked funny upside down. A kid would probably love this view—and be able to spot a dozen different images in the white, puffy clouds.

She decided to take a break and sat crossed-legged between the rails. If she listened hard, she could hear shouts in the distance. The search party. They'd brought dogs along, she decided.

She hoped the howls didn't scare Birdie.

Birdie. Where are you, little girl?

Remy removed her hat and used the hem of her white blouse to wipe the sweat from her eyes. Her mascara left an odd blotch that almost looked like a heart.

A heart.

She looked up, her pulse quickening. "Birdie," she called.

She didn't hear an answer, but a thicket of dried limbs moved near the trunk of a tree. No. Twin trees growing from a shared based, their branches united to create a sort of heart shape. "Birdie," Remy cried, nearly tripping over her feet as she clamored down the weed-choked levy of the railroad bed.

She yanked the limb aside, ignoring the thorns that pierced her skin and left long red gashes on her hands. She didn't feel a thing because a second later a head with long red braids tentatively emerged from the hollowed-out base of the tree.

"Birdie," Remy cried. "Are you okay, sweetheart? I'm Remy. I'm a friend of your daddy's. He's close by. With your mommy. Everybody is looking for you, Birdie. Can I help you out of there?"

The child shook her head as if offended by the suggestion. Independent, even in her obvious fear. She wiggled free of the small space and stood, brushing dirt and twigs from her clothes. She was dressed in jeans and very grubby sneakers. Her T-shirt was faded and torn in spots—an obvious hand-me-down.

"Are you hurt?" Remy asked.

Birdie shook her head, making her braids bounce. "You're the one bleeding."

Remy looked down. "Oh," she said, making a face. "I am." She turned and sat on the level spot at the crux of the twin trees. She pulled a tissue from her bag and wet it with water from her bottle.

"Can I have a drink?" Birdie asked.

"Of course. Have the bottle."

She dabbed at the bloody streaks on her hand. Shallow scratches. Nothing to worry about. She looked up a moment later to see Birdie staring at her.

"I know you."

"You do?"

Birdie nodded. "I saw you in my dream one time. You made me not so afraid."

Remy didn't know what to say—what Jonas would want her to say. Fortunately, she didn't have to answer because a second later, two men in uniforms crashed through the thick underbrush to emerge a few feet away from them.

Birdie didn't hesitate for a second. She launched herself into Remy's arms. Remy hugged her tight and closed her eyes, marveling at the rightness of the feeling. When she opened her eyes, she caught a faint glimmer of a figure she couldn't quite make out. But a voice in her head said, "Mama."

BY THE TIME JONAS HAD the volunteers organized as he wanted them, each group of four equipped with a communication device of some sort and a basic understanding of where they were supposed to search, a good hour had passed. Brother Thom had checked in with him twice, relaying the disappointing, but not surprising, news that Birdie was not in the compound.

"I was also able to get hold of Mick—the man who was leaving when you pulled in. He stopped at a rest area and turned the camper inside out, making sure she hadn't slipped in when they were packing up."

Jonas looked toward the motor home, where the remaining GoodFriends, including Cheryl, were supposedly praying for Birdie's safe return.

Jonas could honestly admit to himself that he was

wrong about Brother Thom. He'd let his worst fears take him down a dangerous road. He owed the man an apology but that wouldn't come until Birdie was safe. If not for Brother Thom and his charismatic persona, Cheryl and Birdie never would have been in this particular hellhole.

He grabbed the last water bottle from the sack in the backseat and took a swig. Two things hit him at once. There should have been more bottles and he hadn't seen Remy in quite a while.

"Remy?" he called out, looking around for her bright-colored pants.

It had crossed his mind earlier that she'd been trying to tell him something when the cops arrived, but he'd brushed her off. Maybe, he thought, she'd found a quiet spot to hunker down and do a little lucid dreaming. Not that he was completely clear on how that worked.

He started toward the GoodFriends's bus. He didn't think for a second Remy would want to be around Cheryl, who had nearly attacked her. But she might have told Brother Thom—her supposed half brother—where she was going.

Half brother. Jonas had spent a good chunk of his life thinking he was her brother. This whole twisted, convoluted mess was the thing of fiction, not real life. Or was it? His mother used to say they were all connected in one way or another.

He had his hand raised to knock on the side of the motor home, when the door suddenly opened. Thom trotted down the steps. "I want to volunteer. Cheryl's resting.

We got her to take another pill." He rubbed a hand across his face and sighed. "You do know she needs to be institutionalized for at least a short time, don't you? I blame myself for not recognizing the signs of her breakdown sooner, but depression has been the norm around here lately. I underestimated the extent of hers."

Jonas didn't want to talk about his ex-wife. "Have you seen Remy?"

"No. Not since we talked in the chapel."

Jonas turned on one heel and started toward the center of the plaza. "Remy?" he called at the top of his lungs. The word echoed off the dilapidated loading dock.

"Damn," he cussed. "Now, we have two people missing."

"She probably joined one of the search parties," Thom said, watching Jonas intently.

The theory made sense. Why had Jonas immediately thought the worst? He looked at Thom. "I was wrong about you. I've been wrong about a lot of things lately."

The man put a hand on Jonas's shoulder. "You've lost your faith. That can happen when the people you should be able to count on let you down."

His father, for instance. His mother and Remy's. Two women he'd trusted and believed. Even Cheryl, who hadn't been truthful about her health issues when he married her. And then there was Remy.

"I got lost when I was a kid. I ran away from home and fell in a well. Remy found me. Or, so her mother claimed. Remy saw me in her dream and told the police where to find me."

"God isn't greedy with his gifts, but most people aren't brave enough to cultivate them. It takes a special kind of person to come to peace with being different. Maybe she's following another dream to find your daughter."

Hope—almost as painful as fear—blossomed in his chest. "I can't stand around and wait."

"You can always try prayer."

He could...if he believed. But his trust in a higher power died when his father took his own life. Where was God when his dad had needed a source of hope? Where was Dad when Jonas and his mother needed him?

A voice cackled to life over the walkie-talkie one of the cops had given him. Jonas hurried back to his car, where he'd left the small, high-tech device. "Galloway, here. What have you found?"

"Two lovely ladies. One, Remy Bouchard. And a Miss Brigitte Galloway. ETA in ten. Over."

Jonas was grateful for the hood of his car because his knees gave out a second later. His daughter was safe. And Remy had found her. He didn't know how. He didn't care how. All he knew was he had his life back. Or would very soon. And he wasn't ever going to let Birdie—or Remy—out of his sight again.

CHAPTER SIXTEEN

THE RETURN TRIP TO THE GoodFriends's compound took about half the time as her trek along the railroad tracks had. Apparently, the piece of land the church group owned was pie-shaped. The men who found them had beat down a fairly accessible path that took them straight back to the cluster of buildings.

Jonas met them halfway. He scooped Birdie up into his arms and hugged her so fiercely Remy was afraid the child might snap in two, but Birdie only laughed. And cried. She seemed very tiny and young in her daddy's arms.

"Birdie, Birdie, Birdie," Jonas cried, touching her hair, her face, then holding her chin steady so he could look deep into her eyes. "I missed you so much. I was so afraid I wouldn't be able to find you."

Birdie threw her arms around his neck. "It's okay, Daddy. I knew you'd come. I was looking for a town so I could call you."

He squeezed her again. "Oh, my sweet, brave girl. I love you so much. I'm never going away again, honey. Never."

Remy felt swamped by emotions she couldn't completely describe and was half-afraid to acknowledge.

She was happy for Jonas. And grateful that Birdie was safe and sound and reunited with her father. She'd come to care deeply for the little girl with the crooked smile and bright red hair. She could almost bring herself to acknowledge that, deep down, the thought had crossed her mind that Birdie could have—should have—been hers. Might have been…if things had been different.

"Is Mommy okay?" Birdie asked.

But things were the way they were.

Remy didn't wait to hear Jonas's answer. Instead, she followed the others. Cheryl was Birdie's mother and she would always be a part of Jonas's life. An immutable fact that Remy had thought she was prepared to accept. But was she? She wasn't sure. She wasn't sure about anything. Except that she was happy to see Birdie safe in her father's arms.

Birdie let out a high-pitched giggle a moment later. Remy glanced over her shoulder to see the child clinging piggyback to her father's back. Arms locked behind him to keep Birdie safe, Jonas jogged to catch up with Remy. He looked happy and relieved—as if the weight of the world had been lifted from his shoulders.

"Wait, Rem," Jonas called. "I haven't had a chance to thank you. You did it," he said, his smile identical to his daughter's. "There simply aren't words enough to ever tell you how much this means to me."

"I'm just glad she's safe."

"She is now, and once I get her home…" He let the thought languish. Remy had no idea what came next;

did he? From the expression on his face, she didn't think so.

They met up with one of the other search parties a few seconds later. Jonas shook hands with every member and introduced them to Birdie, who suddenly turned shy and kept her chin buried in her father's neck. Remy understood the feeling completely. She did her best to remain out of the limelight, too.

A cackling order over one of the walkie-talkies got the group moving again. Remy and Jonas wound up walking side by side. "You didn't tell me how you found her," Jonas said. "One minute you were standing by the car, the next thing I knew, you were gone. Scared the you-know-what out of me."

He gave her a stern look. Fatherly, maybe? She started to explain that he'd been too distracted to listen so she followed her hunch, when he added, "You shouldn't have left like that, Remy. If you'd gotten lost in the woods, we might have needed to set up a second search party."

She doubted that he meant his words to sound like criticism. The intensity of the situation made people say things with less diplomacy than they might use later on. She got that. What she didn't appreciate was him bringing this up in front of strangers. "I was never in any danger, Jonas. The railroad tracks are as good a navigational tool as a compass. Even Birdie figured that out and she's only seven."

"And a half," his daughter put in.

Birdie looked at Remy from her perch on her father's back. Her skinny arms were fastened tight around Jonas's neck. Her gaze was intelligent and watchful. She missed nothing, Remy decided. *The same way I was at her age.*

"Seven and a half," Remy corrected, giving Birdie a little wink. "And a very smart seven and a half, too."

"I agree. But going off alone could have compromised the search. What if you'd fallen and broken your leg? Or bumped into an alligator? Or got bit by a poisonous snake?"

She stopped abruptly, reached into her purse and pulled out her phone. "I would have called someone," she said, trying hard to keep her emotions under control. "Maybe even you. Or not," she added under her breath.

Jonas seemed a little taken aback by her reaction. He reached out as if to touch her, comfort her, maybe. But Remy didn't want his apology. Or his thanks. Or anything else. She didn't know what she wanted at the moment, but she was pretty sure whatever it was, he couldn't provide it.

"My feet hurt," she said, spinning to leave. "I need to get these scratches cleaned before they get infected."

"What scratches?"

"The bush attacked her, Daddy. The one I pulled in front of my hidey-hole in the tree. Remy's hands are bigger than mine. The thorns poked her."

Jonas caught Remy's arm and made her stop. "Good grief, Remy. Why didn't you say something? We have a medic here."

One more criticism. Unintended, perhaps, but the straw that made her snap. Her fingers closed around the phone in her hand. Her phone. "You guys go on ahead. I need to call Jessie and let her know we found Birdie."

"Can't it wait? Your hand needs immediate attention," Jonas argued.

She looked ahead. A couple of members of the search party were still in view. "Come on, you two," one of the men called out. "We're almost there."

No, she thought, the gash on her hand was nothing compared to the one that was going to appear on her heart when she watched Jonas's family reunite. Birdie was safe; Cheryl was alive and presumably well enough to go back to Memphis. Jonas was free to rebuild his life any way he wanted.

"I'll catch up in a minute, Jonas. Go on. Please. Those people deserve a chance to see Birdie and celebrate."

"But…"

"I have to go potty, Daddy. And I wanna see Mommy."

Remy held up her phone and wobbled it. "I'll be right behind you. I promise."

Jonas started walking but with obvious reluctance. Remy watched until he was out of sight before she let out a long, deep sigh. She needed a minute or two alone to get control of her emotions. Being snappish and defensive wasn't her usual style. But, understandably, she was worried about what was going to happen next.

She couldn't picture herself hanging around, waiting while Jonas figured out exactly how she fit into his old life. The GoodFriends were in transition, too. As much as she wanted to know about Thom, now wasn't the time.

Besides that, Remy felt different. Changed. Something

happened to her when she found Birdie. Maybe it was simple validation. She'd listened to her instincts, correctly interpreted the images in her dreams and made something good happen.

Would the searchers have found Birdie eventually? Yes, Remy had no doubt. *But I got there first.* Why? Because she hadn't let self-doubt trip her up. The revelation felt big but fragile, like a piece of blown glass that hadn't completely cooled. She knew she wasn't ready to answer the inevitable questions that would come during the wrap-up phase of this search. Jonas was the cross-every-T kind of guy. He could handle the paperwork. She was going home.

She dropped her phone into her purse. She could have called any of the Bullies and asked them to come pick her up, but she didn't plan to. From listening to the search-and-rescue guys, she knew that the closest big town was under thirty minutes away. She'd catch a ride with one of them, then rent a car.

That would free up Jonas to collect his family and go wherever he needed to go. The thought brought a swift, knifing pain, but no tears. So much had happened. She'd learned more than she could possibly have hoped to learn from this quest. In truth, she couldn't wait to get home and call Jessie and tell her everything.

Home. The word had a certain ring to it.

JONAS HATED THE IDEA of leaving Remy behind, but she'd been adamant. And, in truth, it gave him a few minutes alone with Birdie—something he'd been waiting much too long for.

He felt her wiggle back and forth. "You can go behind the tree, if you need to," he told her.

"Nobody will see?"

Modesty. He smiled. "I'll guard the spot. I promise."

"Okay."

They moved off the path until she found a likely spot. "Turn around, please."

Nice manners. Had she always been this polite? He couldn't remember. He turned his back on her but didn't move away. "I missed you something fierce, honey girl. I thought about you a million times a day while I was in Iraq. No, a zillion."

"A bagillion-trillion?"

"At least."

"Me, too."

A second later, she was back at his side, fumbling with the clasp on her jeans. The pants looked too small. "Are these yours?" he asked.

She shook her head. "I took them from my friend, David. I decided I needed pants in case I got chased by a gator."

He made a face of pure horror. She laughed and tossed her head in a way that made him fight back tears. His poor baby girl. His very special, brave little girl.

"Where's David, now?"

She shrugged. "He and his mommy left today. She used to be Brother Thom's special friend, but then she decided she didn't want to live here anymore so they left. I didn't want to be the oldest kid, Daddy. So, like Remy said, I followed the railroad till I got tired."

He took her hand and they started walking. "You were smart to hide, but I would have found you sooner if you hadn't run away."

"I know, but you ran away once. Grandma Charlotte told me. You fell in a well and nobody could find you. Until a little girl told them where you were."

"Grandma told you that story?"

She nodded seriously. "She said her and Grandpa were *soo* worried. Grandpa walked around so much he wore a hole in the bottom of his shoe."

Jonas seriously doubted that. In his mind, his father hadn't even been involved in the search. Dad had been out of town at the time. Jonas let the subject drop. "Well, I'm glad you were hiding in a tree, not in a well."

"Me, too. Where's Remy?"

Jonas looked over his shoulder. "She's coming."

"She's nice, Daddy. I like her."

"I agree." *And I owe her more than I can ever repay.*

They entered the compound and were greeted by a resounding cheer. Strangers rushed up to them, eager to shake Jonas's hand and clap Birdie on the shoulder. He did his best to thank everyone personally, but he could sense Birdie's disquiet. Her grip on his hand intensified.

"One sec," he told the situation commander when he

approached. "What do you need, sweetheart? Are you thirsty? Hungry?"

"I wanna see Mommy."

"Oh, sorry. I forgot."

"I'll take her," a deep voice said. Brother Thom. "Will you go with me, Birdie? Your mother has been resting in the motor home, but I believe she's awake now."

Birdie swallowed hard but nodded her willingness to go with him. She took Thom's hand and they walked away. The gesture reconfirmed how wrong Jonas had been about the man.

He turned his attention to the situation commander and tried to answer all the questions that came his way. The one he couldn't explain with any detail was how Remy beat the seasoned searchers to Birdie. He spotted her walking across the plaza a moment later but decided not to call her over. Instead, he excused himself. "One minute. I need to check on something."

The man didn't look happy but Jonas didn't care. Something was up with Remy and he needed to make sure she was okay.

"Hey," he said, jogging up to her as she walked to his car. "Is everything okay?"

"Great. Is Birdie with her mother?"

"Uh-huh. Can we talk? What's going on? Is it Jessie? Did you call her?"

She shook her head. "No. I decided to call everyone later. I'm bushed. I need a shower and some serious, dream-free sleep. I'm going home, Jonas."

"Of course. I'll drive you. It'll take a little while to wrap things up here, but—"

"Really, Jonas? You think that's a good idea?" She tilted her head. "You, me, Birdie and Cheryl in the same car? Now? After everything you've been through?"

His Adam's apple lifted and fell. "I don't know what Cheryl's plans are. Thom seems to think she needs to be in a facility for a while."

"Then, you'll be busy figuring that out. I don't need to be part of that."

His eyes narrowed and he shook his head. "But..."

She headed toward his car. "I'm going to catch a ride into town with one of the search teams," she said. "I did what you hired me to do, Jonas. I found your daughter." She opened the rear passenger door and sat, kicking off her shoes with a moan of relief. "I hate athletic shoes," she said, glancing up.

As she peeled off her socks, she told him, "Don't worry. We'll be in touch. You promised me a glowing recommendation, remember?"

The chaos in his mind returned. He could see the situation commander frowning at him from across the plaza. Brother Thom exited the bus, Birdie right behind him. He had so much to juggle and now Remy was leaving. "You can't just leave. What about Thom? I thought you wanted to get to know him?"

She yanked on a pair of sandals and stood. "You mean, get to know my brother the serial killer?"

Jonas's cheeks turned hot. "I admit I jumped to the

wrong conclusion. I already apologized to him. He accepted."

Her gaze traveled toward the motor home, where
Thom and Birdie were talking to the two women Jonas
and Remy saw when they first arrived at Big Stump. "Of
course, he did. He's a man of the cloth. What would Jesus
do, right? But, I'm not sure an 'Oops, I made a mistake'
works for me."

She took a deep breath and let it out before answering.
The look in her eyes told him he wasn't going to like
what she had to say. "I've come to the conclusion that
for some reason, Jonas, the glass is always half-empty
for you. Or maybe a more accurate analogy is the glass
is half-filled with arsenic."

He took a step back. "That's not true."

"You believed the worst when Mama told us she had
an affair with your father."

"But she was my mama. I trusted her. And, besides, I
didn't have anybody else to ask. You got on a plane with
your mother and never said a word about what happened.
Why, Jonas? Why did you give up on us so easily?"

"Marlene made us promise to keep her secret. I was a
kid, for God's sake. What was I supposed to do? Break
my mother's heart?"

"No. You broke mine, instead," she told him, her tone
too flat and cold to be Remy. "And for fifteen years,
I thought I loved you enough to overlook that. Maybe
I could have…if you hadn't assumed the worst about

Thom. Suddenly it became clear to me that you have trust issues that don't have anything to do with me—or with our mothers' lies. I want what Mama was holding out for—someone who will love me no matter what."

She touched her hand to his cheek. "Your daughter and her mother need you, Jonas. I'm a big girl. I can find my own way home."

Then she took her suitcase and computer bag and walked to the closest SUV. The driver noticed and rushed to unlock the door for her.

Jonas stood without moving. His brain couldn't make sense of what was happening. She blamed him for what her mother—and his—did fifteen years earlier? Remy was mad at him for drawing a faulty conclusion from facts that certainly would have raised suspicion about a man who was no perfect angel? If this was her idea of undying love, then who the hell needed it?

He stalked to the big table someone had dragged from inside the old store. He'd wrap up the paperwork, then take his daughter home. Screw love.

Remy watched Jonas storm to the command center. She knew he was mad. She didn't blame him, but she also knew this was the best choice she could make at the moment. She pushed her bags over to give her room to sit. She'd just reached for her seat belt when she heard a high-pitched voice call her name.

"Remy!"

Birdie raced across the plaza, her bright red braids

bobbing behind her. She reached the SUV, breathing hard. "You can't go without saying goodbye. You found me."

Remy got out and went down on one knee. "You were never lost, sweet girl. Just misplaced for a moment. You and your daddy have a special bond. He would never let you disappear for good."

"When will I see you again?"

Remy gave her a squeeze. "I'm going to be working at Shadybrook, where your grandma Charlotte lives. Maybe we can see each other when you come to visit her."

Birdie looked over her shoulder toward the big motor home. "My mommy doesn't feel good."

"I'm sorry."

"It's nobody's fault. I wanted it to be Brother Thom's fault, but Daddy says it isn't."

Remy was glad to hear that. "Nobody likes to be sick, Birdie. I hope your mother gets better soon."

The two search-and-rescue volunteers returned. The driver got in, but the passenger held back, waiting for Remy and Birdie to finish their conversation. "I have to go, now, Birdie. It was wonderful getting to meet you. You're a very special person."

Acting on impulse, she quickly reached behind her neck and undid the clasp on the chain she always wore. "Here, Birdie," she said, motioning for the little girl to turn around. "Your daddy gave this to me a long time ago. I want you to have it."

"Why?"

"Because sometimes you need something tangible to remind you that even when you're lost, someone who loves you will find you."

She dropped a quick kiss on the top of Birdie's head. "Take care, sweetheart, and be good for your daddy."

Big shiny tears sparkled in Birdie's eyes when she turned to look at Remy, but she didn't weep. She touched the little St. Christopher medal, then she smiled and raced to where her father was standing, Thomas Goodson at his side.

Remy felt guilty about not telling her half brother goodbye, but his long-distance nod told her they'd talk again when the time was right. Jonas, on the other hand, didn't acknowledge her leaving in any way. He picked up Birdie when she reached him and walked away.

Remy honestly couldn't say that she blamed him. She wasn't the same girl he thought he'd loved—either in high school or present day. But, finally, she knew who she was—Remy Bouchard. The Dream Girl. And she was done apologizing for being special.

CHAPTER SEVENTEEN

"How did Remy take the news that her half brother wasn't a serial killer like you thought?"

Jonas killed his shot of rum before answering. The bittersweet taste reminded him of sharing a drink in Remy's kitchen. He missed her so much the ache turned physical some nights. But, hopefully, he'd see her soon. If she was done being mad at him for being the world's biggest jerk.

"She accused me—quite accurately, I fear—of being a cockeyed pessimist. She said I was a reactionary who saw the world as half full of poison...or something like that," he told the man sitting across from him.

The blues bar was Leonard Franey's idea. He'd called Jonas the day before to set up the meeting. "I'll be in town on business. Thought we could tie up a few loose ends."

Leonard fiddled with his glass of beer, a smile working at the corners of his mouth. "Optimists are like that," he said, his tone a great deal less businesslike than usual. It sounded a bit wistful, actually, Jonas thought. "But I prefer to think pessimists are actually realists in sheep's clothing."

Jonas smiled but he wasn't sure he understood. Fortunately, the man went on without expecting a response. "The thing that's key is balance. Ying and yang. When two extremes meet in the middle, you can create harmony and beauty."

The markedly Eastern philosophy sounded strange coming from this man in black. "That's very…Zen," Jonas said.

"I speak from experience, Jonas. You are a good man. A well-trained logician. You like things to fit in nice tight boxes that can then be filed away Case Closed. So do I. But life isn't like that, my friend. And people like us need people like Remy to keep from becoming completely jaded."

Too late. He'd snatched a few meaningless facts from a file and immediately concluded an innocent man was a killer. Jonas did not like what that said about him. It was probably the main reason he presently sat on a fence, immobilized by fear. His dilemma was likely the main reason he'd agreed to hire a babysitter to stay with Birdie today. This was the first they'd been apart since her rescue three weeks ago.

"She told me I wasn't the man she thought I was and left—right in the middle of everything. I heard later from one of the search-and-rescue guys that they hung around the rental-car place to make sure she got off safely and that she rented a bright red convertible and drove off, smiling like she didn't have a care in the world."

The image continued to haunt him. Especially at night. God, he missed her.

Leonard let out a big, heartfelt laugh. "I can picture it.

That girl has spunk. And heart," he added meaningfully. "Believe me, Jonas, my biggest regret in life is giving up too easily on my Remy. Her name was Belle, by the way, and she predicted that I would wind up rich and alone if I didn't realign my priorities. 'Realign your priorities.' Who says things like that? I went back to work and she went away."

"What happened to her?"

"She lives in South Beach, where she's married with two kids. She teaches yoga and jogs on the beach. She seems very happy and content. I know this because I'm a highly sought after private investigator, who lacks any real life so I live vicariously through my friends. Even old friends who have moved on with their lives."

Jonas was surprised by the man's candor. Surprised and not sure what to make of his cautionary tale. "And you're telling me this because…"

Leonard took a small, token sip of beer. "You remind me of me, Jonas. Except for the hair." He rubbed his bald pate and grinned. "Plus, I was in the Black Hills, visiting my pal Shane Reynard this past weekend and bumped into Remy's sister, Jessie."

Jonas inhaled sharply. "Really? Should I have checked to see if you're armed?"

Leonard chuckled. "She told me about her threat to castrate you. She's a feisty one, that Jessie. But, no, I'm not here to do you bodily harm. In fact, she asked me to give you this card."

Like a magician, he suddenly produced a glossy business card, which he nudged across the table. Jonas picked it up and studied it a moment. "A web designer and marketing person? What do I need that for?"

"Jessie said to tell you the only way you were going to get back in her sister's good graces was by giving her what you promised when you hired her."

"What did I promise? Oh, wait. You mean, a glowing recommendation?"

Leonard shrugged. "She said you'd know."

Jonas turned the card over and saw a handwritten note. *Think testimonial.* What the hell did that mean?

He heaved a sigh and tucked the card in his shirt pocket. "Too late," he said. "Remy already has a job. I got an email newsletter from the rest home where my mother lives. It included a big spread about welcoming back Remy to a full-time position, blah, blah, blah. She doesn't need my reference."

Leonard didn't say anything for a few minutes. Jonas polished off his shot, nearly gagging on the harsh sweetness. The bitter truth was Remy didn't need a thing from him. But that didn't mean he wasn't tempted to intrude in her life and beg her to give him a second—or was it a third—chance?

"They're closing my department at work," he said. "I can stay in Memphis if I want a desk job or I can transfer to a bigger market. Say…New Orleans."

Leonard's poker face betrayed nothing.

"And I put my condo on the market—just to see if there was a market and it sold the next day."

"So…what are you waiting for? A neon arrow telling

you where you need to be—and who you're supposed to be with?"

"She's beautiful. Single. Good. I have enough baggage for three people. What could I possibly bring to the table to make up for that?"

Leonard shook his head indulgently but his grin was kind—hopeful, even. "People like Remy—and my Belle—aren't blind to the bad stuff that you and I see, Jonas. They simply choose to look beyond it. And, as to what you bring…well, check out that card." He shrugged and reached for his phone that was sitting to one side like a gun. "Or you could sleep on it. Some people get their answers from dreams, I'm told."

He rose, then leaned across the table to shake Jonas's hand. "It was good meeting you. Maybe I'll see you at the engagement party."

Jonas stood, too. "What engagement party?"

"Jessie and her rancher fiancé. Gonna be a big affair in Sentinel Pass. All the stars of the show will be there. I'm handling security. In fact, Shane booked a private plane for me and my crew. N'Awlins isn't too far out of the way if you need a lift." He winked. "Just saying. First, you gotta convince Miss Remy that you're the man to provide her heart's desire. Better get hopping, son. The party's in three weeks."

"I'M SORRY, JESS," Remy repeated for the fourteenth time. "I want to be there, but I can't afford to come. I don't start back to work until next week and I spent my disposable stash on paint and other stuff because I wanted to have the house done before I start working full-time."

She shifted her recyclable bag from her right shoulder to her left so she could pick up the mail on her way into the house. A large manila envelop that didn't quite fit in the funky black mailbox was sticking up. Her heart rate sped up when she spotted the return address.

The paternity test. She'd forgotten all about it.

She grabbed the mail and hurried inside, telling her sister, "I need to pinch pennies so I can come to your wedding. What's more important? An engagement party or being your maid of honor?"

Jessie huffed and muttered on the other end of the line. Not surprising. She was living the fairy tale. She'd come to expect things to work out the way she wanted them to—right down to a glamorous, star-studded street party in Sentinel Pass to celebrate her engagement to Cade.

"Hey, guess what?" Remy asked. "The results from that test Jonas and I took are back. Wanna know what it says?"

"I already know. So do you, obviously. What's the big deal? The real test comes when you talk Brother Thom into donating a swab of DNA. When's that going to happen?"

Remy didn't know. "I've left a couple of messages on his cell phone, but he hasn't called back. Not surprising, I guess, given the fact he was in the middle of losing his land. He might be homeless, for all I know."

"At least, he isn't a homeless serial killer."

Remy groaned and shook her head. She'd told her sister everything, of course. To Remy's surprise, Jessie had been more sympathetic toward Jonas than Remy would have expected. "I could see myself jumping to the same conclusion," she said. "People aren't all sweet and charitable like you, Rem. Jonas was prepared for the worst. That's a good thing in my book. It shows he cares."

They'd argued for miles—Remy behind the wheel of her bright red convertible—Bluetooth in place, Jessie kicking back in her pool, exercising her ankle in preparation for her surgery.

"How's your foot?"

"Ugly. I don't want to talk about it. Tell me what the paternity test says."

Remy set her purse and computer bag on the table. She'd spent the afternoon at the library, doing research into opening a small business. She wasn't sure she was brave enough to actually hang out a shingle, so to speak, but if she decided to start offering lucid dream consultations, while working on her master's degree in psychology, she needed to be prepared.

She skimmed down the cover letter. "Blah, blah, blah, cover my ass so you don't sue me— Hey, I could use this format to protect myself if I decide to go into the dream business."

Jessie didn't say anything. A first. Her sisters had been supportive of Remy's decision to return to college, but, surprisingly, Jessie had been lukewarm about the idea of turning Remy's penchant for lucid dreaming into a business.

"Okay. Here it is. There is a ninety-nine-point-nine percent chance that Jonas is not my brother. Which, of course, means there is zero chance that his father is our father. Pretty anticlimactic, right?" She skimmed to the bottom of the page. "I wonder if they sent a copy to Jonas. Probably, huh?"

"You're dying to call him, aren't you?"

"No," Remy lied.

Jonas was probably busily fitting all the loose and wobbly pieces of his life back into the perfect, white-carpet image he thought he wanted. She missed him. There was no denying that. And Birdie. She would have loved to get to know that beautiful child better, but she hadn't heard from him since that fateful day at the Good-Friends's compound. And she wasn't about to call.

"Men suck."

Jessie's laugh didn't sound the least bit sympathetic. And she immediately changed the subject. "What did you dream about last night?"

Remy walked into her living room—with its newly painted butter-yellow walls and sat on the love seat she'd picked up at that new consignment store in town. "My dreams? Seriously? Why do you want to know?"

"Just tell me."

Remy let her head fall against the cushion. She stared at the ceiling a moment, thinking. "I was planting a garden. Pepper plants. You were there. You laughed and said there were better ways to get some spice in my life."

She smiled. "I ignored you. As usual. And when I looked up, you were gone and Birdie was there, instead."

"You were planting a garden." Jessie sounded speculative. "Hmm…really. That's interesting."

Remy's radar went on high alert. "What's going on, Jess? What aren't you telling me?"

"Cade gave me an iPad for an engagement present. I'm looking at that online dream encyclopedia you told me about. According to it, planting a garden can mean you are open and receptive to new things. You are preparing to reap the bounty of your earlier investments. You are ripe with—"

Remy shot to her feet. "Stop. I know what it means. My job starts next week. I've filled out an application for grad school and picked up the paperwork I need to open my own business. I'm looking ahead and trying to get on with my life, Jess. What more do you want from me?"

Her sister didn't answer right away. When she did, Remy's inner twin sense went on high alert. Jessie was planning something—something that had to do with Remy. "Listen, Rem, no matter what happens, you know I love you, right? And I want you to be as happy as I am. Are we clear on that?"

Clear as mud, she almost said. One of her mother's favorite sayings. But, she didn't have time to formulate an answer, because there was a loud, firm knock on her door, followed by an excited, little girl voice calling her name.

"Remy. Remy, are you home? It's me, Birdie."

CHAPTER EIGHTEEN

BIRDIE WAS SO EXCITED she nearly wet her pants. Her brand-new Hannah Montana panties. Her daddy had taken her shopping a few days after they got home and bought her more clothes than she had before her mommy took her away. She'd picked out her prettiest dress to wear today. To see Remy.

She pressed her face to the old screen door and called Remy's name again. "What if she isn't here, Daddy?"

"Her car is here. Call again."

He was standing a few steps back, the yard sign they'd picked up that morning after visiting Grandma balanced on the porch beside him—the front pressed against his leg so it would be a surprise for Remy.

Daddy had been planning this surprise ever since the day he quit his job and sold their condo. He'd sat beside her on the big leather sofa and explained everything. "I have a job opportunity in New Orleans, which is driving distance from Baylorville. That's where Grandma lives, remember?"

"And Remy," Birdie had put in. She dreamed about Remy nearly every night. Her soft voice and nice smile. Birdie felt safe around her. Not Daddy-safe—like he could beat up anybody who tried to her hurt her, but

I-won't-ever-leave-you safe. Her mommy wanted to be that kind of person, Birdie knew, but her sickness didn't let her.

Darla, the therapist, explained the whole thing nearly every time Birdie saw her. The whole thing was getting old, which was another reason Birdie was glad to move. That, and she wanted her daddy to be happy. In her dreams, Daddy smiled a lot. And laughed. With Remy.

"Remy," she cried one more time, her hand automatically touching the little medal on the chain around her neck.

And, suddenly, she appeared, her golden hair falling softly around her shoulders and face. She was wearing a dress, like Birdie. Only, hers was white. She could have been an angel. Except, angels weren't supposed to cry, were they?

"Birdie," Remy said, pushing the screen door out so she could open her arms. "You're here. I saw you in my dream last night. I've missed you."

"Me, too," Birdie sobbed, her words lost in the warm, safe arms of her personal angel. *Me, too*.

JONAS HAD HIS SPEECH all planned. Unfortunately, the words evaporated the instant he saw his daughter throw herself into the arms of the woman he loved with every ounce of his being. He'd come full circle. He'd run away to escape his fears and had nearly lost everything he held dear. He was stepping a million miles or so outside his comfort zone to try to convince her that his glass would be brimming over if she'd give him another chance.

"What are you two doing here?" Remy asked, looking first at Birdie then Jonas.

His throat closed up at the way she tenderly touched Birdie's cheek before redirecting an errant lock of bright red hair. He sucked at braids and every other nuance of girl's hair care.

"Me and Daddy brought you a present, Remy."

"A present?"

"Sort of," Jonas said. His fingers drummed across the top of the metal sign he was now embarrassed to show her. The idea had sounded playful, optimistic and fun a couple of weeks ago when he'd run the plan past both Jessie and Leonard. They'd given him a green light. How come neither of them saw the downside to this idea, he suddenly asked himself. *What if she thinks I'm trying to control—*

"Jonas?"

Her inflection told him he'd missed something. "Huh?"

"Do you want to come inside?"

"Yes?" He looked at Birdie, who looked worried. Damn. He hated it when she worried. That was his job. "Yes," he said, trying to sound decisive. "But first, we want to show you your gift."

"It's only part of it," Birdie said.

Remy looked confused but she smiled prettily. "Okay."

He motioned for Birdie to stand in front of him, then together they turned the sign—its two long metal stakes squeaking against the porch. "Ta-da," Jonas said, holding his breath.

Remy looked down, turned a ghostly shade of white, slapped one hand to her chest and stumbled back. "I don't believe it. How did you know?"

Birdie looked up at him. He'd been prepared to lie if asked, but he changed his mind. "It came to me in a dream."

Remy blinked, her jaw falling open. A second later, she threw back her head and laughed. "A dream. I love it. Oh, my gosh, it's perfect. You are both perfect. Come in."

Birdie didn't hesitate for a second. She raced across the threshold and disappeared into one of the rooms. He knew he should scold her for making herself at home but he didn't say a word. He couldn't. The look in Remy's eyes made his throat close tight and his heart beat so hard he was afraid it might explode.

She stepped close enough that the sign brushed against the hem of her dress. She put her arms around his neck and pressed her chest to his. "I don't believe you, and you can tell Jessie I said so, but…" She let the word hang while she kissed him. "I'm glad you're here."

Relief on par with what he felt the moment he spotted Birdie in the forest standing beside Remy surged through him. He wrapped his arms around her and kissed her hard, with all the emotion he'd kept tamped down for so long. Fear. The kind that came from losing a man he loved but never understood. Of worrying that whatever overwhelming passion or pain drove his father to take his own life might reappear in Jonas's life if he felt too much—loved too much—still lingered in the far recesses of his brain. But Jonas understood now that love wasn't to blame for his father's suicide. Any more than it would be to blame if Cheryl took her own life.

Her doctors claimed she wasn't suicidal. She might even rebuild a fairly normal life for herself someday—within the safe structure of the mental-health community. Her instincts had been sound when she sought the communal life of the GoodFriends. Routine and security were key. And Jonas would make sure she had that—for Birdie's sake.

"Daddy," Birdie called from inside the house. "Come see the pretty colors. Can we paint our walls this color? Please, Daddy. Grandma won't care. She told me so."

Remy moved back and tilted her head. "Grandma Charlotte?"

He pushed a lock of hair behind her ear. "Birdie and I are moving into Mom's house." He coughed and amended the statement. "Or will be as soon as the contractor I hired rips out all the ugly white carpet and installs new bamboo flooring." He thought a moment. "Maybe now would be a good time to paint. I should hire a consultant. Know anybody local?"

Laughing, she stepped back and picked up the sign. The turquoise background was bold but it served as a perfect foil to the yellow, black and white lettering that read: Remy Bouchard, Consultant—www.thedreamgirl.com.

"Consultant," Remy said, chuckling softly. "Appropriately vague, since I have no idea what I'm doing. Good choice."

"It wasn't my idea."

"I knew it," she exclaimed. "Jessie."

Jonas shook his head. "Nope. You're wrong." But he didn't explain until after he walked the sign to the middle of the yard and stuck it in the ground, facing the street. Then he was back on the porch, leading the way inside. "Where's your laptop?"

Remy's heart was racing and her head was spinning and she couldn't stop grinning long enough to answer questions. Jonas and Birdie were moving back to Baylorville. She wanted to ask about Cheryl. And his job. But the less practical side of her—Mama's side—was content to enjoy the moment.

The minute Remy was seated, Birdie raced across the room from her post at the bay window and jumped on the sofa beside her. A happy, little-girl move that made Remy smile. "You look wonderful, Birdie."

Birdie took hold of both her braids, which Remy had to admit looked as though a man had braided them. "I wanna cut my hair. What do you think?"

Remy glanced at Jonas, who was fiddling with her computer at the dining-room table. "You know what my mama always said? It's your hair, and unless you're Orna Bascomb, it'll grow back."

"Who's Orna Bascomb?" Birdie asked.

"An old woman who only had about seven individual hairs on her head. Still, she came to Mama's shop every week to have her hair washed and styled." She rearranged

Birdie's braids to mimic a pageboy look. "I think you'd look adorable with short hair. Maybe I'll get my hair cut, too. Change is good, they say."

Birdie suddenly threw herself against Remy and wrapped her skinny arms around her fiercely. "I love you, Remy. I told my daddy I want him to marry you someday so you can be my other mommy. Will you, Remy? Please?"

Jonas hurried to the couch. "Whoa, partner," he scolded in a very gentle, almost laughing, tone. "Now, who can't keep a secret?" To Remy he said, "She was positive I was going to blow the rest of our surprise by emailing you to get your feedback."

"Feedback on what?"

He held out his hand to help her up. "You'll see." To Birdie, he said, "I think I left the hard copies in the car. Would you get them for me, sweetheart?"

"Sure, Daddy." He bent down to kiss his daughter's cheek before he handed her the keys.

The second she raced from the room, he hustled Remy to the chair sitting in front of her open laptop. "I wanted you to have a minute or two to process this without Birdie breathlessly waiting for you to 'ooh' and 'ahh.' It's a prototype, Rem. That's all. Nothing is written in blood. The web designer is a friend of your sister's. Her name is Rachel Grey. She's been super easy to work with and she promised to change anything—everything—to your specifications."

Remy heard all of his disclaimers but immediately discounted them as irrelevant. The website was the most beautiful thing she'd ever seen. A more muted, easy-on-the-eyes version of her street sign made up the background. Only, there was a lightness and fluidity to the design that she couldn't quite put her finger on. It seemed to move and change…like a dream.

"It's amazing, Jonas. Absolutely gorgeous, but…" She saw him brace for some negative comments. "Do you like it?"

"Yes. I was blown away when I first saw it."

"How could anyone not be? It's a work of art. The *but* I was going to say had to do with the fact it's meant to sell a service I'm not certain I'm qualified to sell. My lucid dreams are one thing, but doling out advice to strangers… I'm not sure I feel comfortable doing that without more training. So I'm studying for my master's in psychology."

He pulled up a chair and sat close enough for their knees to touch. He took her hand and said, "I know— Jesse told me. And I'm proud of you. Education is always a good thing. But when I hired you to find my daughter, how did you say I could pay you back?"

"Two weeks of salary and a glowing recommendation. The check you sent is on my desk." She glowered at him. "I don't know who you asked, but I've never earned that much in my life."

He lifted her hand and kissed her knuckle. "Consider it seed money."

The image of her dream—the gardening dream she'd told Jessie about—returned. Jonas had been there, too, she realized. Holding an umbrella. You didn't need a lot of training to figure that image out. He was her protector, the one who looked at the sky and worried about the weather so she could garden in peace.

"And, as I told Leonard Franey a couple of weeks ago, you didn't need a recommendation because you already had a job. Do you know what he said?"

She shook her head.

"What did he say, Birdie?"

Breathless but grinning, ear to ear, Birdie handed him the folder and answered, "So give her a test—a testi-ment?"

He pulled his daughter into the tiny space between them and bussed the top of her head. "Testimonial. A personal, rather moving—if I do say so myself—testimonial of your ability to interpret dreams to achieve very specific goals."

"Me," Birdie chirped. "You found me. And you and Daddy found each other, too, right? And we'll never be lost again."

Remy smiled her answer because she was too choked up to speak. She and Jonas had a lot more to talk about, but she knew the important stuff. He loved her. He might never be the cockeyed optimist she was, but he wasn't beaten down by fear and cynicism, either. Together, they'd make a better team than they ever would have in high school because, now, they truly understood—and finally appreciated—the gifts they'd been given. She would probably never understand fully why their mothers lied, but finally she felt some degree of peace with what happened.

"Is Birdie asleep?"

"For now," Jonas told her, joining her in the kitchen of his mother's old house. A vast array of paint samples were spread across the table, along with the library of home-makeover magazines she'd acquired. "She's been having nightmares. Her therapist said this was normal. She's working through some issues."

His willingness to seek counseling for his daughter instead of merely assuming she'd recover from her trauma told Remy a lot about the man he was. A good, involved, connected father.

"What about Cheryl? What's going to happen to her?"

He walked to where she was standing. "Do we really have to talk about my ex-wife right now? She will always be a part of Birdie's life, and I'll try to make that reality as painless as possible for all of us. But the family counselor Birdie and I spoke with said it's important to know your limits. I'm not responsible for Cheryl's choices. I never was."

He took her hand and led her into the backyard. The landscaping lights, which were either set on a timer or triggered by the fall of darkness, had turned the area into a small, green oasis. A padded glider that had been covered in gardening tools the last time she was here had been cleared off and dusted.

They sat there, shoulder to shoulder, comfortable and relaxed. He took her hand and ran his thumb across the faint scar left from her scratches. "When I fell into that well, I tried everything to get out. I was at the point of giving up when I felt a presence in the well with me.

An angel. She wasn't a little girl, like you were. She had beautiful blond hair and a kind smile. She's the one who handed me the St. Christopher medal. I'd stomped it down into the mud and, in my panic, I'd forgotten about it."

She put her free hand to her chest without thinking. Gone. He fished something out of his pocket and held it out to her in the palm of his hand. "I know you gave mine to Birdie, so I bought you one of your own."

She held the shiny silver medallion up to the light. A perfect little diamond winked back at her. This was more than a necklace, she realized, it was a promise. One they'd announce to the world when the time was right.

"I felt naked without it."

He fumbled with the clasp at her neck, but a moment later looked down and tenderly positioned it just where he wanted it. His fingers set her skin on fire like a spark to dry tinder.

She pulled in a quick, shallow breath that made him look up. His lopsided grin reminded her of the boy she'd loved with all her heart. Still loved.

"Speaking of being naked…I have a mosquito-free, king-size bed inside. With a lock on the door and a child monitor on low in case Birdie needs me. Are you interested?"

She smiled and let out a sigh. "You had me at mosquito-free. Let's go."

"I'M ALMOST AFRAID TO touch you," Jonas said, leaning against the door he'd closed and locked behind them. "What if you're a dream?"

She touched her fingers to the necklace he'd given her. "I thought the same thing in Florida the first night we were together."

He walked to where she was standing. "You are the most beautiful woman in the world. To me," he added when she gave him a droll look of disbelief.

She looped her arms around his neck and pulled him closer. "Kiss first, talk later." Her tone was teasing, not imperious, but it was exactly the kind of shorthand communication they'd shared in high school, completing each other's thoughts, humming the same tune at the same time.

He felt a surge of emotion, so raw and deep, it seemed to come from the seat of his soul. Love, loss, sadness for all the time and experiences they'd missed out on, but a need, too, so intense it almost wiped the slate clean. There was no going back, but there was now. And now was the greedy joy of watching Remy unbutton her blouse with fast, nimble fingers; her skirt quickly followed.

She cocked her head and looked at him. "Clothes. Off."

He let out a low chuckle and complied with her demand. His shirt stuck to him from the humidity; it fought back, but he won. "I should shower. I've been moving junk all afternoon."

She ran her fingernails across his shoulder and down one pec, making his nipple turn hard as a nail head. Her tongue followed, teasing his nipple with her tongue. She licked his skin before running the tip of her tongue back and forth across her bottom lip. "Yum. The salty taste of hard work. That's the taste of a good man. I like it."

Then she cozied up against him, putting her hands on his hips. He'd lost a few pounds since the last time he'd worn these particular cutoff fatigues. The waistband was loose, leaving plenty of room for her to work her hand inside the zipper.

His mouth went dry and he forgot to breathe. "Oh, man."

She nuzzled his chest. "I agree. Man, oh, man. You have the most amazing body."

He took her face in his hands and kissed her hard, plundering with all the pent-up need and desire he'd known since their first night together. He'd been crazy to think he could live without this. Without her.

Her tongue matched his urgency. He might have wanted to make this slow and perfect for her, but that idea disappeared the minute she touched him.

"I need—"

"No. I need," she cut him off. "Now."

She unfastened her bra and tossed it over her shoulder, then yanked off her panties.

Jonas's brain was missing a good portion of its normal blood supply and he couldn't make his hands work the damn snap on his fatigues quickly enough. She brushed his hands aside and placed them behind her back. "Later," she said. "Hold me."

She flattened herself against him, wiggling with a wild, demanding urgency that made him pick her up. Her legs locked behind him. Her breasts were in exactly the right place to kiss, nip and suckle. She ran her fingers through his hair while her hips ground in a slow, intense circle that nearly unmanned him.

"Holy...I don't know what..." he murmured. "You are the hottest woman I have ever held in my arms, but if we don't hit the bed in the next three seconds, we're going to wind up on the floor."

She laughed and pointed. "The bed. Now."

He held tight and timed his roll to land with her on top so he didn't squish her. Her hair came loose from the knot she'd had it in, dropping like a golden veil over them both. She arched her back, tossing her head as she laughed. "That was a crazy ride. I loved it. But we have to do something about these pants."

She moved off him and knelt on the mattress to finish what Jonas had started. He lifted his hips when she started to tug them down. One final flick sent them flying, the same way she'd discarded her bra.

"Ah...now, that's more like it," she said, her gaze fixed on his groin.

Jonas wasn't the shy type but there were things he'd planned to tell her before they got this far into making love. Like how much he loved her and couldn't imagine going through the rest of his life without her and that she was the only woman in the world he wanted in Birdie's life and would she marry him. Please? But none of those things made it anywhere near his mouth once her mouth lowered to taste a different part of him.

Remy wanted to savor this moment forever. She wanted to laugh and squeal with triumph and shake her fists in the face of Fate. *He's here. He's mine. We're together.* And the best way she could think of to seal the deal was the one thing she'd never been brave enough to try with him in high school.

She held his body in her hands and gently ran the tip of him back and forth across her cheek, her nose, her other cheek. She inhaled deeply before letting her tongue touch and taste.

His muscles tightened, his breathing sped up. He was turned on to the max even before her mouth closed around him. She heard his low, gruff moan. She tested his response to her teeth and almost smiled. She loved the power it gave her to pull back, suckling the way he had at her breast.

"Oh, geez, Remy, *stop.* No. Yes. Wait."

She knew exactly what he meant. She stopped, but only long enough to put her body where her mouth had been. She guided him into her and settled against him, feeling an instantaneous reward. Tiny shivers exploded from the inside out. She lifted her hips in shallow, dipping circles, drawing upward until he cried out for her and anchored her hips with his hands, driving them both to that explosive point beyond this plane of existence. Once, twice. Again. At last.

She sank against him, their bodies still connected, their hearts racing as their breathing slowly began to return to normal. She closed her eyes and let herself simply enjoy.

Beautiful. Fabulous. Perfect. The words seemed too mundane to describe something so...dreamy.

She might have stayed there forever, but a soft whimper a few minutes later made them both startle fully awake and present. "Birdie?" Remy asked, rolling to one side.

"Uh-huh. I'd better check on her."

He pulled on his army shorts and left the room.

Remy used the time to freshen up in the adjoining bath. She looked at her reflection in the mirror, seeing a well-loved woman.

Jonas was sitting on the end of the bed when she returned.

"Is she okay?"

He nodded. "Fine. If I touch her arm, her shoulder, she stills right away and drops back to sleep. I think she needs that reassurance that I'm here and I'm not going to leave her."

She sat beside him and put her arm around him. "You're a good dad."

He swallowed. "Thanks. Speaking of fathers…did you get a copy of the DNA results?"

"This morning. No surprise, right?"

He took her free hand in his with a solemnity that made her heart rate spike. "What?"

"I want to be related to you, Remy. By marriage. Will you marry me?"

She kissed him on the lips—a sweet kiss filled with promise. "Someday. When Birdie's ready. I can wait. I've waited this long." A thought hit her. "And Jessie is announcing her engagement this coming weekend at a big party in the Black Hills. We can't rain on her parade, so to speak."

His eyes lit with laughter and he pulled her into his arms, rolling them both backward. "The party. I almost forgot. Leonard offered to give us a lift. In a business jet. He's in charge of security. Shall we go? Jessie might hunt us down and hurt us if we don't. Remember her threat?"

He put one hand over his groin and wiggled his eyebrows. Remy laughed and kissed him. "Well, since you put it like that, there's only one thing I can say. Sentinel Pass, here we come."

EPILOGUE

"HAVE A GOOD TIME AND stop worrying about stealing your sister's thunder, Remy. Jessie is going to be dancing on her crutches the minute she sees you," Leonard said, his tone the voice of authority.

Remy believed him. She did. Jess would be ecstatic to see them. And pulling off this sort of surprise seemed like a minor miracle, but Remy still felt some misgivings. Partly because everything happened so fast. Her new job, her dream-consulting business, her as-yet-undisclosed engagement. Well, they'd told Birdie—and Miss Charlotte. And Leonard.

"Thanks, Leonard. For everything. We'll see you at the street party later, right?"

"Wouldn't miss it. Now, go rub shoulders with the stars of *Sentinel Passtime*. I need to check out my command post at the Tidbiscuit Café. Man, can that woman make a mean biscuit and gravy."

The impressive black van pulled away and disappeared behind the Sentinel Pass volunteer fire department. Half a block ahead was the spot Remy remembered all too well. Her sister had nearly fallen to her death after a maniac had sabotaged her stunt. Luckily, Cade had been there to catch her.

"Looks like something's happening over there," Jonas said.

"Is that a dinosaur?" Birdie asked, pulling Remy to walk faster. "Can I ride on it?"

"That's Seymour, the town's mascot. The girl sitting on it is Shiloh—Cade's daughter. And there's Jess," she exclaimed, fighting back a smile because her sister's lime-green halter dress clashed something fierce with the dinosaur.

"Cool," Birdie said. "She's pretty. But you're prettier."

Jonas looked at Remy and winked. "I agree."

"Come on, you two. I think it's starting."

They were still making their way through the people milling about when a sudden shriek of joy and surprise filled the air. "Remy," Jessie yelled at the top of her lungs. "You came. You big sneak. I hate you. Wow. I can't believe you pulled this off."

Remy looked at Jonas. He smiled and let go of her hand so she could weave through the crowd. Jessie shoved her crutches at Cade the second before Remy reached her. "You came," she cried again. "I love you, Rem. Thank you so much. It wouldn't have been the same without you. I really can't believe you're here."

Jonas reached them a moment later, Birdie safely hoisted in his arms. Jessie gave him a hug, too. "Good job, Jonas. You brought her and I didn't even have to threaten you with great bodily harm. Way to go."

Cade stepped in to hand Jessie her crutches. "You promised the doctor you'd be good," he reminded her, before shaking hands all around. "You must be Birdie," he said. "My daughter, Shiloh, has been dying to meet you. Do you want to check out Seymour the dinosaur?"

She nodded vigorously causing her adorable new bob to dance with abandon. Taking Birdie to Marlene's House of Beauty for her first haircut had been one of the most beautiful, full-circle moments of Remy's life. They'd sniffled a little, laughed a lot and gabbed with the stylists, who had talked Remy out of going short. Ultimately, she'd settled for a just-past-the-shoulders style that seemed smart and grown-up—totally befitting her new, professional image.

Remy felt a tug on her heartstrings. Everyday, she noticed the little girl blossoming, becoming more outgoing and sure of her place in the world.

Jonas set her down. "I'll be right here, sweetheart. Have fun."

"Remy," a familiar voice exclaimed. "You're here. That is so cool. Jack. Come see. Remy's here."

"Kat, this is Jonas. Kat is Jessie's future sister-in-law. I worked for her husband, Jack," she said, looking around, then pointing at where she spied the man. "Over there standing with Mac and the boys. How are you, Kat? Ready for school to start?"

Kat's grin broadened. "You won't believe this. After all the time and effort it took to get my teaching credential, I didn't even apply for a job."

"Why no—" She didn't finish the question. The answer was in Kat's eyes. "You're pregnant."

"Yep. For real," she added, although Remy didn't know what that meant exactly. "Jack is over-the-moon excited. Even his mother's happy." She gave a small sigh that said a lot, then she spun around and dashed toward the dais. "I forgot. I'm supposed to bring this microphone to Libby."

Jonas leaned close and asked, "By Libby, does she mean Libby McGannon? Wife of Cooper Lindstrom?"

Remy nodded.

Jonas looked impressed as he faced toward the podium. After a couple of seconds of controlled chaos, a woman whose face regularly appeared on magazine covers held the mic to her lips and said, "Hi, everyone. It's me, Libby. Thank you all for coming. It's high noon, so let's get this show on the road."

A thunderous response made Birdie hop off the dinosaur and run back to her father. Jonas hefted her to his shoulders, then put his free arm around Remy. Remy noticed Jessie watching and was gratified when she saw her sister grin.

"Cooper? Where are you? Give Gannon to Morgan and get your much-photographed behind up here."

A second wave of clapping rocked the area but Cooper quickly quelled it once he reached the mike. "Now, now, this isn't about me." He gave the crowd a droll look. "Although, come to think of it, we wouldn't be here today if I hadn't answered a certain beautiful lady's online ad."

He winked at his wife, then turned more serious. "Libby and I are here today for two reasons. First, and foremost, we're celebrating the engagement of Jessie

Bouchard to Cade Garrity. Jessie is one of the coolest stuntwomen on the planet, and don't let that cast on her leg fool you. She may look harmless but she can still kick your butt. I guarantee it."

Everyone laughed, including Jonas.

"Cade, you told me you'd like to meet the man who bought the climbing tower Jessie swan-dived into your arms from, so…here he is. Shane Reynard and his soon-to-be wife, Jenna Murphy."

Two more people joined them on stage—a George Clooney-handsome man with black hair, holding the hand of a beautiful redhead.

"My heartiest congratulations, Cade and Jessie," Shane said, giving Cooper a friendly punch to the shoulder and kissing Libby's cheek. "The tower was a gift to Jenna. We both felt terrible when we heard someone sabotaged your stunt, Jess. But, hey, all's well that ends with a diamond ring, right? Right?"

As if on cue, Jessie held up her left hand, flashing her bright, glittery diamond. Remy probably clapped the loudest because she was so happy for her sister. She couldn't wait for some alone time to compare notes.

Shane looked into the crowd and made a come-here motion to someone. "Morgan, bring the baby up here. I want to ask Gannon something."

"That's Morgana Carlyle," Jonas said under his breath.

"Jessie doubled for her in every show. Cool, huh?"

The glamorous blonde caused a stir in the crowd as she climbed the stairs—toddler in arms, shadowed by the man Remy had seen earlier. "The man behind her is Libby's brother, Mac. He stopped to help me when Yota's tires blew out. He's a firefighter and a miner."

The group crowded around the microphone. The baby reached for his mother, but managed to grab a handful of Jenna's hair in the process. She let out a little yelp, which caused a giant dog sitting at the base of the stage to give a deep, loud bark. The baby startled visibly and burst into tears.

Cooper hurried over to comfort his son. He scowled at the handsome, tricolor dog. "Luca, we've had this discussion before. Stop scaring my kid."

"Your kid started it," Shane countered.

Jenna exchanged amused looks with the other women on stage. "Boys, please, a modicum of order and dignity. Just while we finish the introductions."

Jenna returned the mike to Shane, who continued, "Thanks, my love. Now, as I was saying, from the beginning, Coop and I knew we wanted *Sentinel Passtime* to be about more than one life and one love affair. On screen, Cooper and Libby have become the nucleus of a large, diverse, slightly whacko family and community. As the name implies, our setting plays a huge part in the story line and that means getting *our* Libby out from behind the barred windows of the post office. And because nobody wanted to see Morgana get hurt—" the audience gave a collective cry of horror "—we turned to Jessie Bouchard for help."

Shane clapped, which produced another swell of cheers.

"Jessie," he said, addressing her directly. "You have been a consummate professional. You're a dazzling athlete and your public and your profession are going to miss you. Heal fast, my friend."

Remy could tell her sister was choked up, but Cade was there to give her a hug, and a moment later, she managed a little bow.

"I don't think I asked…have Jessie and Cade set a date?" Jonas asked. The warm whisper of his breath near her ear gave her a shiver of pleasure. "Will it be before or after ours?"

They'd discussed the timing of their wedding at length, but Birdie wound up picking the date when she told them, "Daddy, do you know what I want for my birthday? A wedding."

October.

The date would certainly fall before Jessie and Cade's. Would that be a problem? Remy wondered. As she looked at her sister sharing a private moment with Cade, she decided Jessie would be happy for her. Period.

A sudden commotion to her left brought her out of her reverie. A tall, robust man, carrying a three-story birdhouse made to resemble a Bavarian castle plunged through the crowd, leading the way for his wife or girlfriend, who was carrying an intricately carved pole about five feet in length. "Sorry. Engagement gift coming through."

The pair scaled the steps, moving toward the front of the dais, while the others spread out. "You artist types," Libby scolded, her tone resigned. "Are you ever on time?" To the public, she said, "Everyone, it's my honor to introduce Rachel Grey and Rufus Miller."

Remy turned to Jonas. "That's Rachel," she exclaimed softly. "I can't wait to talk to her in person. Her design for my website is unbelievable. This is so exciting."

Rachel took the microphone and waved at Jessie. "Hey, you two. I wanted you to know that everyone up here—plus, Char and Eli, who couldn't be here today because they are on their honeymoon—" she gave a little squeal that made everyone smile "—as well as William and Daria, who are standing in the back, trying to look cool and British..." Heads turned, but Remy couldn't see who she was talking about. "Anyway, we all went in on this amazing new DreamCastle that Rufus will be selling soon, as well as his totem pole, which, when you look closely at it you'll see that it combines the stories of both your lives into one."

She lifted the pole overhead and carefully passed it into the audience. Cade retrieved it and carried it to his future bride. "Oh, my God," Jessie exclaimed. "Remy, come here. You have to see this."

Remy smiled but stayed where she was. As she guessed, a low chant started. "Speech. Speech. Speech."

Cade scooped Jessie into his arms and carried her to the podium. She was blushing like crazy, but Remy could tell she was happy, too. "If we get any more people up here, the stage is going to collapse. We're talking a true YouTube moment. So, I have one question for y'all. Do you have your SAG cards?"

Amid laughter and joking, the entire group filed off

the dais. Jessie looked at Cade and said, softly, "Alone at last."

That drew hoots and catcalls from the audience.

Shoulder to shoulder, the couple faced the gathering. Remy and Jessie made eye contact. Remy knew her sister was nervous, but she'd always been good at meeting anything that scared her head-on.

Jonas held his breath, waiting for Jessie to speak. He knew how close the sisters were and he hoped that by coming here today, he'd helped to lay the first plank in the bridge that would unite their two families. He couldn't wait to get to know Cade and Shiloh better, as well as his future sister-in-law.

He only half-listened as she thanked everyone for coming. There were more introductions, but he basically tuned everything out until he heard Remy's name. "And some of you probably remember my twin sister, Remy," Jessie said, gesturing toward where Remy and Jonas were standing.

"Remy came to the Black Hills a few months back because something told her I was in trouble. That something is a bond we've shared since the womb. It's called love." She smiled at her sister, and Remy blew her a kiss.

"The best part of having Remy here was she kept me honest. She made me face my fears—especially when it came to admitting how much I cared for our landlord, Cade Garrity."

She looked perfectly at home on the arm of the tall,

lanky guy in cowboy boots, jeans and white shirt with snaps, not buttons.

Jonas thought the two looked amazingly perfect together, which made for an interesting conundrum, considering Remy and Jessie were twins and Jonas didn't look anything like that cowboy.

He was still marveling over the concept when he heard his name mentioned on the speakers. He looked at Remy for help. "She asked about your intentions."

He swallowed hastily. "Oh." To Jessie, he called out, "I love her. Always have. Always will."

Jessie let out a delighted hoot. "It's about time, Galloway. It's about frigging time."

Jonas agreed. "And, I hate to steal your thunder, but face it, you're twins. You do things alike. Remy and I are getting married in October. Everyone is invited. It's going to be at my mom's place."

"Your mom's house?"

"Nope. Shadybrook."

Jessie burst out laughing. She whispered in her fiancé's ear, making him grin. He brought the mike closer to his lips and said, "An old folks' home? That's original, Remy. I like it."

"And, of course we'll be there," Jessie put in. "This is the best—" She hesitated a moment then gestured toward the birdhouse and totem pole. "I mean, second-best engagement gift, ever."

She clapped her hands to get everyone's attention. "Enough. Enough talking. I'm an action kind of gal, so everybody get a drink and fill your plate while the band sets up. We Louisiana girls are going to show you how to party. To heck with my cast. So, as we say in our neck of the woods, *laissez les bon temps rouler!* Let the good times roll."

Jonas had his hands full for the next hour or so, meeting and greeting friends, strangers and Remy's family. He somehow managed to pull his daughter away from her newfound pals long enough to join him and Remy for a buffalo burger with all the trimmings.

Then, finally, at long last, the band was playing a song that made him smile. "Dance with me?"

Remy turned on the picnic bench to look at him. She tilted her head. "Oh. Yes. I do want to dance with you. But, wait, we need Jessie and Cade, too."

He understood and patiently followed her to a group standing in front of a landmark deeply ingrained in the American TV viewer psyche—the Sentinel Pass Post Office.

"Jessie, they're playing our song," Remy called.

Jonas watched her sister react with almost eerie similarity. Her smile was a lot like Remy's, too, although a tad more cautious. He could understand that. Life left indelible impressions on a person. Some good, some bad. But, with luck and the right person at your side, you could weather nearly any storm.

The four of them walked to the area roped off for dancing. He'd overheard someone say this was the exact spot Jessie dropped from the sky into Cade's arms. He didn't know if he believed that but he knew all too well not to discount the influence of Fate—and timing.

Who knew what might have happened if he and Remy had gotten together in high school as they'd planned. He wouldn't have had Birdie, that was for sure. He might not have finished college or achieved the success he had in his career. He might not have joined the National Guard or helped to ensure the safe return of the men serving under him.

He didn't know where that other road might have led him, nor did he care. There was no reclaiming the past. They were together now and that was all that mattered.

He pulled her close and pretended to waltz with her—the same way he had when they were kids in high school.

Her laughter was pure happiness and it made everything right. "I love you," he murmured in her ear.

Before she could reply, a shoulder bumped his shoulder. He looked sideways.

"Sorry," his future brother-in-law said. "I'm no dancer." He poked out his hand to shake. "I'm Cade, by the way. Looks like we're going to be family."

Jonas returned the courtesy, immediately liking the guy. He was real and grounded—exactly what Jessie needed. He looked at her and said, "Congratulations. I'm happy for you."

"Thanks. I'm happy for both of you. I know Mama is up in heaven looking down, smiling from ear to ear. It took us a while, didn't it, Rem? But we both figured things out on our own."

Remy nuzzled her cheek against Jonas's shoulder.

"Mama might have missed out on her chance at a happily-ever-after, but she always told us dreams do come true. And here we are—living proof."

More friends and family members joined them on the dance floor, swaying to the sound of Cass Elliot crooning, "Dream a little dream of me."

Jonas closed his eyes and sighed with a contentment he hadn't felt for years. As far as he was concerned, the dream was just beginning.

* * * * *

COMING NEXT MONTH

Available June 14, 2011

#1710 FINDING HER DAD
Suddenly a Parent
Janice Kay Johnson

#1711 MARRIED BY JUNE
Make Me a Match
Ellen Hartman

#1712 HER BEST FRIEND'S WEDDING
More than Friends
Abby Gaines

#1713 HONOR BOUND
Count on a Cop
Julianna Morris

#1714 TWICE THE CHANCE
Twins
Darlene Gardner

#1715 A RISK WORTH TAKING
Zana Bell

You can find more information on upcoming
Harlequin® titles, free excerpts and more at
www.HarlequinInsideRomance.com.

HSRCNM0511

REQUEST YOUR FREE BOOKS!
2 FREE NOVELS PLUS 2 FREE GIFTS!

Harlequin®

Super Romance®

Exciting, emotional, unexpected!

YES! Please send me 2 FREE Harlequin® Superromance® novels and my 2 FREE gifts (gifts are worth about $10). After receiving them, if I don't wish to receive any more books, I can return the shipping statement marked "cancel." If I don't cancel, I will receive 6 brand-new novels every month and be billed just $4.69 per book in the U.S. or $5.24 per book in Canada. That's a saving of at least 15% off the cover price! It's quite a bargain! Shipping and handling is just 50¢ per book in the U.S. and 75¢ per book in Canada.* I understand that accepting the 2 free books and gifts places me under no obligation to buy anything. I can always return a shipment and cancel at any time. Even if I never buy another book, the two free books and gifts are mine to keep forever.

135/336 HDN FC6T

Name	(PLEASE PRINT)

Address	Apt. #

City	State/Prov.	Zip/Postal Code

Signature (if under 18, a parent or guardian must sign)

Mail to the **Reader Service**:
IN U.S.A.: P.O. Box 1867, Buffalo, NY 14240-1867
IN CANADA: P.O. Box 609, Fort Erie, Ontario L2A 5X3

Not valid for current subscribers to Harlequin Superromance books.

Are you a current subscriber to Harlequin Superromance books and want to receive the larger-print edition?
Call 1-800-873-8635 or visit www.ReaderService.com.

* Terms and prices subject to change without notice. Prices do not include applicable taxes. Sales tax applicable in N.Y. Canadian residents will be charged applicable taxes. Offer not valid in Quebec. This offer is limited to one order per household. All orders subject to credit approval. Credit or debit balances in a customer's account(s) may be offset by any other outstanding balance owed by or to the customer. Please allow 4 to 6 weeks for delivery. Offer available while quantities last.

Your Privacy—The Reader Service is committed to protecting your privacy. Our Privacy Policy is available online at www.ReaderService.com or upon request from the Reader Service.

We make a portion of our mailing list available to reputable third parties that offer products we believe may interest you. If you prefer that we not exchange your name with third parties, or if you wish to clarify or modify your communication preferences, please visit us at www.ReaderService.com/consumerschoice or write to us at Reader Service Preference Service, P.O. Box 9062, Buffalo, NY 14269. Include your complete name and address.

HSR11

Harlequin® Blaze™ brings you
New York Times *and* USA TODAY *bestselling author*
Vicki Lewis Thompson with three new steamy titles
from the bestselling miniseries SONS OF CHANCE

Chance isn't just the last name of these rugged
Wyoming cowboys—it's their motto, too!

Read on for a sneak peek at the first title,
SHOULD'VE BEEN A COWBOY

Available June 2011 only from Harlequin® Blaze™.

"THANKS FOR NOT TURNING ON THE LIGHTS," Tyler said. "I'm a mess."

"Not in my book." Even in low light, Alex had a good view of her yellow shirt plastered to her body. It was all he could do not to reach for her, mud and all. But the next move needed to be hers, not his.

She slicked her wet hair back and squeezed some water out of the ends as she glanced upward. "I like the sound of the rain on a tin roof."

"Me, too."

She met his gaze briefly and looked away. "Where's the sink?"

"At the far end, beyond the last stall."

Tyler's running shoes squished as she walked down the aisle between the rows of stalls. She glanced sideways at Alex. "So how much of a cowboy are you these days? Do you ride the range and stuff?"

"I ride." He liked being able to say that. "Why?"

"Just wondered. Last summer, you were still a city boy. You even told me you weren't the cowboy type, but you're...different now."

He wasn't sure if that was a good thing or a bad thing. Maybe she preferred city boys to cowboys. "How am I different?"

"Well, you dress differently, and your hair's a little longer. Your face seems a little more chiseled, but maybe that's because of your hair. Also, there's something else, something harder to define, an attitude…"

"Are you saying I have an attitude?"

"Not in a bad way. It's more like a quiet confidence."

He was flattered, but still he had to laugh. "I just admitted a while ago that I have all kinds of doubts about this event tomorrow. That doesn't seem like quiet confidence to me."

"This isn't about your job, it's about…your…" She took a deep breath. "It's about your sex appeal, okay? I have no business talking about it, because it will only make me want to do things I shouldn't do." She started toward the end of the barn. "Now, where's that sink? We need to get cleaned up and go back to the house. Dinner is probably ready, and I—"

He spun her around and pulled her into his arms, mud and all. "Let's do those things." Then he kissed her, knowing that she would kiss him back, knowing that this time he would take that kiss where he wanted it to go. And she would let him.

Follow Tyler and Alex's wild adventures in
SHOULD'VE BEEN A COWBOY
Available June 2011 only from Harlequin® Blaze™
wherever books are sold.

Finding Her Dad

Janice Kay Johnson

Jonathan Brenner was busy running for
office as county sheriff. The last thing on
his mind was parenthood...that is, until
a resourceful, awkward teenage girl shows
up claiming to be his daughter!

*Available June
wherever books are sold.*